ALSO BY ELAINE VIETS

Dead-End Job Mystery Series

Shop till You Drop
Murder Between the Covers
Dying to Call You
Just Murdered
Murder Unleashed
Murder with Reservations
Clubbed to Death
Killer Cuts
Half-Price Homicide
Pumped for Murder
Final Sail
Board Stiff
Catnapped!
Killer Blonde
(an e-book novella)

Josie Marcus, Mystery Shopper Series

Dying in Style
High Heels Are Murder
Accessory to Murder
Murder with All the Trimmings
The Fashion Hound Murders
An Uplifting Murder
Death on a Platter
Murder Is a Piece of Cake
Fixing to Die
A Dog Gone Murder

Francesca Vierling Mystery Series

Backstab
Rubout
The Pink Flamingo Murders
Doc in the Box

Checked Out

A DEAD-END JOB MYSTERY

A DEAD-END JOB MYSTERY

Elaine Viets

AN OBSIDIAN MYSTERY

OBSIDIAN
Published by New American Library,
an imprint of Penguin Random House LLC
375 Hudson Street, New York, New York 10014

This book is a publication of New American Library. Previously published in a
Obsidian hardcover edition.

First Obsidian Mass Market Printing, May 2016

Copyright © Elaine Viets, 2015
Excerpt from *The Art of Murder* © Elaine Viets, 2016
Penguin Random House supports copyright. Copyright fuels creativity, encourages
diverse voices, promotes free speech, and creates a vibrant culture. Thank you for
buying an authorized edition of this book and for complying with copyright laws by
not reproducing, scanning, or distributing any part of it in any form without permission. You are supporting writers and allowing Penguin Random House to continue
to publish books for every reader.

Obsidian and the Obsidian colophon are trademarks of Penguin Random House LLC.

For more information about Penguin Random House, visit penguin.com.

ISBN 978-0-451-46633-4

Printed in the United States of America
10 9 8 7 6 5 4 3 2 1

Penguin
Random
House

For the librarians who gave me
so much entertainment between the covers

ACKNOWLEDGMENTS

John Singer Sargent really did abandon society divas to paint *Muddy Alligators* and landscapes. You can view his alligator watercolors by appointment at the Worcester Art Museum in Worcester, Massachusetts, or see one online at www.worcesterart.org/collection/American/1917.86.html. Don't you love its primeval power?

Thank you, Kate Dalton, Worcester curatorial assistant, who checked auction results from the last ten years to determine the price of the mythical watercolor in *Checked Out*. There is no evidence that Clark Gable ever owned *Muddy Alligators*, but he did play poker.

To help research this book, I shelved books for my local library, the Galt Ocean Mile Reading Center, part of the Broward County Library. Librarian Marlene Barnes, circulation supervisor Larry Cosimano, and library aides Vicki LaRue and Brittany Christopher helped me understand the inner workings of a reading room. The Galt Ocean Mile Reading Center in no way resembles the Flora Park Library and its staff, except they both have lots of books.

I'd need another book to name all the librarians who helped me with *Checked Out*. Thank you all. It's true: Librarians are search engines with hearts.

I appreciate the many librarians who told me the interesting and appalling things they've found in library books.

Special thanks to retired librarian Doris Ann Norris, who helped with the mysteries of the Dewey Decimal System. To librarian Dave Montalbano, Imperial Point Branch Library, Fort Lauderdale. Jill Patterson, branch manager of the Orange Country Public Libraries. Thank you, Anne Watts, assistant director of the Boynton Beach City Library, for your help and for lending me your six-toed cat, Thumbs, for this series.

I'd rather write a whole book than a title, but three mystery writers brainstormed and named *Checked Out* on the way to a signing at the Ivy in Baltimore. Thanks, Marcia Talley, Frances Brody and Hank Phillippi Ryan.

Former Fort Lauderdale commissioner Tim Smith, who owns T.L.C.'s Greenery, helped me with the details of Phil's undercover lawn care.

Thank you, Detective R. C. White, Fort Lauderdale Police Department (retired) and licensed private eye. You answered my e-mails, even on New Year's Eve. Thanks to Houston private eye and mystery writer William Simon and poison expert Luci Zahray, who fortunately uses her powers for good.

The real Margery Flax is much younger than Helen's landlady, but both love purple.

Thank you, Donna Mergenhagen, Well Read Bookstore and Gallery, Fort Lauderdale; Molly Weston, Dick Richmond, Richard Goldman and Mary Alice Gorman, who knew of John Singer Sargent's Florida connection. Thanks to Jane K. Cleland, author of the Josie Prescott Antiques Mysteries. Deborah Sharp let me use Himmarshee, Florida, the imaginary home of her Mace Bauer series.

Café Vico is a real Fort Lauderdale restaurant and I recommend the tiramisu.

Thank you to senior editor Sandra Harding, her assistant, Diana Kirkland, and publicist Kayleigh Clark, as well as my agent, David Hendin, and Don Crinklaw, my award-winning husband and reporter. (Yes, he's both.)

Thanks to supersaleswoman Carole Wantz, who can sell string bikinis in a Siberian winter.

Thank you, Femmes Fatales Charlaine Harris, Dana Cameron, Marcia Talley, Toni L. P. Kelner, Kris Neri, Mary Saums, Hank Phillippi Ryan, Donna Andrews, Catriona McPherson and Frere Dean James/Miranda James for your encouragement and advice. Read our blog at www.femmesfatales.typepad.com.

Thanks also to my fellow bloggers at The Kill Zone for your entertaining writing advice. Read us at killzone blog.com.

All mistakes are mine. You can reach me at eviets @aol.com.

CHAPTER 1

. . . .

"I need your help," Elizabeth Cateman Kingsley said. "My late father misplaced a million dollars in a library book. I want it back."

Helen Hawthorne caught herself before she said, "You're joking." Private eyes were supposed to be cool. Helen and her husband, Phil Sagemont, were partners in Coronado Investigations, a Fort Lauderdale firm.

Elizabeth seemed unnaturally calm for someone with a misplaced million. Her sensational statement had grabbed the attention of Helen and Phil, but now Elizabeth sat quietly in the yellow client chair, her narrow feet in sensible black heels crossed at the ankles, her slender, well-shaped hands folded in her lap.

Helen studied the woman from her chrome-and-black partner's chair. Somewhere in her fifties, Elizabeth Kingsley kept her gunmetal hair defiantly undyed and pulled into a knot. A thin, knife-blade nose gave her makeup-free face distinction. Helen thought she looked practical, confident and intelligent.

Elizabeth's well-cut gray suit was slightly worn. Her turquoise-and-pink silk scarf gave it a bold splash of color. Elizabeth had had money once, Helen decided, but she was on hard times now. But how the heck did you leave a million bucks in a library book?

Phil asked the question Helen had been thinking a little more tactfully: "How do you misplace a million in a library book?"

"I didn't," Elizabeth said. "My father, Davis Kingsley, did."

"Is it a check? A bankbook?"

"Oh, no," she said. "It's a watercolor."

CHAPTER 2

Elizabeth sat with her hands folded demurely in her lap, a sly smile on her face. She seemed to enjoy setting off bombshells and watching their effect.

"Perhaps I should explain," she said. "My family, the Kingsleys, were Florida pioneers. My grandparents moved to Fort Lauderdale in the 1920s and built a home in Flora Park."

The Kingsleys might have been early local residents, Helen thought, but this pioneer family hadn't roughed it in a log cabin. The Kingsleys had built a mansion in a wealthy enclave on the edge of Fort Lauderdale during the Florida land boom.

"Grandpapa Woodrow Kingsley made his money in oil and railroads," Elizabeth said.

"The old-fashioned way," Phil said.

My silver-haired husband is so charming, only I know he's calling Woodrow a robber baron, Helen thought.

"For a financier, Grandpapa was a bit of a swash-buckler," Elizabeth said, and smiled.

Helen decided maybe Elizabeth wasn't as proper as she seemed.

"He enjoyed financing silent films. He often went to Hollywood. Grandmama was a lady and stayed home."

The old gal was dull and disapproving, Helen translated. Grandpapa had had to travel three thousand miles to California to go on a toot.

"Grandmama would have nothing to do with movie people. She dedicated herself to helping the deserving poor."

Heaven help them, Helen thought. Their lives were miserable enough.

"Grandpapa put up the money for a number of classic films, including *Forbidden Paradise*—that starred Pola Negri—and Erich von Stroheim's *The Merry Widow*."

Films with scandalous women, Helen thought. Did Grandpapa unbuckle his swash for some smokin'-hot starlets?

"Impressive," Phil said. "Von Stroheim was famous for going over budget. He ordered Paris gowns and monogrammed silk underwear for his actors in *Foolish Wives* so they could feel more like aristocrats."

A tiny frown creased Elizabeth's forehead. She did not like being one-upped.

"When he was in Hollywood, Grandpapa would drink scotch, smoke cigars and play poker," she said. "He played poker on the set with the cast and crew, including Clark Gable."

"Wow!" Helen said.

"Oh, Gable wasn't a star then," Elizabeth said. "Far from it. He was an extra and Grandpapa thought Gable wouldn't get anywhere because his ears were too big. Many men made that mistake. Until Gable became the biggest star in Hollywood."

There it was again, Helen thought, that glimpse of carefully suppressed glee.

"Gable was on a losing streak that night," Elizabeth said. "He was out of money. He'd lost his watch and his ring. He bet a watercolor called *Muddy Alligators*."

"A painting?" Helen said. "What was Gable doing with that?"

"I have no idea, but he was quite attached to it," Elizabeth said. "He thought gators sunning themselves on a mud bank were manly. Grandpapa won the painting with a royal flush, but he didn't trust Hollywood types. He made Gable sign it over to him. Gable wrote on the back: *I lost this fair and square to Woodrow Kingsley— W. C. Gable, 1924.* Gable's first name was William. He changed his stage name to Clark Gable about then.

"Grandpapa admired the watercolor, and was surprised that a roughneck like Gable owned a genuine John Singer Sargent."

"Sargent painted muddy reptiles? I thought he did portraits of royalty and beautiful society women," Phil said.

"He did, until his mid-forties," Elizabeth said. "Then he had some kind of midlife career crisis and painted landscapes in Europe and America. Sargent painted at least two alligator watercolors when he stayed at the Florida home of John D. Rockefeller."

"Sargent switched from society dragons to alligators," Helen said, then wished she could recall her words. Elizabeth's grandmother was definitely a dragon.

"Dragons in training, usually," Elizabeth said, and again Helen caught a flash of well-bred amusement. "Most of his society belles were young women.

"Grandmama refused to display the painting in her house. Grandpapa couldn't even hang it in his office. She said it was ugly. I suspect it also may have been an ugly reminder of his Hollywood high jinks. She banished the alligator watercolor to a storage room.

"Sargent died the next year and Grandpapa had a fatal heart attack seven years later, leaving Grandmama a widow with one son. The watercolor was forgotten for decades.

"Until about five years ago," Elizabeth said. "My father,

Davis Kingsley, inherited the family home in the fifties. Papa was eighty when he found the watercolor in the storage room. Sargent's work was fashionable again. He had it authenticated and appraised. The watercolor wasn't worth all that much, maybe three hundred thousand."

Helen raised an eyebrow and Phil gave her a tiny nod. Three hundred K might not be much to Elizabeth, but the PI pair thought it was a substantial chunk of change.

"But it was worth much more, thanks to what the art world calls 'association.' A painting owned—and signed—by a film star brought the price up to more than a million dollars. The story behind it helped, too.

"Papa told everyone he'd discovered a lost family treasure. My brother, Cateman, and I begged him to have it properly stored and insured, but Papa said it wasn't necessary. 'It's in a safe place,' he'd say. 'Safer than any vault.' But we were concerned. Papa suffered from mild dementia by then.

"He died in his sleep six months ago, leaving his estate to Cateman and me. Papa gave me the Sargent watercolor and my brother inherited the family home. When the will was made five years ago, I was happy with that arrangement. I was a single woman with a comfortable income."

Comfortable. That was how rich people said they were rolling in dough, Helen thought.

"Since then, I've had some financial reversals. That watercolor has become important. I need that painting to save my home, and we can't find it."

"It was stolen?" Helen said.

"Worse," she said. "I believe it was accidentally given away. We've looked everywhere in the house, checked Papa's safe-deposit boxes and the safe, but we've found no sign of the missing watercolor. My brother even hired people to search the house. We can only conclude that my father hid it in one of his books that were donated to the Flora Park Library."

"Who gave it away?" Helen asked.

"Scarlett, my brother's new wife. Cateman recently married his third wife. It's a May-December marriage. He's sixty and she's twenty-three."

Did Elizabeth disapprove of her new sister-in-law? Helen thought Elizabeth had made a face, like she'd bitten into something sour, but it was hard to tell.

"Cateman and Scarlett moved into the family home immediately after Papa's funeral, and Scarlett began redecorating.

"Papa had let things slide in recent years. Scarlett doesn't love books the way he did. I doubt she reads anything but the magazines one finds in supermarket checkout lines."

Yep, Helen thought. Elizabeth definitely doesn't like her brother's new wife.

"Her first act was to get rid of what she called the 'dusty old books' in my father's library, which dates back to Grandpapa's time. Scarlett donated more than a thousand books to the Flora Park Library. Most of the books were of little value. Papa was a great reader of hardcover popular fiction, and the Friends of the Library began selling those while they had the more valuable books appraised.

"The Friends put ten mysteries on sale for a dollar each, and the hardcovers were bought within a few days. But a patron found the birth certificate for Imogen Cateman, my grandmama, in her thriller. She returned it to the library. Then a man discovered the deed to property in Tallahassee in a spy novel."

"The Flora Park Library has honest patrons," Phil said.

"People of quality live there," Elizabeth said. "I would expect them to return family papers."

Elizabeth sat a little straighter. She considered herself one of the quality.

"We concluded that my late father hid valuables in his books, and the missing watercolor was in a donated volume."

"Why don't you look for it?" Phil asked. "Don't you know the people at the library?"

"Of course I do," Elizabeth said. "But my job as a facilitator for my college alumni association takes up all my time."

Helen had no idea what a facilitator did, but Elizabeth said it so gravely, Helen felt she should have known.

"I could have taken the books back and searched them myself, but that would cause talk.

"I can only give you a small down payment," Elizabeth said. "But if you find the watercolor, I'll pay you ten thousand dollars when it's sold at auction. The library director is a friend and she's agreed that you can work as a library volunteer, Helen, while you discreetly look for the watercolor."

"Me?" Helen said. A library, she thought. I'd like that. I'd get to read the new books when they came in, too.

"How do you know Scarlett didn't keep the watercolor?" Phil asked.

Helen thought her husband would make a fine portrait—eighteenth-century British, she decided. He had a long, slightly crooked nose, a thin, pale face and thick silver hair. She dragged herself back to the conversation.

"I showed her a picture of one of the alligator watercolors and she said it was 'gross.' She prefers to collect what she calls 'pretty things,' such as Swarovski crystal."

"What about your brother?" Helen asked. "Does he have the watercolor?"

"Cateman is an honorable man," Elizabeth said. "Besides, he has more than enough money."

Rich people never have enough money, Helen thought.

"He actually hired people to search his house. Why would he do that if he was trying to keep the painting for himself?" Elizabeth asked.

"The search was done after the books were donated to the library?" Phil said.

"Of course," Elizabeth said. The frown notched

deeper into her forehead. She was annoyed. "My brother is most anxious to help me find that artwork. He has sufficient means for himself and Scarlett, but he doesn't feel he can afford to support me. His two divorces have cost him dearly."

Now, that's convincing, Helen thought.

CHAPTER 3

. . . .

T he Flora Park Library was as beautiful as its name, Helen thought. The color of dawn light, the two-story building had a sun-warmed barrel-tile roof and graceful arched windows. A curving wrought-iron fence wrapped around the Mediterranean building like an elegant vine.

She parked her car in the library lot, next to Elizabeth's. It was a little after ten in the morning and Helen had agreed to go straight to the library with Elizabeth and get started.

Flora Park was an islandlike enclave on the New River, at the edge of Fort Lauderdale. Helen decided the library looked like an estate in the south of France.

"Gorgeous, isn't it?" Elizabeth said. "Stately."

"Stately seems so formal," Helen said. "This library is inviting."

"Flora Portland would certainly welcome us," Elizabeth said as they passed through the open gates surrounding the library gardens. Rustling palm trees shaded the thick, velvety grass. "This was Flora's house for almost twenty years. It was built to her specifications."

"She must have been quite a woman," Helen said.

"Flora was no fragile flower," Elizabeth said, her heels clicking on the walkway pavers. "She was as strong-willed as she was beautiful. In the early 1890s, she defied her parents to marry the man she loved. Turned down two proposals."

"Young women didn't do that back then," Helen said.

"Especially not rich, well-brought-up ones," Elizabeth said. "Grandmama told me the story. She admired Flora greatly. The Portland family was in railroads, and she had many suitors. Flora refused to marry a titled Englishman. It wasn't a love match. He needed pots of money to restore the family home. But Flora learned he'd impregnated a teenage maid and refused him, even though his family did the right thing and married the maid to the second gardener. Flora's refusal ruined her mother's attempt to get into London society. She took her troublesome daughter home to New York, where Flora turned down the banker her father favored.

"Instead, Flora eloped to Paris with her college tutor, Lucian Humboldt. Her parents disinherited her, but Flora had a handsome trust from her maternal grandmother. She and Lucian lived in style abroad until the mid-twenties, when she built this mansion."

Elizabeth opened the library's etched glass door and she and Helen stepped into a light-filled lobby. Sunlight danced in a crystal chandelier and burnished the sweep of the grand staircase.

But Helen was drawn to the full-length portrait of a brown-haired beauty in a slim lavender gown. She wore her big-brimmed mauve hat at a rakish angle and looked straight at the world.

"Hello, Flora," Helen said. She studied Flora's surprisingly modern face with its high cheekbones. A strong woman, she decided. And a smart one.

"This picture was painted right before she eloped, wasn't it? I can see the triumph in her face."

"Perceptive," Elizabeth said. "Flora crowned herself queen of Flora Park when she and her husband moved here in 1925. This was a happy house. The couple hosted literary discussions and musical evenings. When the widowed Flora died in 1941, she left this mansion, their books and a generous trust to Flora Park for a community library—with one stipulation. That picture would stay in the lobby."

Elizabeth nodded toward a series of arches behind the staircase. "Much of the popular library is back there. The director's office is down this hall. Alexa Stuart Andrews agreed to meet us at ten thirty this morning."

"Before we meet Ms. Andrews, please explain these library titles and organizations," Helen asked. "I'm going to be a volunteer. Does that make me a Friend of the Library?"

"You could be a Friend," Elizabeth said. "The Friends are a nonprofit organization dedicated to supporting the library. Our dues are ten dollars a year. We have our own board, and decide how our fund-raising will benefit the library. Of course, the library staff has some input."

Helen didn't want to think about the genteel power struggles those words implied.

"Last year, the Friends gave this library eighty thousand dollars to create a children's section," Elizabeth said.

"You have that many children in Flora Park?" Helen asked.

"We have very few young families," Elizabeth said, "but lots of grandchildren. The Friends bought children's books and DVDs and child-sized furniture.

"You could pay the dues and become a Friend, but for your investigation you'll be a volunteer. You'll work for the library staff and be subject to the library's policies for volunteers."

"And Alexa, the director, is the boss?" Helen said.

"You make her sound like she wears a hard hat," Elizabeth said, but softened her remark with a faint smile. "Alexa is definitely in charge. Most definitely."

Helen followed Elizabeth down a rather dark hall with lustrous wood floors, carved Spanish tables and curlicued cabinets. "The furniture is from Flora's time," Elizabeth said. She stopped at a glass door to a book-lined room with a thick pink-and-gray Oriental rug. "Alexa's office is the former morning room," she said. "It overlooks the ground floor and has a view of the back gardens."

Alexa Andrews was frowning at her black desktop computer. Helen guessed the library director was about her age—early forties. She looked like a successful CEO. Alexa's shoulder-length dark hair had a dramatic white streak that framed her fine-boned face. Her pale blue suit was soft and stylish.

"Ms. Hawthorne," she said, and shook Helen's hand. Helen and Elizabeth sat in the button-tufted barrel chairs opposite her desk, and Alexa got down to business.

"Elizabeth has explained her dilemma to me," she said, "and I've agreed to let you work here as a volunteer, even though my decision will make some people very unhappy."

"Why?" Helen asked.

"Volunteer positions at our library are highly coveted," she said.

I should have known, Helen thought. The rich want to do their civic duty, but prefer not to get their hands dirty. Raising money for a worthy cause with a fashionable gala was acceptable. Mixing with actual unfortunates was not. Genteel library volunteer positions would be in demand.

"Seraphina Ormond, who belongs to a Flora Park first family, believes she is entitled to the next volunteer position."

"What's a first family?" Helen asked.

"Seraphina's great-grandparents bought one of the first houses in Flora Park."

"And that real estate deal gives their family the right to rule Flora Park forever?" Helen asked.

"Of course not," Alexa said, but her smile wasn't quite as bright. Helen decided to back off. She didn't want to get into an entitlement debate.

"But they've been here so long, the first families have certain expectations," Alexa said. "I believe these positions should be given on merit. Seraphina and her friends will be quite annoyed when you get the post."

"Couldn't you say I'm only here temporarily?" Helen asked.

"Oh, no," Alexa said. "We must keep your true mission confidential.

"I've asked the Friends of the Library to hold off selling the other books from Mr. Kingsley's library until they've been examined. I've said it was a legal issue."

"Which it is," Elizabeth said. She was wringing her hands and Helen thought she seemed defensive.

"Exactly," Alexa said. "The last thing we want is someone creating a stir. It's bad enough we have a ghost."

"A what?" Helen said.

Alexa sighed, and tugged on her white streak. "I was going to call in a private eye anyway, and I've heard that you're very discreet. Some people believe the ghost of Flora Portland is haunting this library. I think it's ridiculous. I don't believe in ghosts. Flora was a fine woman and I'm sure she's resting in peace, not roaming this library. Besides, I've seen signs that a human is behind this alleged haunting."

"What are the signs?" Helen asked.

"Food is missing from the staff break room, books reshelved in the wrong places and three emergency flashlights have disappeared."

"The flashlights could have been stolen," Helen said. "I worked at a bookstore and stock was mis-shelved all the time. As for the missing food, I've worked at offices where my colleagues swiped my lunch or ate my snacks."

"All true, but our hurricane kit was taken, and that was a substantial loss."

"What was in it?" Helen asked.

"The usual: jugs of water, juices, peanut butter, break-fast bars, canned fruit, raisins, chips, a can opener, paper plates and plastic utensils, trash bags, blankets and pil-lows, toiletries, wipes, a tarp."

"Why a tarp?" Helen asked.

"In case there are holes in the building."

"Right," Helen said. Floridians were all too familiar with blue tarps after Hurricanes Wilma and Katrina.

"The biggest losses were a battery-operated televi-sion and five hundred dollars in small bills to purchase additional supplies."

"And you haven't found any peanut butter jars, juice bottles or food wrappers in the library?" Helen asked.

"Nothing that wasn't left behind by patrons. The TV has disappeared, along with the blankets and pillows."

"It is October," Helen said. "And hurricane season is still on for a month."

"All true, Ms. Hawthorne. But I still don't believe in ghosts. Nor do I believe our patrons would steal from us. And our staff is completely trustworthy."

I've heard variations on the "everyone here is honest" theme before, Helen thought. The client is usually sur-prised when a trusted person turns out to be a crook.

"Has Flora always haunted the library?" she asked.

"Certainly not!" Alexa said. "The haunting started about a month ago, after a heated library board meet-ing. This is a well-built historic home, Ms. Hawthorne, and Flora Portland's trust is enough to maintain it. But historic homes do not have reinforced floors, and books are heavy. An average hardback weighs close to a pound, and we have several hundred thousand pounds of books in this building.

"At first, we kept the bookshelves along the walls, but as the collection grew, we put a bookcase in the middle of the floor, then another, and, well, they kept multiply-ing. Now the floors upstairs are sagging and we have problems with the first floor, too.

"We hired an engineer to evaluate the problem. At

the board meeting, he told us the cost of reinforcing the floors in this historic building would exhaust the rest of Flora Portland's trust. The library would have to be closed for at least a year. We were shocked.

"Then the engineer said it would be less expensive to have a new purpose-built library with floors that could bear the load, and new plumbing and heating systems away from the collections. You can imagine the response that got. Our board president said that Flora would turn over in her grave."

"Would this building be torn down?" Helen asked.

"Oh, no," Alexa said. "It's historic. It would be turned into a community center. I'd hate to move, but a new building would have reinforced floors, accessibility ramps, a delivery dock. I love this building, but we might be able to serve our patrons better with a new library. Right now, the board is split—three members want to renovate and three want to build a new library. But our heritage is important. If the library could come up with the money, the vote would be unanimous to renovate."

"Where do you stand on the matter?" Helen asked.

"I'm completely neutral," Alexa said. "The matter is still being discussed, but shortly after the meeting, some of our patrons and staff said that Flora Portland was haunting her library. A week later, a patron—a rather excitable older woman—reported seeing a slender young woman with brown hair running through the stacks. Then Lisa, the president of the library board, said she saw the same thing and the so-called ghost was wearing a long lavender dress. Lisa is an influential person here.

"That story made our community paper, the *Flora Park Gazette*, and since then, the sightings and rumors have been running wild.

"I want these rumors stopped, Ms. Hawthorne," the director said, and glared at Helen as if she'd started them. "I want you to find that so-called ghost. The library will pay your regular rate. Bring the contract back by five this afternoon and I'll sign it."

"Certainly," Helen said. This is a dream job, she thought. I get to work at this gorgeous library and hunt for a ghost.

"You can smile, Ms. Hawthorne," Alexa said, "but your work will not be easy or pleasant. I believe this ghost started as a prank, possibly by someone who doesn't want the library to change. But now it's a nuisance. It upsets the staff and patrons and disrupts the library. People are jumpy and edgy. Someone has already been hurt.

"Lisa actually hit a patron with a heavy brass bookend because she thought Flora's ghost had 'jumped out at her.' The poor woman was simply reaching for a reference book in the upstairs study room. She was young, had brown hair and wore a purple sundress. She needed six stitches in her scalp. Fortunately, she did not have a concussion.

"It's a delicate situation. The board runs this library, and I serve at their pleasure. I have to tread carefully. I can't offend Lisa, but I can't have our patrons attacked, either.

"Someone is playing a dangerous game, Ms. Hawthorne. I want it stopped before an innocent person dies."

CHAPTER 4

. . . .

"**D**id you get the job?" Phil asked.

Helen's husband and PI partner had been pounding the computer keys in the Coronado Investigations office when she walked in after the library visit. She paused to admire her new husband. She liked his long, silver white hair, tied back in a ponytail, his thin aristocratic nose and his blue eyes. She kissed the little worry wrinkle on his forehead.

"Job? I have two jobs," Helen said. "Three, if you count my highly coveted volunteer job at the Flora Park Library. But only two are paid: I'm searching for the missing million-dollar alligator art, and now the library wants me to be a ghost buster."

"The library's haunted?" Phil asked. "Who's the walking dead?"

"Flora Portland," Helen said, rooting through a gray metal filing cabinet. "Do you know where we keep our standard contract form? It's either under *C* for contract, or *S* for standard."

"I thought we put it under *F* for form," Phil said. "Is Flora Park named for Flora the ghost?"

"No, but she donated the library to the city. It was her

home, and the library opened in the forties, after she died. Ah, there it is," Helen said, pulling out the contract form. "I have to take this back to the library before five o'clock."

"Flora's been haunting the library for nearly sixty years," Phil said, "and they're finally doing something about it?"

"No, she hasn't. Flora's been dead quiet," Helen said.

Phil groaned.

"The haunting started a month ago, according to Alexa, the director, after the library got bad news. The floors in the old building can't take the heavy load of books anymore. The repairs are so expensive, they'll eat the trust fund Flora left behind and the library will have to close for a year during construction. The other choice is to build a new library. The library board president said Flora would turn over in her grave at that prospect."

"Instead, she got up and started walking the halls?" Phil said. He wandered to the kitchen for another cup of coffee. His fourth, judging by the foam cups lined up next to his computer. "Coffee?" he asked Helen, holding up the pot.

"Water, please," Helen said. Phil opened a bottle from the fridge and handed it to her.

"Some people believe Flora has suddenly risen from her grave," she said, "but Alexa doesn't. She's paying me to find the so-called ghost."

"What if you don't find her?" Phil said.

"I will," Helen said. "I bet I'll track down Flora's ghost in three weeks. She'd have felt at home in our office in the forties."

The one-bedroom apartment had smooth art moderne curves, a speckled terrazzo floor and a slatted-glass jalousie door. The two private eyes used the former living room to meet with clients, and worked in the back room. Phil swore that Sam Spade would drink bourbon in an office like this, so he hung a brooding Bogart poster over his desk.

But the office was too cheerful for dated noir romanticism. Coronado Investigations was clearly a successful small business.

"I thought you'd be working on our other case today," Helen said, sipping her water.

"I'm enjoying my last day of freedom before I go undercover," he said. "We worked the Coakley case as much as we could together."

"I thought that case would be easy," Helen said. "A twenty-thousand-dollar necklace was stolen at Bree Coakley's twenty-first birthday party, and a golf cart went missing. We've been interviewing the Coakley family and their daughters' snotty friends for weeks, and not a single lead."

"Most of the partygoers were too out of it to remember anything," Phil said. "That's why I have to go undercover as a gardener and get to know the Coakley staff. I'm not looking forward to yard work in the Florida heat."

"Not even in ritzy Peerless Point?" Helen asked.

"Sun's just as hot for the poor folks as the rich ones," Phil said. "I've been updating my list of dicey pawnshops where the stolen ruby-and-diamond necklace could be sold and places that would sell that stolen golf cart."

"You still think the cart has been stolen and the crimes are connected?" Helen asked. "I figured the cart was dumped in a canal after a drunken joy ride."

"I think it was the getaway car, or cart," he said. "Everyone gets around that neighborhood by golf cart. No one would notice. The driver could take it outside the gates and load it into a pickup."

"Golf cart rustling," Helen said. "What a ridiculous crime."

"At least stealing a ruby necklace is ordinary enough," he said.

"Why do you think the necklace was sold at a pawnshop instead of at a bar?" Helen asked.

"The family thinks the staff took it," Phil said. "I'm not sure anyone working there has fencing contacts."

"It's too easy to blame the staff," Helen said. "There were more than fifty people at Bree Coakley's twenty-first birthday party, not counting crashers. The thief could have been a guest or a family member."

"I'm not ruling out the family, either," Phil said. "But I need to spend time with the staff to learn about the home owners."

"Mansion owners," Helen said. "The Coakley home has eight bedrooms, six baths, two pools and a living room with a walk-in fireplace."

"You don't like them," he said.

"No, I don't," Helen said. "Amis, the husband, is condescending. Ashler, the wife, is a snob. When I called her Ashley, she said that name was common and Ashler was a family name. Bree, the so-called victim, is snippy. I guess she's named after the family cheese."

Phil laughed.

"It's not funny," Helen said. "Bree's little sister is another piece of work. Chloe is so jealous of Bree she can hardly see straight. I've had enough of them and their friends. They have this inborn sense of entitlement."

"Their parents gave them that," Phil said. "And their private schools. Don't let your prejudices blind you to the facts."

Helen shrugged. "I still don't like the whole bunch," she said. "I'd rather chase ghosts at the library."

"You can," Phil said, "but I need you to talk to Chloe Coakley again."

"Again? Do I have to?" Helen knew she was whining, but she didn't care.

"Yes," he said. "You caught that Chloe was jealous of Bree. I didn't see that. I'm an only child. You're better with the family dynamics. If Chloe is really that jealous, maybe she took the necklace. If she didn't, she was still at the party. She could have seen something useful. Just one more interview and then you can go ghost hunting."

"Might as well get it over with," Helen said. "I'll call and see if she's home now."

She made the call and reported, "Ashler says I can see Chloe now. I'll stop by the Coakley house before I go to the library."

Phil propped his feet up on his dented desk, and his chair squeaked. "Do you believe in ghosts?" he asked.

"I believe there are things I don't understand that seem supernatural," Helen said. "So far, this haunting can be explained in earthbound terms: Flashlights and a hurricane kit have been lost or stolen. Food is missing from the staff break room."

"Ghosts don't eat," Phil said.

"No, they don't," Helen said. "And that gorgeous full-length portrait of Flora Portland in the lobby helps suggest suggestible types see Flora flitting through the halls. They say the ghost has brown hair and wears a long lavender dress."

"Just like Flora in the picture," Phil said.

"Right. Even though Flora didn't move into that house until the 1920s, she's ghosting in 1890s clothes," Helen said.

"Did Flora die in the library?" Phil asked. "I mean, when it was her house."

"Yes, but peacefully, when she was nearly ninety," Helen said. "If anyplace should be haunted, it's this office. A woman was murdered here. Have you ever felt her presence?"

"Never," Phil said. "Margery let us rent this unit for our office for a dollar a year because our landlady didn't want to say what happened to the last tenant."

"Once people start saying a place is haunted," Helen said, "even normal things look spooky.

"I think there's a logical explanation for Flora's haunting. My big problem will be finding the ghost before someone gets killed. Lisa, the jittery library board president, already hit a woman with a brass bookend."

"A reader?" Phil asked.

"Yep. Knocked the poor patron silly. Lisa said she jumped out at her when the woman simply reached for a book. The woman got six stitches. Now the library director's worried someone will get killed."

"I don't envy you working with jumpy, nervous people," Phil said.

"Don't forget resentful," Helen said. "Alexa says that Seraphina Ormond is upset with me because I'm the new library volunteer. Seraphina feels she was entitled to that job."

"You stole a free job?" Phil said. "Now it's definitely dangerous."

CHAPTER 5

. . . .

Helen flew straight down the Coronado stairs and slammed into a young man.

Oof!

She caught flashes of curly black hair and a well-stretched black T-shirt before they tumbled onto the sidewalk.

She heard Phil clattering down the steps after her. "Helen!" he called. "Are you hurt?"

Helen sat stunned on the sidewalk, the breath knocked out of her, unable to answer.

The man she'd run into was definitely breathtaking. Helen guessed he was Latino and in his late twenties. He had smoldering romance-cover good looks, until he smiled at her. That was no sultry-surly pout. He seemed too good-humored.

"Are you okay?" Helen asked him. "I'm so sorry. I have to deliver a contract and I was rushing to my car."

"Not your fault," he said, standing up. "I should have been watching where I was going." Helen caught a trace of an accent. Cuban?

Phil was at her side, but the unknown hunk held out

his hand and helped Helen up before her husband could. "You're hurt," the man said.

Helen brushed off her skirt. "Just a skinned knee," she said. "That should make me look younger. About eight years old."

He smiled at her. "I'm Markos Martinez," he said. He shook her hand and held it until Phil cleared his throat. Helen had forgotten her husband was standing next to her.

With a vivid swish of purple fabric and a swirl of cigarette smoke, Margery Flax, the Coronado's landlady, materialized next to Markos. Margery was seventy-six, with a swingy gray bob and a face full of wrinkles. They seemed more like marks of achievement than signs of age.

"I see you ran into our new resident, Helen," she said. "Markos is moving into the downstairs apartment that Cal the Canadian used to rent.

"Markos, this is my prize pair of private eyes, Helen Hawthorne and Phil Sagemont. They live here on the first floor and their office, Coronado Investigations, is upstairs in 2C."

Phil shook the newcomer's hand. "Martinez," Phil said. "Any relation to Marcos Martinez, the Spanish race car driver?"

"Only that we both drive too fast," Markos said, and grinned. "I have a common Cuban name. My family's been here since the Mariel boat lift in 1980. I was born in Fort Lauderdale."

"Can we help you move in?" Phil asked.

"Thanks, but I'm already moved in," Markos said. "The apartment was furnished, and all my belongings fit in the trunk of my car. It was easy. All I had to do was carry in some clothes, books and my laptop."

"I've been giving Markos the grand tour," Margery said.

She waved her Marlboro like a wand at her kingdom,

the Coronado Tropic Apartments. The harsh Florida sun brought out the best in the art moderne building: the swooping iceberg white curves, fresh turquoise trim and the sapphire swimming pool. The two-story L-shaped apartments were set around the pool, and shaded by palms and broad green-leaved elephant ears. Ruffled purple bougainvillea spilled around the pool. The walkways were a triumphant imperial purple march of impatiens and spiky salvia.

"I can't believe apartments built in 1949 are so beautifully preserved," Markos said. "I'm lucky to live here."

"We just finished an extensive renovation," Margery said.

Our landlady didn't mention that the Coronado had almost been torn down because the repairs were so expensive, Helen thought. Maybe some night when we're drinking wine around the pool we can tell Markos the full story.

"Are you interested in architecture, Markos?" Phil asked.

"A little," he said. "I like to know my city. But I'm really interested in food service. I'm working on my bachelor's degree in restaurant food and beverage management at Reynolds-White College."

"Impressive," Phil said.

"The one in Fort Lauderdale?" Helen asked.

"You've heard of it?" Markos asked. "Are you a foodie?"

"Uh, I like to eat," Helen said. "But I'm not much of a cook."

"Reynolds-White has a four-year program," he said. "But I want to know the restaurant business inside and out. I'm also a waiter at Fresh and Cool. They specialize in low-calorie healthy food."

"I love that place," Helen said.

She saw Phil's face was a frozen mask of politeness. My man loves those evil-looking orange chips and other unnatural foods, she thought. He thinks ketchup is a vegetable.

"You can tell us all about it at tonight's sunset salute around the pool," Margery said, "when you can meet the rest of the menagerie."

"Good," Markos said. "I'll make my special mojitos and bring the appetizers. I'll make kale chips and gluten-free taco wraps stuffed with lentils."

"Can't wait till sunset," Helen said, "but I have to deliver that contract now."

"Kale chips?" Phil said, as if trying out the words for the first time.

Helen figured he'd probably never said that phrase before.

CHAPTER 6
. . . .

Helen didn't like the Coakleys, but she admired their home. It was in Peerless Point, a small rich community that bordered Fort Lauderdale.

Between Peerless Point and Flora Park, I'm definitely working the area's extravagant side, she thought. No mean streets for this PI.

The Coakleys' winding pink-paved drive, lined with red hibiscus hedges, ended at a three-tiered fountain in a cool green garden.

Helen parked the Igloo in front of the white coral rock mansion. Creatures from long-vanished seas were etched in its surface. Millions of years ago, they were laboring for the Coakleys' pleasure.

The pale front door was sheltered under a pillared portico. Ashler Coakley met Helen at the door. A thin generic blonde in her forties, she was expertly exercised and exquisitely nipped and tucked. Helen had seen dozens of women like her in the society pages, clinging to their wealthy husbands' arms, smiling tentatively. Ashler had brought up the Coakley daughters and run the vast household, but now that the daughters were nearly grown, she had no job security. Amis could replace her with a younger, thinner blonde, and she knew it.

"Helen," she said. "Good of you to stop by. Have you found the necklace?"

"We're hot on the trail," Helen said. "I'm glad Chloe's home and can see me."

"She's on the terrace. I'll take you there." Ashler gave Helen a Stepford wife smile, and her heels pattered across the vast white marble floors. Helen followed her through a living room and dining room so white she was nearly snow-blind by the time they reached the terrace. It opened out onto a hundred-foot deepwater dock and a spectacular view of the Intracoastal Waterway.

Chloe was blond like her mother, but she looked bored instead of eager to please. She was stretched out on a blue-striped chaise, wearing a bikini. Helen sat in the matching striped chair across from her.

"Would you like something to drink?" Ashler said, running her hands through her hair. "Ana can bring iced tea, coffee. . . ." Her voice trailed off and she turned to her daughter. "Honey, anything for you?"

"More iced tea," Chloe said, as if addressing a servant.

"Ice water, thank you," Helen said.

Chloe and Helen talked about the weather until the housekeeper, a generously built Latina in her fifties, bustled in with the drinks and a plate of cookies. Chloe ignored Ana. Helen thanked her and received a dazzling smile.

When they were alone, Chloe said, "Sorry about that. Mom fusses."

"That's what mothers do," Helen said.

Chloe shrugged, and the bikini bra quaked. "Are you really a private eye?" she asked, and sipped her iced tea.

"Class C license," Helen said. "My partner, Phil—you talked with him last time—is also a detective."

"He's hot," Chloe said.

"He's my husband," Helen said, marking her territory. "We work together."

"That's so cool. You and your husband are, like, equals. My mom doesn't work," Chloe said.

Helen decided to forgo the lecture about women working in the home.

"All Mom and her friends do is play bridge and go to lunch and now they're old."

Old, Helen thought. My age. Maybe.

"I don't want that to happen to me," Chloe said. "I'd rather die than live like her. Being a private eye must be exciting."

Helen heard that all the time. "It's not like TV," she said. "I spend a lot of time sitting in a car."

"Do you drive a Porsche?"

"You have been watching TV," Helen said. "I drive a white PT Cruiser."

"Boring," Chloe said.

"I need a car that blends in," Helen said. "Porsches are too flashy. That's what a good private eye does—blends in so she can tail people. I don't want to be noticed, and I can't do too many car chases with a four-cylinder engine."

"Ew. That's like a . . . Neon." The private eye profession was quickly losing its romance.

"My computer's fast," Helen said. "I do a lot of research on the Internet."

"I'm good at Snapchat, Pheed, Tumblr, Instagram, Twitter, Vine and Vimeo," Chloe said.

"All useful," Helen said. "There are social media investigators. You'd be surprised what people put on Facebook."

"I can do Facebook," Chloe said, "but only old people use it."

Ouch, Helen thought.

"Do you have a gun?" Chloe asked. Helen got that question a lot, too.

"I'd need a Class G license to carry a weapon," Helen said. "To get your PI license, you'll need to take a certification exam and you'll probably have to work as an intern, which won't pay much. But once you get your license, it's a good job."

"How much do you make?" Chloe asked.

"Enough," Helen said. "Phil and I live where we want and we can afford what we want." She didn't add that a big house or a housekeeper were out of their price range.

"Am I old enough to start now?" she asked.

"Not quite. You have to be twenty-one in Florida. You're eighteen, right? And your sister, Bree, is twenty-one."

"Bree." Chloe snorted. "She gets everything. My parents think she's perfect. She got a better birthday party than I did. Just because she's three years older." Red resentment flared in her eyes.

There's no mistake this time, Helen thought. Chloe is definitely jealous of her older sister.

"Now that I'm eighteen, my parents said they'd get me VIP tickets to the next Ultra Music Festival in Miami."

"Impressive," Helen said. "Those tickets are, like, what—eleven hundred for a three-day pass?"

Like? she thought. Did I just say *like*?

"Eleven hundred forty-nine," Chloe said. "They spent thousands on Bree's birthday party and got her a new Beemer and a diamond-and-ruby necklace. I'm still driving Mom's old silver Acura and they think they can buy me some cheap tickets and I'll be happy. I'll get my own."

"Can you afford them?" Helen asked. "Is your allowance that good?"

"My allowance barely covers my clothes," she said.

And your clothes barely cover you, Helen thought. She wished Chloe would put on a cover-up or a T-shirt. She wished her chair faced the water instead of Chloe's nearly naked body.

"I wanted a boob job but they said no. All the girls in my class got boob jobs at sixteen, but Mom wouldn't let me."

Helen knew that outrageous statement was true. Big breasts were replacing the traditional sixteenth birthday gift of a new car. She felt sorry for Chloe, who maybe wasn't so different from her mother after all.

"You need brains, not boobs, to be successful," Helen said. "But if you're making enough money to buy eleven-hundred-dollar tickets, you must be successful."

"I'm a partner with my boyfriend," she said. "We work together, sort of like you and Phil."

Helen recognized an opening. "Do you have a job?"

"Not a *job* job, where we wear stupid uniforms and say, 'Do you want fries with that?' But we're partners. Last Friday we made two hundred dollars."

"Impressive," Helen said. "That's more than I made last Friday."

"We can make a couple hundred every weekend," Chloe said. "More during spring break and in the summer, when school's out."

"Sounds interesting," Helen said. "What do you two do?"

"I can't tell you without his permission. I promised," Chloe said.

"Is it legal?" Helen asked.

"What he does is legal," Chloe said.

Why did she word that so carefully? Helen wondered.

"You could guess, but you'll never figure it out." Bree's little sister liked to play games.

Helen tried a lie. "This is probably old-school," she said, "but I used to sell things my mom stashed in the back of the cabinet—old silver and stuff that she never used. She never missed it. I sold it at a pawnshop."

Chloe wrinkled her nose. "Pawnshops are so gross. I only go in one if I'm with my boyfriend. He bought a ukulele at one, some kind of collectible. I wouldn't touch anything in those places. They're dirty."

"I can see that," Helen said. She let the silence stretch, until Chloe couldn't contain her curiosity.

"I can't tell you what we do until I check with him,"

Chloe said. "But I'll give you three clues: Rex, Crown, Jewel. Meet us there at nine o'clock any weekend night and you'll know."

She gave Helen a sly smile. I'm not getting anything else out of her, she thought, and I have to get to the library. Time to finish this. "I stopped by to ask: Who do you think took your sister's necklace?"

"Bree did," Chloe said. She didn't hesitate. "She took the necklace. I bet she sold it at a pawnshop. She'll keep the money and get all that attention. My parents were boo-hooing with her. She eats that stuff up."

"You don't think anyone at the party took it?" Helen said.

"A necklace with a big, fat, stupid ruby and a bunch of diamonds? That's jewelry for old ladies."

Helen heard the scorn in Chloe's voice and saw the want in her eyes.

"What about the golf cart?" Helen asked.

"One of the lawn guys," Chloe said, and shrugged. "I can't remember their names. They're Mexicans or something. They hate us, you know."

With good reason, Helen thought.

CHAPTER 7
· ·

Helen inhaled the Flora Park Library's special perfume that afternoon. The scent of old leather-bound books, sunlight, dust and vanilla mixed with the sharp tang of new books.

The library smell transported Helen back to her favorite summer reading nook in her grandmother's honeysuckle-scented yard. For a moment, she could see the red metal lawn chair and the green summer grass, and taste the sweet-sour lemonade.

Then she was back in the sunlit library entrance, and she swore the portrait of Flora Portland gave her a saucy wink.

Helen hurried down the hall to the director's office, clutching the Coronado Investigations contract. Alexa Andrews was still frowning at her black desktop computer, as if she hadn't moved since this morning.

She looked up, smiled and said, "Hi, Helen."

"Reporting for duty," Helen said.

"You're overdressed," the director said. "Tomorrow, I'd like you to shelve books and DVDs. You'll also be searching through the dusty old Kingsley books for that missing watercolor. Wear nice pants and a washable blouse, and leave those heels at home. I'm an executive, so I have to dress professionally. You'll be running all over this building.

"I have your check for the deposit," she said. "Let me sign the contract and then we'll take the tour."

Alexa signed both copies in black ink with bold, oversized strokes, and Helen put her copy and the check in her purse.

"We'll start with the popular library," Alexa said.

Helen thought that was an odd term for bestsellers. What were the other books—unpopular?

"Flora Park is more of a reading room than a true library," Alexa said. "Most of our residents are older, and until a few years ago, few lived year-round in Florida. Flora Park is their winter home. Our patrons want to read the latest novels, biographies and periodicals. They like our educational programs, too.

"You've already seen the lobby and Flora's portrait," she said as they passed under the arches behind the wrought-iron staircase. "Our popular library was Flora's main salon, where she and Lucian had their musical evenings and book discussions. It overlooks the garden."

The walls were painted silvery violet and lined with warm cherrywood bookshelves decorated with carved lions' heads. Six patrons sat in cool, lavender-cushioned wicker wing chairs, reading books and magazines. A white-haired man in a dark suit was deep into Sunday's *New York Times*. Two college-age students had their iPads set up at a dark wood library table with lions' paws. A fortysomething businesswoman was typing on her laptop.

"It looks like a private club," Helen said.

"In many ways it is," Alexa said. "That's Gladys Gillman behind the checkout desk. Come meet our head librarian."

The leggy Gladys looked like an MTV dancer, with

long, glossy dark hair, red lipstick, a pleated red miniskirt and black boots with buckles. Helen guessed Gladys's age at thirty.

Helen almost said, "She's a librarian?" but stopped herself in time. That stereotype is a hundred years out-of-date, she reminded herself.

"Really pleased to meet you," Gladys said as she shook Helen's hand. "Volunteers make my life so much easier. Thanks for helping."

A woman impatiently rang the bell at the checkout desk, and Gladys ran back to help her.

"As you can see, we're short-staffed," Alexa said. She led Helen down a back hall. "The public restrooms are here." She opened the door marked WOMEN. The bathroom sinks were thick, old-fashioned porcelain ovals and the stall dividers were brownish marble. The only modern touch was two hot-air hand dryers.

"This is where I saw evidence of our so-called ghost," Alexa said. "I came in early one morning and water was splashed everywhere: the mirror, the floor and, especially, the sink. Someone took a sink shower. No one else was in the building yet. The rest of the staff and the volunteers hadn't arrived."

"Any other signs of a real human besides the missing hurricane kit and the flashlights?" Helen asked as they climbed the stairs to the second floor.

"Food disappears from the staff break room, but that could be a hungry staffer or volunteer. Last Tuesday, my chicken salad sandwich was missing from the fridge, but Blair might have thrown it away."

"Blair?" Helen said.

"Blair Hoagland, head of the Friends of the Library. She's compulsively neat and has this thing about food going bad."

"The Friends go into the staff break room?" Helen asked.

"The Friends are powerful at this library," Alexa said. "The money they make selling used books funds our Spanish, Hebrew and French language programs. They refurbished the chairs in the popular library and bought books, DVDs and furniture for our small children's section."

They were at the top of the stairs now, in a pleasant light-filled room with shelves of DVDs, more books and those inviting wicker wing chairs with the plump cushions. Helen wished she could curl up in one and read.

"We keep the reference books, cookbooks and biographies up here," Alexa said, and they walked through another arch into the next room.

"This was Flora's formal dining room. It's our computer room. We had to take out her Waterford chandelier, but we left the paintings."

Helen studied the pictures of nineteenth-century women watching the patrons on the computers. "The paintings look familiar," she said.

"They're by Mary Cassatt, the Impressionist painter. Flora Portland collected them. Actually, these are good copies. The originals were sold at Flora's death to provide part of the library's endowment."

A long, sturdy table with lions' paws held twelve computers. "The computers are free to everyone for thirty minutes. If there's a crowd, patrons have to sign up again. I may ask you to supervise when the library gets busy. Hello, Ted."

Ted was typing at a monitor, a fat, dirty-gray backpack at his side. His skin was baked brick red and Helen caught the sharp pong of body odor as she got close to him.

"Hi, Alexa," he said. "I'm applying for a grant to get into a group home."

"Let me know if I can help," she said. "I'll be happy to be a reference. This is Helen. She's a new volunteer."

"Hi," Ted said, and went back to work.

"The elevator is back this way," Alexa said, and Helen followed her down a dark hall with a maze of small rooms. "These were servants' quarters, closets and pantries in the original house." Helen saw a bewildering number of closed doors.

"We use them mostly for storage now, but we can't keep too much in them until the floors are reinforced. Ted is our homeless person. He's schizophrenic, but he's on medication. He spends his days here at the library and sleeps in a shelter at night."

"And you don't mind?" Helen asked.

"Why should I? He follows the rules."

"You have homeless people, even in ritzy Flora Park?" Helen said.

"We have homeless people everywhere in the United States," Alexa said. "We just don't see them." Helen recalled how she'd looked away when she saw a homeless woman pushing a shopping cart on upscale Las Olas Boulevard, and felt uneasy.

"You don't think he took that sink shower?" she asked.

"No. Ted always cleans up after himself—when he remembers," she said. "He'd never leave a mess."

"And you don't think Ted ate the food in the break room?"

"I've never seen him back here in the staff area," Alexa said.

The hall ended with two beige steel doors. "This is the Beast, our vintage fifties elevator," Alexa said.

The massive doors slid open and swallowed them. The elevator lurched, then groaned all the way to the first floor. Helen grabbed the railing.

"Relax," Alexa said. "The Beast is noisy, but it does the job."

The elevator jolted to a stop near the back door. "When you come tomorrow, please use the staff entrance," she said. "And check for foundlings. Ah, here's a box on the doorstep."

She opened the back door and picked up a musty cardboard box piled with tattered paperbacks and children's books with torn pages and chewed covers.

"Ew," Helen said. "Why would anyone donate trash to the library?"

"They've cleaned out the garage and can't bear to throw the books away," Alexa said.

"The Friends can't sell those," Helen said. "I wouldn't touch them."

"They'll probably get shipped to Better World Books," Alexa said. "They recycle and sell old books. These go into the Friends' intake room to be evaluated and sorted."

Behind the grand foyer and the popular library was another honeycomb of rooms. Alexa opened the first door and Helen was slapped with the overpowering stink of mold and decaying paper. Boxes of books were piled six feet high. Drab books with stained covers and curled paperbacks were stacked on a long table. Library carts labeled SELL and BETTER WORLD were lined up next to it. A covered plastic bin was labeled DISCARD.

"This is our intake room," she said. "The donated books are kept here away from the collection while the Friends of the Library check them for mold, silverfish, bedbugs or bodily fluids. The books that make the cut are moved to another FOL room."

"Are the Kingsley books in here?" Helen asked.

"No, I've had those moved down the hall into a locked room," Alexa said. "You'll have to sort through them. We'll have the only keys." She handed Helen a skeleton key.

"This isn't secure," Helen said. "Any skeleton key will fit those old locks. We should have a new lock on this door."

"It's the best I can do," Alexa said. "If Jared, our janitor, puts on a new lock, it will attract too much attention. I'll show you the Kingsley books tomorrow. Let's visit the staff area and then you can go. Blair's probably back there on break. I should warn you—she's quite annoyed with me because of you."

"Why?" Helen said. "What did I do?"

"She feels her friend Seraphina Ormond was entitled to your volunteer position."

"You can't say I'm temporary?"

"No, I explained why that would interfere with your investigation. I didn't want to give that position to Seraphina. She may be a Flora Park first family, but that doesn't mean she's entitled to a volunteer position."

"My volunteer job is that important?"

"To Seraphina," Alexa said. "Flora Park society revolves around this library, its programs and fund-raisers. It's the key to the local social life. But I still run this library. Seraphina is a fabulous fund-raiser. Her parties are the talk of society. Fund-raising is her great strength. But I want volunteers who will help the patrons, and Seraphina doesn't have the patience to deal with people."

"Will this decision cost you a good fund-raiser?" Helen said.

"I think I can bring her around," Alexa said, but her smile was uncertain. "Seraphina is hot-tempered, but she doesn't stay angry for long. She's a great believer in retail therapy. After she has a major disappointment, she usually goes out and buys something outrageous. Last time, after she had a big fight with her husband, she bought herself a beach house in Aruba and flew twelve of her closest friends to the island for a weeklong party. Then she was her old self again. My job will be to find her a fund-raiser that challenges her."

"What if she raised the money for the renovation of the Flora Park Library?" Helen said.

"That's what I've been thinking," Alexa said. "By the time the board makes its final decision, she'll have cooled down. I'll ask her to run the whole show. She'll be the toast of Flora Park.

"Meanwhile, be prepared for her to snap at you."

"Can't wait," Helen said.

"Our tour is nearly finished," Alexa said. "This is the staff break room. It used to be the old kitchen."

The huge, high-ceilinged room was painted a pleasant coral. An old Magic Chef stove squatted next to an industrial sink and a white fridge. A microwave sat on a cabinet. A round oak table cluttered with paper napkins, plastic utensils and piles of mustard and ketchup packs dominated the room.

Helen saw a thin, lanky woman in a drab green pantsuit sipping a mug of tea and reading *Masterpieces of the Frick Collection* at the table. She looked like Helen's idea of an old-school librarian: horn-rim glasses, no makeup and dark brown hair in a tight bun.

"Helen Hawthorne," Alexa said, her voice too cheerful, "let me introduce you to Blair Hoagland, head of the Friends of the Library. We couldn't function without our Friends' support."

Blair put down her tea and glared at Helen. "You're the new volunteer? What are your qualifications? Do you live in Flora Park? Have you ever been in this library?"

The attack surprised Helen, even after Alexa's warning, but she tried to remain cool. "I like to read and I'm a good worker," she said. "I'll do my best to help."

"Hmpf! We have a perfectly good candidate for your position," Blair said, "someone who's lived her whole life in Flora Park. But Alexa chose to ignore her."

"Blair, please," Alexa said. "We need our volunteers. If you have issues with my decisions, please discuss them with me."

"I already did," Blair said. "You told me Seraphina wasn't a people person. She's very good with people, but that doesn't mean she has to put up with cretins."

"Blair . . ." Helen heard the warning in Alexa's voice. Blair ignored it and rushed on.

"I know what you said, but I was there that day. The woman was standing in front of the *G* section and she asked Seraphina where she could find Sue Grafton's mystery *S Is for Silence*. It was right in front of her. Right in front! Seraphina said if she couldn't see how close the book was, she was too blind to read."

"We don't speak to our patrons that way," Alexa said.

"Seraphina tells it like it is," Blair said. "We could use some plain speaking around here. Instead, you brought in this stranger." She glared at Helen.

"Nice meeting you," Helen said. "It's getting late. I'll see you tomorrow, Alexa."

Helen forced herself to walk slowly down the corridor and out the back entrance. The garden was cool and shady, even in the late-afternoon sun.

As she trotted toward her PT Cruiser, a gleaming white Beemer roared into the lot. A woman with long blond hair unfolded herself from the driver's seat. She was a little taller than Helen, maybe six feet one, with square white teeth and a leathery tan. Her hot-pink-print Lilly Pulitzer top and white clam diggers looked odd on her lanky frame, but Helen knew they were the mark of old money.

"You're Helen Hawthorne," the woman said. It was an accusation.

"I am."

"I'm Seraphina Ormond," she said, her voice an upper-class bray. "You took my job. It's mine. I'm entitled to it. A nobody like you! You'll pay for this."

CHAPTER 8

. . . .

"Contract signed, sealed and delivered?" Phil asked as Helen entered her Coronado apartment. He was sipping a cold beer.

"With a threat," Helen said, kicking off her heels. Her blouse felt sticky and her pencil skirt was rumpled, but she was too tired to change them. She snuggled next to Phil on her turquoise couch.

"At a library?" he asked, putting down the sweating bottle. His smile vanished. Helen's partner was tense and alert. "Who threatened you?"

"Seraphina Ormond, the woman who wanted my volunteer job," Helen said. "She confronted me in the library parking lot. She said a nobody like me wouldn't get away with that."

"Whoa! That's extreme. Did she threaten you physically?"

"Her glare could have stripped off my skin, but she kept her fists balled up at her sides. She's an inch or so taller than me—and very angry."

"Maybe I should have a talk with Seraphina," he said.

"No need," Helen said. "I can take care of myself. She startled me, but she looked more silly than scary.

I've never been threatened before by anyone wearing a hot-pink top dotted with blue elephants."

"Sounds like you need a drink," Phil said. "How about a cold beer?"

"Ice water," she said. "I want to try Markos's mojitos at the sunset salute. Beer and rum don't mix."

Phil fixed Helen a frosty glass of water in her tiny kitchen, and handed it to her. "What else happened today?" he said.

She took a sip of cool water, then said, "Blair Hoagland, the chief Friend of the Library, wasn't very friendly. I stepped on a lot of toes when I took this library job."

"Do you want to tear up the contract?" he asked.

"Hell, no," Helen said. "I'm not going to be intimidated by ladies who lunch. This is a good case. I'm sticking with it."

"You're tough," he said, and kissed her.

"Damn right," Helen said. Thumbs, their six-toed cat, jumped up on the couch next to her. The big-pawed cat had golden green eyes and white fur with patches of brown tabby. She scratched his thick fur and said, "I don't get it, Phil. Library volunteer isn't even a paid position. Why are those two so upset?"

"It's about power, not money," Phil said. "You entered their little world and walked off with a coveted prize—and your family isn't even important."

"They are to me," she said.

Phil gave Helen a beery kiss and said, "Let me help you out of those sweaty clothes."

"So we can get sweatier?" Helen said, and kissed him back.

"Exercise is a good tension reliever," he said, kissing her neck.

"And I thought you were in my apartment because you wanted to see me," she said.

"I do," he said. "All of you. Bedroom's this way."

Forty minutes later, Helen was singing off-key in her shower. She and Phil had been married more than a year now, and they still had honeymoon sex. Once he started working undercover as a gardener at the Coakley mansion in Peerless Point, there wouldn't be time for love in the afternoon.

Helen and Phil had kept their separate one-bedroom apartments at the Coronado after their wedding. Helen's terrazzo-floored apartment was furnished with the original midcentury modern furniture. She had learned to appreciate its clean, quirky style. Now she thought the bright orange and turquoise colors fit the tropical landscape. She knew decorators would sigh over her turquoise Barcalounger and lamps shaped like nuclear reactors.

In the phone-booth-sized bathroom, she blow-dried her shoulder-length hair, added a slash of lipstick and slipped into a cool white cotton top and shorts.

Phil whistled when she came out in a cloud of steam. "You look hot," he said. "And that glow didn't come from makeup."

"Let's go meet Markos and his mojitos," Helen said.

"I'm sticking with beer," Phil said. "And I'm not looking forward to gluten-free tacos and kale chips."

"Where's your sense of adventure?" she said.

Phil pulled on an imaginary cowboy hat and drawled, "Back at the ranch, little lady. I like my red meat."

"Veggies won't kill you," Helen said, following him out the door.

"Beer is strictly vegetarian," Phil said. He hoisted his bottle. Then the two private eyes headed toward the Coronado pool.

The palm trees rustled in the cooler evening air. The turquoise pool was surrounded by waterfalls of purple bougainvillea. Margery waved and raised a tall glass brimming with lime wedges and mint. She was stretched out in a chaise, her summer lavender dress the same shade as the slanting shadows.

"Our landlady has a mojito," Helen said. "The sunset salute has started."

Black-haired Markos, the new tenant, had set up a bar on an umbrella table. He looked like a Chippendale with his bronze skin and tight white trunks.

Peggy, their elegant red-haired neighbor, was fanning herself with a handful of colorful cards, but Helen suspected Markos was causing the heat. Pete the Quaker parrot patrolled Peggy's shoulder and said, "Woo-hoo!"

Peggy raised an icy mojito topped with lime and mint.

"I'm celebrating," Peggy said. "I bought five scratch-off lottery tickets and just won a thousand dollars."

"A thousand bucks," Phil said. "Always wanted to live in a rich neighborhood."

"Congratulations!" Helen said. "You've been buying tickets forever. Is this your first win?"

"At long last," Peggy said. "Today, I'm basking in my success. Later, you're going to help me figure out how to spend it."

"We'll need liquid inspiration," Helen said. "Your mojitos look fabulous, Markos."

"Taste them and find out," he said, and handed her a glass. The cold burned Helen's hand, and she inhaled the summery scent of lime and mint.

"Phil? One for you?" Markos asked.

"Thanks, but I'll stick with beer," Phil said.

"Then have a kale chip and garlic dip made with Greek yogurt," Markos said. Helen scooped up one and popped it in her mouth, then tried the gluten-free taco.

"Yum," she said. "These are good. Phil?"

Phil gingerly tasted the snacks and said, "Interesting." Helen knew that was his polite way of saying he hated them. Markos smiled and showed his white teeth.

Helen sipped her mojito. The first taste was a cool explosion of sweet and citrus with the slightly bitter taste of rum. "Amazing," she said. "Is this an authentic Cuban recipe?"

"No, I learned it in bartending school," he said.

"Most bartenders hate making mojitos, but I love them. The key is muddling the lime, mint and sugar."

"What's muddling?" Peggy asked. She sounds a bit muddled herself, Helen thought.

"You crush the mint, lime and sugar in the bottom of the pitcher." He held up a fat glass pitcher. "With this muddler." Helen thought it looked like a small wooden baseball bat.

"It's an essential bar tool," Markos said. "I also have a plastic muddler, but the wooden one works better with mint."

"Why are you crushing sugar?" Helen asked.

"I use raw sugar—turbinado. Sugar doesn't dissolve well in cold drinks. You muddle the ingredients before you add the rum and club soda."

"That's a lot of work," Phil said.

"It's why bartenders hate to make mojitos, especially on a busy night."

"Sure is good," Peggy said, holding up her empty glass. "I'll take another. I don't have a long drive home." She slurred her last words.

Markos took her glass and pulled another frosted one out of a foam cooler.

"You could have used the old glass," Peggy said.

"Never!" Markos said as he built another mojito and carried it to Peggy. He held out a piece of fresh kale.

"Can Pete have this?" he asked.

"He can, but Pete usually likes fattening food like pecans and potato chips. He's on a diet. He's never had kale before. Try it."

"Kale is a nutritional powerhouse," Markos said. "I love it. A cup of chopped kale only has thirty-three calories."

Pete grabbed the green leaf and nibbled it. "Awk!" he said, and dropped it on the concrete.

"Pete!" Peggy said. "That's not polite." She'd finished her second mojito and tried to hide a yawn. "I think I've overcelebrated. Markos, I enjoyed meeting you and your mojitos. See you all. Think about ways I can spend that thousand dollars—and nothing boring like paying bills."

"Night!" Pete said as Peggy walked carefully to her apartment.

"Another drink, Helen?" Markos asked. He shook the pitcher of mojitos, and the ice, limes and mint did a seductive little dance.

"I'll take a rain check," Helen said. "I have to work tomorrow."

Despite the relaxing poolside drink, she felt a gnawing worry about going to the library tomorrow. Seraphina had been dead serious when she'd threatened Helen. She'd downplayed her fear to Phil.

What did Seraphina mean when she said Helen would pay for taking her job? Pay how? And would her friend Blair Hoagland help?

CHAPTER 9

"I have proof our ghost is alive," Alexa said. "I found it this morning."

The library director was waiting at the staff entrance when Helen arrived at ten o'clock.

"I'm glad you're on time," Alexa said. "The proof is in the women's restroom. I've hung an out-of-order sign on the door so the evidence won't be disturbed."

Helen followed the director down the hall to the restroom, Alexa's tailored coral suit a chic beacon.

"I came in early at seven thirty to get some work done," Alexa said, "and found this." She threw open the restroom door with a flourish. "There are four reasons why our ghost is a human. Do you see them?"

Helen wished Alexa wouldn't test her this morning. She woke up headachey and cotton-mouthed. Last night, Markos's mojitos had knocked her out after one round.

Helen smelled industrial disinfectant and saw a slightly dated public restroom.

"Jared Kobek, our janitor, told me he cleaned this restroom last night," Alexa prompted. "Then he locked up and went home."

"Did he set the library alarm?" Helen asked.

"We don't have one. This is a small community with few young people. The police watch it on their patrol rounds."

Helen studied the oval sinks and marble stalls and saw the first sign that something was off. "The toilet seat in the first stall is down, but the others are still up," she said. "Someone used this restroom after the janitor cleaned it."

"Good," Alexa said. "There's more."

Helen checked the sinks. They were white and shining. "I see water spots on the mirror over the second sink," she said.

"That's two," Alexa said. "I found two more."

Helen touched the soap dispenser. "No liquid soap splashed onto the sink," she said, "but there are lots of paper towels in the trash and some look damp."

"Excellent," Alexa said, a teacher ready to give her A-student a star. "One more."

Helen felt like she was looking at a "Find What's Out of Place" puzzle—and failing. She checked the toilets again, then the sink, the trash and the sealed window. Nothing stood out, except the room's exceptional cleanliness.

"Your cleaner is thorough," Helen said. "He gets in the corners."

"Jared Kobek is new. The board hired him after our old janitor retired. He does good work, but he's, well, bitter."

"He's mad at the library?" Helen asked. "Maybe he's the ghost."

"No, no, Jared is an excellent worker. But he expected to retire at seventy-two after Davis Kingsley died. I'm not spreading gossip. Jared tells everyone who'll listen. He worked for the Kingsleys for fifty years, and he thought old Mr. Kingsley would remember him in his will. Jared got a bequest of five thousand dollars, and he can't make ends meet on Social Security. He has no love for the Kingsley family, but he'd never make trouble for the library."

Jeez, Helen thought. You have to be connected to clean toilets in this town. No wonder Seraphina is so mad I took her volunteer job.

"I realized something else," Helen said. "Our ghost is a she. She used the women's restroom and put the seat down."

"Good," Alexa said. "Now we have a gender. I didn't think of that."

"She washed her hands and probably wiped the sink afterward," Helen said.

"A logical deduction," Alexa said.

Helen peered into the tall trash can. "But this can is half filled with paper towels. She didn't need that many to dry her hands and clean the sink."

"Also correct."

"This is a real brain basher," Helen said.

Or a rum deal, she thought. Thanks to that mojito, I'm not in mint condition this morning. Stop with the stupid puns, Sherlock. You have work to do.

She stared at the room again, looking for something else out of place. Toilets. Sinks. Floor. Trash can. Mirror. Window. Hand dryers.

"The dryer!" Helen said. "The one closest to the sink has its nozzle pointing up."

"You got it!" Alexa said, and clapped her hands. "I knew you were good. The ghost took a sink shower and dried her hair. That's why the nozzle was pointing up. I came into work earlier than usual and must have surprised her. She ran out of here before she could completely clean the restroom."

Helen leaned against the sink, wishing she could collapse from relief.

"You did good," Alexa said. "I already knew to check the hand dryer. Homeless people using the facilities are a problem for many libraries. We librarians talk about what to do and how to help them. Fortunately, our library's homeless man abides by the rules."

"Looks like you have a homeless woman who doesn't," Helen said. "Where is she now?"

"Vanished," Alexa said.

"Very ghostlike," Helen said.

"Yes. I know ghosts don't wash their hair, but after I discovered this, the silence was creepy. I didn't hear footsteps or doors slamming. I did a quick search of the library, but didn't find anyone. Paris, the library cat, followed me, but she didn't act spooked."

"You can't go by a cat's reaction," Helen said. "You shouldn't have searched the library alone. Next time, call the police. Your library has an intruder. She could still be here."

"If I called the police, the ghost would be in the *Flora Park Gazette* again," she said. "The paper's already made jokes at the library's expense."

"You could have called me," Helen said.

"And you're trained to handle an attacker?" Alexa raised one eyebrow.

Helen remembered her conversation with Phil last night, when she'd downplayed Seraphina Ormond's threat in the parking lot.

"At least there'd be two of us," Helen said. "Are there any patrons you don't recognize in the library now?"

"Let's go see," Alexa said. They walked through the popular library, the silvery lilac room with the lovely wicker wing chairs. Two gray-haired women were reading novels and the same white-haired man in the dark suit was reading the *New York Times*. Today he had the "Review of Books" section. The rest of the paper was carefully stacked on the table by his elbow.

"Did that man stay overnight?" Helen whispered.

"No, Mr. Ritter likes to savor the *Times*. He'll read it all week. Gladys usually referees at least one disagreement when someone tries to claim a section he's already read. And I know both those women."

Alexa smiled and waved at them.

Upstairs, a portly man in a tropical Tommy Bahama shirt was searching the DVDs. He grabbed six out of the *S* section and it collapsed into chaos.

Alexa sighed. "That's Ed," she said softly. "The bane of our shelvers. He always messes up the DVDs."

In the computer room, two older men and a business-woman were using the library computers.

"Let's take the Beast down to the break room," Alexa said. "Then I'll show you the Kingsley donations."

The old elevator shuddered and groaned on its slow journey to the first floor, but this time Helen ignored it. When the Beast crash-landed on the first floor, Helen followed Alexa into the high-ceilinged break room.

Alexa held up the coffeepot. "This coffee looks pretty fresh."

"I take mine black," Helen said.

Alexa poured them both a cup and they sat at the round table. "Most of our volunteers work about an hour a day," Alexa said. "We don't want to burn them out."

"I'm not really a volunteer," Helen said. "I need to be here most of the day. How about if I shelve books or do other library chores for an hour? Then I'll hole up in the room with the Kingsley books."

"That will work," Alexa said. "I know we've barely started today, but will you take your lunch at eleven, after you see the Kingsley room? Gladys can talk to you about shelving, and then you can grab some lunch. I'll watch the desk while she's at lunch."

"Sure," Helen said. She felt better after the caffeine infusion. She drained her cup and washed it. Then the two women strolled down the hall to the Kingsley collection room.

"Brace yourself," Alexa said, and unlocked th old door. "It's small."

Small was a relative term. The room was bigger than Helen's living room, but with a twelve-foot-high ceiling, it was almost as tall as it was wide. Dented beige metal bookshelves filled with dated bestsellers lined the walls, their dust jackets torn and faded.

"Nothing looks sadder than yesterday's sensation," Helen said.

She waded through a maze of dusty, taped cardboard boxes, all labeled KINGSLEY COLLECTION.

"How many books are in this room?" she asked.

"Roughly a thousand, in three hundred boxes," Alexa said. "As you can see, many of the boxes haven't been opened yet."

She patted a stack of books at least two feet long on a sturdy wooden table. "These have to be evaluated by experts. They could be valuable, depending on their condition."

On top of the stack was a pair of white cotton gloves. "If you want to examine them, wear these."

"Those are the biggest coffee table books I've ever seen," Helen said. "That one on the bottom could be a coffee table if it had legs."

"These are elephant folios," Alexa said. "The biggest book on the bottom is a double elephant.

"Nowadays, most coffee table books are at least twelve inches high and fourteen inches wide, but there's still a lot of variation. But publishers used to love these outsized books."

She patted the top folio. "This book is a first-edition elephant folio of Raphael's work called *Stanza della Segnatura* ~~art~~. And the old brown beauty with the gold ~~ver~~ is an elephant folio of Goethe's *Faust*."

~~t~~ in the skyscrapers of dusty book boxes.

~~here~~ to start," she said, and sneezed.

~~one~~ box at a time," Alexa said. "I had

~~ed~~ and stacked in numerical order,

~~undred.~~ The first ones are over here

"I'll get started right after lunch," she said.

As Alexa locked the heavy door with the skeleton key, Blair Hoagland came running down the hallway and planted herself in front of Alexa.

"That . . . that animal is in the popular library," she said, her face pale with rage. Her thin body shook like a sapling in a storm.

Helen's bleary brain searched for a title to go with the furious face. Blair Hoagland. The unhappy, powerful president of the Friends of the Library.

"You know I hate cats," Blair said, and Helen swore the woman hissed. Her brown-striped pantsuit made her look rather like a scrawny tabby cat. Blair's brown eyes were narrowed and her hands were clenched into fists. At least her claws weren't out.

"And you know that our library cat, Paris, is an important part of our image," Alexa said. "That calico is the spitting image of Flora Portland's pet."

Helen wondered if Alexa used that pun on purpose.

"Paris the cat is on our posters," Alexa said, "and she goes to our French language programs. That's why we call it 'Paris in the Afternoon.' Patrons love her."

"People are allergic to that stupid cat," Blair said.

"No one's complained," Alexa said. She seemed to grow calmer as Blair unraveled. Her dark brown hair was escaping its bun.

"She's sneaky!" Blair screeched, and Helen winced. She was still feeling the effects of last night's mojito. "She brushed up against my pantsuit. I've got cat hair on it."

"That means she likes you," Alexa said. "There's a pet hair remover in the break room."

"I don't like cats," Blair said again. "That animal is supposed to stay in the back rooms and staff areas."

"Paris is working," Alexa said. "She's an important part of our 'Go Green' program, which you enthusiastically support."

"I fail to see what a cat has to do with recycling," Blair said.

"She's our organic mouse catcher," Alexa said. Helen thought she saw a trace of a triumphant smile. "No harmful pesticide chemicals, remember? Now, if you'll excuse me, I have to return to briefing Ms. Hawthorne."

"You've spent an hour giving that woman a tour of this library. If you'd let Seraphina volunteer, she would have started immediately. She was born in this town and grew up in this library. She knows Flora Park. Instead, you've wasted an hour."

Finally, Blair looked Helen in the eye. "Exactly what are you doing next, Ms. Hawthorne?"

"Going to talk to someone pleasant," Helen said. "Good afternoon."

CHAPTER 10

. . . .

"Wanna see my tattoo?" Gladys asked.

"Depends on where it is," Helen said.

"Chill," Gladys said. "It's on my arm."

The librarian took off her yellow plaid suit jacket. She wore a short A-line skirt, white knee socks, and black suede double-strap Mary Janes.

"Your yellow suit looks familiar," Helen said. "I've seen it on someone famous."

"Iggy Azalea," Gladys said. "She wore it in the video of 'Fancy.'"

"The Australian rapper," Helen said. "Nice kicks. They're Miu Miu, right?"

"I like shoes," Gladys said. "Another weapon in the fight against the frumpy librarian stereotype."

An expensive weapon, Helen thought. Those shoes cost more than three hundred dollars.

"You get a lot of that?" Helen asked. "Stereotyping?"

"All the time. My name doesn't help. I loved Grandma Gladys, but when people see my name and my profession, they automatically think horn-rims, hair in a bun and dowdy clothes. My tat takes care of that."

Gladys rolled up her sleeve and showed off her biceps: a grinning skull balanced on a stack of books. The eyeless skull wore horn-rim glasses. Underneath, it read *Bad to the Bone* in Gothic type.

"That's one badass tattoo," Gladys said, admiring her body art.

"I love it," Helen said, and glanced at her watch. Ten forty. "I'm supposed to ask you for shelving tips before I go to lunch at eleven," she said.

"We keep the returned books on these carts behind the circulation desk," Gladys said. "I check them in and the computer automatically records the fines and lets me know which books are on hold. Right now, we have a run on the new John Grisham mystery. We only have twelve copies."

"How does a small library afford twelve copies of one bestselling hardcover?"

"We'll buy one or two for the collection and rent the rest from a company called McNaughton," Gladys said. "Then, when the demand is over, the books go back and we aren't stuck with all those extra copies. Lots of libraries use some version of this.

"We're a reading room, so we have some books filed by their Dewey Decimal System numbers, but most are fiction and biographies. They're filed in alphabetical order."

"What do you do about Mac and Mc?" Helen said. "Where would McNaughton go?"

"Under Mc. And Mac is Mac. We don't shelve them together. If I have time, I'll prep the books for you and put them in alpha order, so you can just roll the cart out on the floor and start working."

"This mahogany cart with the brass wheels is a beauty," Helen said.

"They don't make them like this anymore," Gladys said, "and that's a good thing. These old carts are tanks. Good for toning up the arms."

"They'll keep your tattooed biceps show-worthy," Helen said.

"Do you know there are tattooed librarian calendars?" Gladys said. "I'm not the only one fighting the stereotype."

"You sure don't look like Mrs. Brackensieck, my favorite librarian when I was in grade school," Helen said.

"What? Did she keep her hair in a bun and wear twinsets?" Gladys's question was a challenge.

"No, she looked like what she was—a soccer mom," Helen said. "She knew I loved to read and let me check out books that were way above my reading level. I grew up in a St. Louis suburb and used to hide out at the library when my parents weren't getting along.

"The bookmobile came to our neighborhood one Saturday a month, and it provided the best drama in town. We kids used to sit around in the bookmobile and see if anyone would check out The Book. This was the Midwest, so you have to remember two things about that time:

"First, people didn't fling around so many four-letter words back then. Not in public, anyway."

Gladys nodded her dark head. "I'm from a little town in Michigan," she said.

"Second, librarians checked out books with the old Dictaphone system."

"Before my time," Gladys said, "but I've heard of them. The librarians had to say the title out loud and it was recorded."

"Right," Helen said. "The reason we kids hung around the bookmobile was that about once a month, someone would check out The Book. It was an Erskine Caldwell novel. We'd watch the very proper librarian hesitate, take a deep breath, then do her duty and say the book's title out loud. In public. *The Bastard*."

Gladys laughed so loud Helen was afraid a patron would shush her.

"I think the bookmobile librarian wore a twinset," Helen said.

Gladys grinned. "Every once in a while, I see a librarian who dresses like the stereotype," she said, "but we come in all colors, sizes and flavors—Asian, Caucasian, Latino, African-American, men, women, straights and gays. When I started here, Hilary was the head librarian. She's African-American, the daughter of a board member's housekeeper. Hilary left for a better job in Chicago.

"So far, Flora Park hasn't hired a replacement. Instead, they gave me a small raise and now I'm doing the work of two people. I don't know when they're going to replace me—maybe never. Alexa fills in when I take a day off."

"Why won't Flora Park hire someone else?" Helen asked. "It's a rich town."

"And clueless when it comes to libraries," Gladys said. "One of the city council members popped in at eleven on a weekday morning and didn't see any patrons in the library. He assumed we didn't have anything to do. Another council member said we didn't need a library because everyone uses the Internet."

"There's a lot of misinformation on the Net," Helen said. "I need a librarian to help me find the right stuff. You're the real search engines."

"Tell the city council that," Gladys said. "I hear variations on that theme all the time: 'We have Google, so we don't need librarians.'

"Even our library board members are clueless. One donated a hardcover mystery and expected to see it on the shelf the next day. The book has to be cataloged and labeled, put in a special protective cover, given a card pocket, a category and a spine label. And it's even more complicated for big libraries. She was ticked because it took two weeks to get it in the library."

"What do you like to read?" Helen asked.

"Biographies and history. I really do believe that

George Santayana was right: 'Those who cannot remember the past are condemned to repeat it.'"

Helen decided to test her. "I think we're doomed to repeat the past no matter what," she said. "It's part of living. Most kids can't afford to go to Harvard and be misinformed."

"You read Kurt Vonnegut, too," Gladys said. "Good. I read and reread him, and Mark Twain and Edith Wharton and Maya Angelou and Charlotte Brontë and lots more. Plus I read the *Economist*. Their politics are usually wrong, but their features are clever. My pile of books to be read—Mount TBR—is threatening to take over my condo."

"Do you live in Flora Park?" Helen asked.

"No, too white and uptight," she said. "I have a condo in the Ocean Royale."

"Wow. Sweetest real estate in Lauderdale," Helen said. "You can afford that?"

"Barely," Gladys said. "I got a good price on a foreclosed studio with an ocean view. That's why I'm driving my mom's old white Chevy Impala. Talk about a librarian stereotype. Between buying books and clothes and the condo, I've run up some bills, so I'm stuck with the mom mobile for a while, until I can pay off my debts. Then I want to be the first librarian in South Florida to drive a red Ferrari."

"That will smash some stereotypes," Helen said. "Not to be rude, but who did you know in Flora Park to get this job?"

"You have this place figured out," Gladys said, and laughed. "My mom belonged to one of Flora Park's so-called first families. We spent the holidays here. You knew someone to get your job, Helen. Elizabeth pulled some strings."

Helen looked startled, but Gladys said, "I accidentally heard her talking with Alexa about hiring a private eye to recover that *Muddy Alligators* painting. Next thing I know, we have a new volunteer and Seraphina Ormond is pissed off.

"She doesn't know why you got the volunteer job she wanted, but she'll find out. Watch out for Blair. She's Seraphina's best bud, as well as head Friend of the Library."

"Anyone else I should watch out for?"

"Seraphina's college-age son, Ozzie. He wants to be a herpetologist."

"Do you date him?" Helen asked.

"Too young," she said. "And too weird. He invited me to his place so I could watch him feed live mice to his snakes."

"Ew," Helen said. "Disgusting. He keeps snakes?"

"Yeah," Gladys said. "Told me he likes the poisonous ones."

"I gather you didn't go to his place?"

"A date like him is really gonna make my heart beat faster," Gladys said. "Ozzie usually slithers in once or twice a week and puts the moves on me. He hits on any chick he sees, and you'll definitely be on his radar.

"Oh, hell, he's here," she said.

"Ozzie?" Helen asked.

"That's him. Short, stocky, bearded. The little sidewinder is making his way through the popular library. Brace yourself." She started typing on her computer.

Ozzie swaggered up to the desk with a white cardboard box and said, "Gladys, how's my favorite fantasy librarian?"

"Busy, Ozzie. As you can see," she said.

"Wanna go out?"

"No, Ozzie. If I'd spent six months in a lighthouse, I wouldn't go out with you."

He ignored the insult. "Who's your hot friend?" He looked Helen up and down. "Are you a librarian, too?"

"No," Helen said, her voice clipped. Up close, she saw his well-trimmed dark beard gave him the illusion of a chin, and his lips were rubbery pink.

"Wanna do lunch?" He rolled the word around as if savoring it.

"No, thanks. I'm out of circulation," Helen said. "I'm married."

"My favorite kind of woman," he said.

"Are you here for library business?" Gladys said.

"I just stopped by to see Aunt Blair."

"Then go see her," Gladys said. "She's in the back." She walked away from the desk and began alphabetizing books on the cart.

"Aunt Blair?" Helen said, when Ozzie slouched toward the back.

"It's a courtesy title," Gladys said. "The families have been friends forever."

"He's repellent," Helen said, and shuddered. "Does he really get dates with that routine?"

"Not with me. I think he just hits on women for practice. Ozzie dates impressionable high school girls who tell him how wonderful he is. I have to be nice to him because his mother's a big donor."

"You were nice?" Helen said.

"You should see me when I'm rude," Gladys said.

"I guess there are a lot of politics in a small library," Helen said.

"You wouldn't believe," Gladys said. "Some of the stories are better than those novels you're shelving. Actually, the crazy politics have improved since I came here six years ago.

"Back then, the library had a totally different Friends group, a bunch of rich old trouts who spent most of their time fighting over who should run the Friends. There was so much infighting they finally closed the bookstore."

She nodded toward the shelves of used books in the corner. "Nobody would sort the donated books or help sell them. They were too busy backstabbing one another.

"The bookstore is the Friends' primary fund-raising tool, and those old books bring in seventy or eighty thou a year. The Friends' power grabs didn't stop until the woman who ran the group died. Then, six months later, the Friends started up again, this time with a new president and a new, younger board. Blair is in charge, but I give her credit—she actually works, and so do the new Friends.

"I'd just missed the big Flora Park Library sex scandal, but I heard about it from Hilary. The library board censured the library director—an old white guy—because he was having an affair with a staff member. They both were married, to other people.

"The board found out because the two shared a room at a library convention. One of our librarians ratted them out. The director made that librarian's life so miserable she finally quit."

"Why would she tell the board?" Helen asked.

"She thought she'd get his job. Instead, she couldn't take the harassment. She left. Then the censured director quit, and we got Alexa. She's good."

"The old director must have been a heartbreaker," Helen said.

Gladys laughed. "He starred in the epic video *Flora Park, Flower of South Florida Libraries*. The dude was no hunk—short, bald, in his late fifties, and spoke like he had a mouth full of mashed potatoes."

"Wow," Helen said. "I had no idea there was so much going on between the covers."

"Lisa, the current board president, is a bit whack-a-doodle about ghosts," Gladys said, "but she's still an improvement. You're doing a good job as an undercover detective. It must be cool to be a private eye. You've really maintained your cover as a library volunteer. You don't look like a private eye."

"Now who's stereotyping?" Helen asked.

CHAPTER 11

H elen smelled the books before she saw them. She'd passed a fragrant jasmine vine near the library's staff entrance, when she caught the stink of mold and rotting paper.

The half-crushed cardboard box was abandoned on the staff steps. More worthless books for the Friends of the Library, she thought. Do people really think dumping trash here helps the library?

Might as well take it inside. It's part of my new job.

Helen was in a better mood after her encounter with Blair Hoagland. Her lively conversation with Gladys had lightened her outlook. She'd had a sandwich and a soda, and bought treats for Paris, the library cat. It was nearly noon and she was ready to tackle the Kingsley collection.

The abandoned box was piled with tattered medical books and outdated dictionaries. She picked it up gingerly and heard a tiny buzz.

Did someone leave a cell phone in the box? she wondered.

Helen tried not to hold the moldy box close to her

blouse, especially after Alexa said donated books might be infested with silverfish and bedbugs. But the box was too heavy to hold at arm's length. At least it was a short walk to the Friends' intake room.

The top book was thicker than a brick and weighed maybe six pounds. The stained blue cover had a naked skull under the title *Color Atlas of Anatomy: A Photographic Study of the Human Body.*

Helen's stomach flopped like a beached fish. The atlas had full-color photos of real dissected dead bodies. She was definitely not opening that book. The others could have been doorstops. Moldy, smelly doorstops.

She staggered into the Friends' intake room, dropped the box on the table and heard that buzz again.

It has to be a cell phone, she decided. Maybe a doctor's phone. What if someone's calling with a medical emergency? She grabbed the tattered atlas by the corner and saw movement.

Something long, swift and dark darted out and attacked the book. A rat? No, a snake!

Helen screamed and slammed the heavy atlas down on the snake, crushing it, then hit the snake again and again until its midsection was a bloody pulp. She was still hammering the dead snake when Alexa ran in, followed by Blair Hoagland.

"Helen! What on earth!" Alexa said. "I heard you screaming in my office."

"A snake," Helen said, her voice shaking. "I picked up these books at the staff entrance and there was a snake in the box. A live snake."

"Not anymore," Alexa said, looking at the smashed snake. "It's definitely dead."

Helen steeled herself to examine the bloody mess in the book box, then shuddered. "I'm sorry," she said. "I've ruined the books."

"We couldn't have used them anyway," Blair said. "They were infested with silverfish."

"You aren't hurt, are you?" Alexa asked.

"No," Helen said, still breathing hard. "The snake didn't bite me." She gathered her courage and looked at the dead snake again. She hated snakes, and this was no harmless garter snake. The long, yellow fangs were bared. The grayish body was thicker than a garden hose and blotched with dark spots. On its tail was a spike. No, not a spike.

"Is that a rattle on the snake's tail?" she asked, her voice high and thin.

Alexa peered into the box. "Yes," she said. "I believe that's a rattlesnake."

"Do we have rattlers in Florida?" Helen asked.

"You're asking the right person," Alexa said. "I used to work the reference desk, answering patrons' questions. We don't get as many reference questions these days, thanks to the Internet. Follow me to my office and we'll look up Florida snakes on my computer."

"Wait!" Blair said. "What about this disgusting snake? Who's going to remove it?"

"Ask Jared," Alexa said. "We'll be back shortly."

Helen sank into the leather barrel chair in Alexa's office. The room's soothing quiet calmed her while Alexa clacked on her keyboard. Something about that snake incident nagged at her. Something someone said. Alexa? No, it was . . .

"I've found your snake on a Florida wildlife Web site," Alexa said, and Helen saw the hunter's light in the librarian's eyes. She enjoyed tracking down information. "Take a look. It's a pygmy rattlesnake."

Helen hurried over to the computer screen and saw the snake's photo. Coiled on a pile of leaves, heavy-bodied and evil, the rattlesnake was so lifelike Helen backed away.

"That's it," she said.

"The site says the pygmy rattlesnake is 'the most commonly encountered venomous snake in urbanized areas, often in gardens or brush piles,'" Alexa said. "Just like Adam and Eve, we have a snake in our garden."

Snake. Garden. Helen suddenly remembered what had been nagging at her. "Maybe you have a snake in the grass," she said. "When I apologized for ruining the books, Blair said, *We couldn't have used them anyway. They were infested with silverfish.*"

"I heard that," Alexa said.

"How did she know the books had silverfish?" Helen said. "That box was abandoned at the employee entrance. I took an early lunch, came back and found it. Did anyone else go out that entrance?"

"I don't think so," she said. "Our lunch hours start at noon and we've been busy."

"Blair left that snake there for me," Helen said.

"You're upset, Helen," Alexa said. "I admit Blair wasn't very welcoming, but she wouldn't try to harm you."

"Murder me," Helen said. "You can die from snake venom."

"Blair wouldn't do that," Alexa said. "The Friends of the Library are valuable contributors to our library. We need them and we need Blair. I admit she can be difficult, but a killer? Never."

The library director absently tugged on her distinctive lock of white hair. Alexa looked so distressed, Helen said, "You know her better than I do."

I have a ghost to find, she thought. I'll be extra careful around Blair, that's all.

There was a knock on the door and a tall, thin woman with lank gray-blond hair poked her head in. "Alexa, may I speak with you, please?" she said.

"Ah, Lisa," Alexa said. "Helen Hawthorne, meet Lisa Jackson Hamilton, president of our library board. Helen is our new volunteer, Lisa."

Alexa's smile seems forced, Helen thought. Is it the strain of finding that snake, or is Lisa another difficult person?

"Pleased to meet you," Lisa said, and held out a bony white hand with short, polish-free nails.

Lisa looked like a certain kind of old-money type Helen had seen in St. Louis. She was thin and faded, with fine bones and an aristocratic air. At twenty, she would have been dazzling, with a creamy complexion and pale shining hair. Three generations ago, her debutante portrait would have graced the family drawing room.

Lisa had aged, but it was more than that. Something had sucked out her spirit and left this lifeless shell with the no-color hair.

Helen stood up to greet her. "I'll go back to work so you two can talk," she said.

"No, no, I'd like you to stay," Lisa said. "I'll need your participation, too, tonight."

"Tonight?" Alexa said. "What's tonight?" She sounded suspicious.

Yep, Helen thought. Lisa is definitely a thorn in the director's side.

"I want to hold a séance to contact the ghost of Flora Portland," Lisa said.

Alexa frowned.

"I know you believe the library isn't haunted," Lisa said quickly, "but I disagree. I can feel Flora's essence in this building. She is troubled and restless."

Alexa's jaw was clenched. Helen fought to keep hers from dropping. Lisa didn't look like a flake. She was a fiftysomething woman in a well-cut lavender suit.

"Hear me out," Lisa said softly, quickly. "The séance won't cost the library anything. I have a sensitive medium. Melisandra is volunteering her services. I need the people who are here today to form the circle to communicate with Flora. I need you, of course, Alexa, and the new janitor, Jared."

"Jared?" Alexa said. One word seemed to be all she could manage.

"He worked for the Kingsleys and they were friends of the Portlands."

"Jared didn't know Flora Portland and he's angry that Davis Kingsley didn't give him a more generous bequest."

"Even better," Lisa said. "Spirits are attracted to strong emotions. I'll need Blair because she's head of the Friends of the Library, and you, too, Helen. You have a good aura."

"I do?" Helen said.

"I can see it pulsing. It's a lovely shade of indigo," Lisa said. "You are a person of honesty, inner peace and love."

Good thing she wasn't around when I was bashing that rattlesnake, Helen thought.

"I'm essential to the séance because I saw Flora," Lisa said.

No, you *believe* you saw Flora, Helen thought. Instead, you hit an innocent patron in a lavender dress.

"I did see Flora," Lisa said, as if she'd read Helen's mind. "Ghosts can be quite playful."

"That wasn't playful," Alexa said. "Our patron needed stitches. We'll be lucky if she doesn't sue."

"That's why Flora's spirit needs to rest, don't you see?" Lisa's voice was insistent. "She doesn't want to hurt anyone. She's trying to communicate. Melisandra can help reach her and then we'll know what she's trying to say."

Helen remembered Alexa telling her that the Flora Park Library might have to be abandoned and a new one built: *Our board president said that Flora would turn over in her grave.*

"Oh, and one more person," Lisa said. "I saw her working at the checkout desk. Gladys Gillman, our librarian."

"I'll ask her if she can stay," Alexa said.

"I already did. She said she would," Lisa said. "I have everything set for nine o'clock tonight. Please, Alexa. It won't cost anything but a little time. I even found someone to watch Mother.

"My mother is indisposed," she said to Helen.

"I—" Alexa began, and Helen could tell by her expression she was going to refuse.

"I think it's a wonderful idea," Helen said, quickly. "Please forgive me for speaking out of turn, but a séance will be a huge help in getting to the bottom of this mystery."

"Exactly," Lisa said, and showed her tiny white teeth. "Flora is upset by the proposed changes in her library. We need to find out her wishes, and then I promise she'll stop haunting this building."

And you'll have the ammunition you need to get the library you want, Helen thought.

CHAPTER 12

• •

"It's bad enough I had to get rid of the damned dead rattlesnake," Jared said. "But Blair didn't even thank me."

The library janitor was pacing the dusty Kingsley collection room. He'd helped Helen shift the tallest box tower, so she could examine the elephant folios on the table.

Jared might be seventy-two, but he was tough, wiry and strong, she thought. His liver-spotted arms were knotted with muscle.

"Now I'm supposed to haul a G-D mahogany table from upstairs and set it up under Flora's portrait in the lobby. That table weighs a ton."

"I can help you with that," Helen said.

"Ha! I'm not so weak I need help from a woman," he said, and scratched the scraps of white hair on his balding head. "I appreciate the offer, though." His grin showed square yellow teeth.

Jared isn't too old to flirt, Helen thought.

"Then, after I set up that table and seven chairs, I'm supposed to stick around until nine o'clock for a séance.

I won't do it. Don't believe in ghosts and hoodoo. It's not right and it's not my job."

Helen needed Jared at the séance. "I do hope you'll stay," she said. "I think this medium is a fraud and I'd like to have a smart observer."

"I love flattery," he said. "But I work for money, not promises."

He didn't bother to smile. So much for my irresistible charm, Helen thought.

"I made that mistake once," Jared said, "and it was a big one. I believed that old buzzard Davis Kingsley when he said I was his best worker and he'd take care of me in his will. You know what he left me? A lousy five thousand bucks. When he was young, that was a lot of money, but it won't buy nothing now. My brother owns a repair shop and I wanted to work as a grease monkey, but he couldn't afford to take me on. That's how I wound up a janitor when I should be retired."

"Maybe I can get you some overtime," Helen said. "May I ask what you make?"

"Minimum wage," he said.

That's $8.05 an hour in Florida, Helen thought. She'd worked enough minimum wage jobs to know.

"What if you were paid nine dollars an hour overtime?" she said. "In cash?"

"Now, that would be real sweet," he said. "I get off work at six."

"Six to eleven is five hours. Let's say fifty dollars even," Helen said. "That would include an hour afterward to put away the table and chairs, plus a small bonus. I'll ask Alexa for the money, so you won't have to."

"Now, that's right nice of you," he said. "You know about working for a living. A day's work would kill most people here. Alexa's okay, but the others don't know a damn thing about the real world.

"Like that Blair. Told me to drop that dead rattlesnake in the Dumpster, like I was emptying a wastebasket. You don't do that."

"Why not?" Helen asked.

"Because it can still bite. Even a rattlesnake head that was chopped off its body can nail you. I learned that on my granddaddy's ranch in Ocala."

"That's Florida horse country," Helen said.

"See? You know things. These horses' rear ends think horses come from Kentucky, but Florida could put them to shame. We had our share of rattlesnakes on the ranch.

"My granddaddy taught me how to cut off a rattler's head with a shovel, and then the old man gave me a demonstration of what a dead rattler can do, using his cowboy hat. He showed me that a cut-off snake head could still bite all the way through the hat, too. Evil creatures, snakes."

"I won't argue with you on that," Helen said. "What did you do with the snake I killed?"

"Dropped it in an old paint can on my workbench. It will stay there until it's good and dead. Ted, our homeless man, goes through our Dumpster looking for things. Can't risk him getting hurt.

"Lisa, the board president, is just plain silly with her ghost, but at least she offered to buy us all dinner. She's having it delivered at seven."

"That's nice," Helen said.

"Not for me. It's Chinese. Hash with weird gravy. I don't eat what I can't pronounce. Who knows what those foreigners are chopping up? Could be cats, for all I know."

Paris, the library cat, appeared on cue. The calico jumped up on the elephant folio table, and Jared absently scratched her ears. Paris had one black ear, one pale brown ear, yellow eyes and a round, sweet face.

"Can't risk having you served as dinner, can we, girl?" Jared said.

The cat twirled on the tabletop and bumped Jared's hand with her head.

Helen reached for the bag of cat treats and put a handful on the floor. Paris abandoned Jared and crunched the treats.

"See?" Jared said. "You're naturally thoughtful. You understand that even with overtime, I'm gonna lose money. I'll have to buy dinner."

Helen felt her initial admiration for Jared seeping away, but she still needed an ally. "What if I get us a couple of burgers for dinner?" she said.

"With cheese fries?" he asked. "You got yourself a deal." He grinned.

Helen smiled back at the old con artist.

"I'll leave you to your work," he said.

After Jared left, Helen called Phil. "You sound tired," she said.

"I was taking a nap," he said. "This was my first day undercover as a gardener at the Coakley estate. It's hot and I'm sunburned."

"I'm sorry, sweetheart," Helen said. "You go back to sleep. Did you find out who took the Coakleys' ruby necklace and golf cart?"

"I'm getting closer," he said. "How's your investigation? What do you need?"

Helen didn't mention the snake. "I'm going to have to be at the library until after eleven o'clock tonight. The board president wants to hold a séance and talk to Flora Portland."

"What a waste of time," Phil said.

"Maybe not," Helen said. "I want to see if anyone connected with the library is involved in this ghost hoax. Jared the janitor is helping me. He didn't want to stay, but I said the library would pay his overtime. They won't, but I'll give him fifty bucks cash and charge it to expenses. I need to get cash and two burgers for dinner."

"I'll deliver the burgers and cash to the library," Phil said. "And don't say I need my sleep."

"Thanks," Helen said. "I'll meet you at the staff entrance at seven. Don't forget Jared's cheese fries. Would you bring me a fresh blouse, please? Mine is dusty."

Helen spent the rest of the afternoon searching the Kingsley collection. Paris abandoned her mousing duties to curl up at Helen's feet and eat treats.

Helen thought the elephant folios would be the logical place to stash a watercolor, but they held nothing. By six fifty that night, she was ready for dinner. Her back and arms ached and she felt grubby. She washed the grime off her face and hands in the restroom.

Phil met her at the staff entrance with a kiss, a clean blouse and the carryout. "You're sunburned," she said, and hugged him. He winced in pain. "I can't wait to find out what you learned today. Thanks for everything."

Helen and Jared sat in the Kingsley book room, munching burgers.

"You find the painting that crazy old coot left in those old books?" he asked, squeezing more ketchup on his burger. "Don't look so surprised. I heard the family talking to Alexa. I can keep it under my hat."

Helen looked doubtfully at his ragged Miami Heat cap. It had more holes than a colander.

"Good burger," he said.

"I've been through thirty-two boxes of books, mostly mysteries," Helen said, "and all I've found is a paid tax bill from 1967."

"Only two hundred sixty-eight boxes to go," he said.

"Give or take a box," she said, giving Paris a bit of her burger.

"You feed her like that and she'll quit catching mice," he said. "Blair will get rid of her for sure."

"Paris is part of the library's image," Helen said. "Does she really look like Flora Portland's cat?"

"Don't look at me," Jared said. "Flora died before I was born. But there's a photo in the hall that shows Flora as an old woman with her cat. It's hand-colored and the cat looks just like this one. They say Flora named the cat Paris because that's where she and Lucian lived when they were first married. This Paris turned up in the parking lot one day and made herself useful catching mice."

He checked his watch. "One hour till showtime," he said. "I've got the lobby set up for the séance tonight. The medium wanted that table because Flora touched it."

"She lived in this whole building," Helen said.

"But it's been remodeled. The medium wants an object Flora personally touched, and the séance has to be at a round table. The medium even sent a pale purple tablecloth and seven red candles in brass holders for this shindig." He snorted. "She said the light cloth would attract friendly spirits. What a fraud. Even her name belongs to a fraud—Melisandra."

"What do you bet she wears a turban?" Helen said.

"We'll find out in an hour," Jared said.

CHAPTER 13

· ·

I don't believe in ghosts, Helen thought as she carefully slit open another carton of the Kingsley books with a box cutter. But I don't like dabbling in the supernatural. It unleashes strange forces. I wish I didn't have to go to that séance tonight, but I wanted it.

The Kingsley collection room was lit by a single bare bulb, and the ancient water leak on the faded flowered wallpaper looked like a map of Asia. The remodeling had never reached back here.

Helen heard a *crack!* and ran out into the dingy back hall. Nothing.

You have boxes to empty, she thought.

Helen opened another six book boxes after her burger with Jared, and found nothing except a used tissue. Paris prowled the collection, jumping from box to box. When the calico toppled a stack near the door, Helen jumped.

Merr! the cat said.

Helen scratched the calico's ears, and said, "I thought cats were supposed to be graceful. What time is it?" She checked her watch: eight forty-five. "Showtime, cat," she said. She slipped on the fresh blouse Phil had brought her, locked the door and headed for the séance. Paris disappeared down the hall.

Helen had just entered the library lobby when a brunette in a severe charcoal pantsuit knocked on the front door. Alexa unlocked it, while the séance attendees wandered around the lobby. Helen stayed in the shadows and watched the scene like a play.

"I'm Melisandra," the dark-haired woman said. "The medium."

"Alexa Andrews, Flora Park Library director." The two women shook hands like business rivals in a boardroom.

Melisandra, slim, short-haired and stylish, could have been a bank president. The library director, with her fine-boned face and exotic white-streaked hair, looked more like Helen's idea of a medium. All Alexa needed was a gypsy skirt and a turban, Helen decided.

"You already know Lisa, our board president," Alexa said.

"Lisa told me about you," the medium said.

I'll bet, Helen thought. I'll also bet she told you what to say.

Alexa introduced the other participants: Blair Hoagland looked ready to go into a swoon. Gladys Gillman, the hot librarian in the cool yellow suit, said, "This is awesome. I've always wanted to go to a séance."

"Are you a spiritualist, Ms. Gillman?" Melisandra asked.

"I have an open mind," she said.

"That's all I ask," Melisandra said.

Jared silently shook the medium's hand as if she'd handed him a rotten fish.

"And this is Helen Hawthorne, our newest volunteer," Alexa said.

Helen stepped out of the shadows.

"You're more than a library volunteer," Melisandra said.

Helen looked startled, then figured Melisandra must have heard about Coronado Investigations on TV after she and Phil had cracked a tough case. She'd read that smart mediums had good memories and scoured the papers and the Internet for information.

Helen was relieved that the other attendees seemed puzzled by the remark.

Melisandra cocked her head slightly and smiled. "What?" she said. "You seem surprised. Did you think I'd wear a turban, Ms. Hawthorne?"

Helen turned red with embarrassment.

"I'm not a mind reader," Melisandra said, "but I know what skeptics think of mediums."

I'd better not underestimate this woman, Helen thought.

"Now it's almost nine o'clock," Melisandra said. "Let's get ready, shall we? Take a bathroom break if you need to, and please turn off your cell phones."

She marched briskly to the round table under the portrait of Flora Portland. The table was covered with a long, fringed lavender cloth. Seven heavy, oak, lion-pawed chairs surrounded the table. At each place was a thick, red, six-inch-tall candle in a brass holder.

Melisandra pulled a purple-handled barbecue lighter from her briefcase and lit the candles. Next, she removed a small alabaster bowl, filled it with pink pebbles and placed it in the center of the table.

"Himalayan sea salt," she said. "From the highest mountains in the world. Salt is a ritual purifier.

"We have seven people here tonight, a good number. But the conditions are not optimal. I sense negative energy, but we will overcome it with love and strength.

"Blair and Lisa, I need you seated at my left and right hands. Ms. Hawthorne, I'd like you next to Lisa. Alexa, please sit next to Blair."

Jared tried to take the chair next to Helen, but Melisandra said, "No, no, I need Gladys in that chair. The male force is stronger than the female."

Sexism in the spirit world? Helen wondered.

"Jared, you'll sit next to Alexa. I'm still linking two negative forces, but I will draw strength from Blair and Lisa, and neutral Gladys will help counteract the two skeptics. I will say again, these conditions are not optimal, but this is the best I can do."

Paris the cat trotted into the lobby, jumped on the table and settled in next to Helen. *Merp!* the calico said.

"Get that cat out of here," Blair said. "She'll ruin everything."

"Pets don't disrupt spirit activity," Melisandra said. "This one may help. She looks exactly like Flora Portland's animal companion."

"How did you know?" Lisa said. The library board president looked impressed by the pronouncement.

Because our medium saw the colorized photo in the hall, Helen thought. Across the table, Jared rolled his eyes at her.

"That's why we named this cat Paris," Gladys said. "She showed up at the library one day and she's stayed ever since, catching mice for us."

"Excellent," Melisandra said. "She's part of the spirit of the house." She took a flat, round CD player from her briefcase, and said, "I'll play something relaxing while we discuss the goals of this spirit encounter."

Helen heard the sort of semi-Asian music that reminded her of massage therapy.

Finally, the medium brought out a pocket-sized video recorder and set it up on a stand behind Jared.

"I want to record this session," she said, "for reasons I will explain. Please turn off all the other lights and dim the chandelier to the lowest level. I want it just light enough so I can see your faces."

Alexa got up, turned off the lights and turned down the sparkling chandelier until it looked like a distant burned-out sun.

In the flickering candlelight, the seven faces were Halloween masks. Flora seemed to dance in her portrait.

Paris sat on the table by Helen, ears back, yellow eyes alert.

"Now, I need you to grasp each other's hands to raise the energy level," the medium said. Lisa placed her dry, skeleton hand on top of Helen's. Helen reached for Gladys's small hand with the cheerful green nails. That stylish touch helped counteract Helen's case of the creeps.

"We will take a moment to say a private prayer," the medium said.

Helen prayed this séance wouldn't take all night. Lisa's bony hand was tight with tension.

"We are here this evening to call upon the spirit of Flora Portland and end her restless wanderings on the earthly plane," Melisandra said. As she talked, her voice grew lower and husky, almost hypnotic.

"I am an experienced conducting medium. Flora will speak through me. Do not be alarmed by what you see when I invite her to talk. My body may contort and move as my spirit is liberated and leaves my body, and Flora's spirit enters my physical form.

"Although it looks like a death struggle, I will be going into a deep trance. When I reach the full trance stage, I will be unaware of what the spirit is saying or doing. Hence, the video camera to record this session.

"Are we ready?"

A chorus of yeses and nods. *Merp!* Paris said. Helen noticed the soothing music had stopped.

"Good. Let's begin." Melisandra intoned, "Flora Portland, we call upon you to visit us in your beloved earthly home and tell us what is troubling your spirit. Come to us, Flora. Come."

Silence. Helen heard the *plop* of wax dripping from the seven candles. Someone's stomach gurgled.

Then Melisandra moaned and threw her head back. Her body bucked, her back arched and her head whipped from side to side, but she never let go of Blair's and Lisa's hands. The medium squeezed them so hard their fingertips were white, but neither woman said anything.

Helen thought the performance was most unspiritual, more like an amateur porno film than a spirit session.

The medium groaned as if she were in labor, and her eyes rolled back in her head. Paris jumped into Helen's lap and buried her head in Helen's blouse. Helen wanted to comfort the cat, but didn't dare break the circle.

Suddenly Melisandra sat up, shoulders straight, head cocked at the same angle as Flora's in the portrait, as if she were wearing that jaunty lavender hat. But the medium's eyes seemed sightless in the dim light.

"You've called me from my heavenly home." Helen heard a different voice now, lighter, with an upper-class lockjaw accent, coming from Melisandra.

"I feel cold," gullible Lisa said, and shivered dramatically. "Flora's spirit is with us." Helen heard the awe in her voice—and the air conditioner switching on.

The medium's blank eyes turned toward Helen, who was sheltering the calico in her lap. The playful voice sounded eerie. "Is that my cat, Paris?" the medium said. "No, of course not. Paris is with me. It's one of her descendants, continuing her work of caring for the library." Her blank smile was terrifying.

"I named her Paris because of the romantic honeymoon Lucian and I had in the City of Light. We lived there happily for so many years. Lucian is with me now." The medium sighed. "Now we are in the light forever.

"We never had any children, except for this library, my spiritual child, my life's work. I've left my eternal rest because my child is in danger. I need you to save it. You must save my precious baby."

Tears ran down the medium's face.

"She's crying," Lisa said. She sounded like she might weep with her.

"You understand my heartbreak," the medium said, and stared at Lisa with unseeing eyes.

"She touched my arm," Lisa shrieked. "I felt it. Her hand is cold."

Helen saw that the medium was still clutching Lisa's

hand. She also felt the long, heavy tablecloth move slightly.

"I know you are burdened with earthly concerns," the medium said, "but you must find the money to save my baby. My life cannot be in vain."

The medium's heartrending howls raised the hair on Helen's neck. Paris jumped out of her lap and ran out of the room. Helen wished she could join the cat.

"Save her! Save her, please! I beg you, so I can rest again!" Melisandra's eyes rolled crazily and she slumped back against her chair.

"She's fainted," Blair said.

"Don't let go of her hand," Lisa said. "If you break the circle, the evil ones will join us. Remember Melisandra's warning. A séance can be traumatic for a conducting medium. We must give her spirit time to return to her body. She will soon be with us."

Helen studied the faces in the candlelit circle. Gladys looked as if she had a front-row seat at a riveting play. Lisa was concerned, and so tired she looked like a ghost herself. Blair was awed and alert. Alexa seemed skeptical and Jared looked bored.

The candle in front of Melisandra suddenly snuffed itself out. The medium's eyelids fluttered and she moaned softly. Then she sat up, ran her fingers through her well-cut dark hair and said, "Hello. Did anything happen?"

"Oh, yes," Lisa said. "Flora was here and revealed her true wishes."

"Good," the medium said. "I'll review the tape later. Right now, I'd like to close the session with a prayer. Continue to hold hands, please."

Melisandra joined hands again with Blair and Lisa.

"Thank you, Flora, for visiting us tonight from the spirit world," she intoned. "May you now be free from worldly cares, and may we come to know the truth about tonight."

"Amen," Helen said.

CHAPTER 14

. . . .

Helen came home from the séance at midnight. Phil was reading in bed, his face and arms red as raw steak.

"Phil!" she cried. "You're burned even worse than I realized." She dropped her packages and ran to him.

He raised a fat brown bottle of Jamaican Red Stripe beer to his sunburned face and said, "The label is almost the same color as my nose."

"Did you wear sunscreen?"

"Of course."

"What about a hat?"

"My official Clapton Crossroads hat." He pointed to the sweaty-damp ball cap hanging on a bedroom chair.

Helen gently turned his head. "That doesn't protect your neck," she said. The back of his neck was seared a painful deep red, except for an inch-wide white spot his ponytail must have covered.

She hissed in sympathy and said, "Your neck is so red."

"What's wrong with red necks, darlin'?" he drawled.

"Why didn't you wear your hair down to protect your neck?"

"Too hot, sweaty, and dangerous around machinery," he said.

Helen pulled a wide-brimmed straw hat from a bag. "I stopped by a late-night tourist shop and bought you this."

"Nice," he said. He smiled, and his burned face looked like it might crack. Helen hurt looking at him.

"The other gardeners, Charlee and John—that's Carlos and Juan—wear straw hats, but not as good as this one."

He grabbed her wrist and pulled her close. "Come here," he said, kissing her lips. "You worry too much."

She put her arms around his neck and felt him wince. "I also have a topical steroid cream and an aloe vera lotion," she said.

"I love it when you talk dirty," he said.

"You have a fever," she said.

"Because you're so hot. Come to bed, Nurse. You can take care of this burning sensation."

"I don't want to hurt you," Helen said.

"Oh, you'll make me feel much better," he said, unbuttoning her blouse. For a man who looked parboiled, he moved with enthusiasm.

Afterward, when they were sprawled on the sheets, Helen hugged him carefully, her arms wrapped around the unburned parts of his chest. The contrast between his pale skin and seared face and arms was dramatic.

"Did you learn anything today?" Helen said. "I'd hate to have you suffer for nothing."

"It was worth sacrificing some of my hide," he said. "The cook, Ana, brought us cookies and cold drinks when we took our morning break in the kitchen."

"The Coakleys let the help eat in the kitchen?" Helen said.

"The staff kitchen, where Ana does the actual cooking, not the show kitchen in the front of the house. Ana's English is excellent, better than Charlee's. John speaks some English, but understands more. I suspect the two men may be illegal, but it's not polite to ask.

"Ana asked me why a gringo was doing yard work. I said I was on probation for speeding, and they relaxed a bit. I was outside the law—but not seriously. They thought getting arrested for speeding was funny. The real ice-breaker was when Charlee said I was a good worker."

"A high compliment in that world," Helen said.

"The highest," Phil said. "I praised Ana's cookies—they were delicious. She said the Coakleys never said anything good about her cooking."

"Ana sounds like a flirt," Helen said. "It's a good thing I've met her. She's at least fifty."

"With a husband and four kids. Even if she was twenty and hot, you're still sizzling." He kissed the top of her head.

"Ana is old-school Mexican," Phil said, "and none of the Coakleys were home, so she fixed us a traditional *la comida,* a big lunch. We had ceviche, salad, empanadas and *carne en su jugo*—that's meat and beans, like a stew—and hot tortillas. Ana made flan for dessert. Sure beat that health food Markos gave us the other night.

"After lunch, Ana relaxed and was ready to gossip. I asked about Bree Coakley's twenty-first birthday party. Said I'd read about it in the newspaper. Boy, did Ana give me an earful.

"The family hired some big-time celebrity chef from New York because they didn't want Ana's 'peasant food.' That's what they called her cooking. Never mind that she'd trained at one of the best restaurants in Fort Lauderdale, and she doesn't serve Mexican food unless the family asks for it.

"*They hurt my feelings,* Ana said, *but I said fine. I told them I didn't want the extra work. I didn't, either.*

"Maybe not," Phil said, "but Ana was still hurt. She

said the party cost half a million dollars, but Bree was unhappy."

"Why?" Helen said. "You could buy a house for that."

"Bree only got one birthday party, and that party was in Fort Lauderdale."

"So?" Helen asked.

"Bree whined that Paris Hilton had a five-day birthday bash—five parties in five cities and five time zones—London, New York, Tokyo, LA and Las Vegas. Hilton had a different dress for each party, and a twenty-one-tier cake."

"And I really admire Paris Hilton," Helen said. "What a dimwit."

"Which one?" Phil asked.

"Both," Helen said. "Bree forgot that Hilton's daddy has a ton of money."

"No. Bree complained that her daddy was only a partner in a law firm and didn't make 'real money.'"

"Bree wanted Daddy to buy her some celebrity guests, but all he could afford was someone like Vanilla Ice."

"Who's Vanilla Ice?" Helen asked.

"That was the problem. Bree still had a pretty good party with fifty of her closest friends and a twenty-one-tier cake."

"Just like Paris," Helen said.

"Plus Bree's party had caviar, ice sculptures and a champagne fountain. Rich people love champagne fountains. Oh, and lots of drugs."

"Pot and coke?" Helen asked.

"That's like asking if there was beer at a barbecue. Ana said the servers told her they saw weed, coke, heroin, and 'coket,' a mix of cocaine and Special K. Along with mephedrone and MDMA, and the usual abused prescription drugs, including Xanax, Vicodin, Klonopin, Percocet and Seroquel, better known as jailhouse heroin. One more—Desoxyn, prescription speed."

"Good Lord," Helen said. "What a pharmacy."

"There could have been more, but that's all Ana

said the waitstaff recognized. She said it turned into a real orgy, sex everywhere."

"Were Bree's parents home?"

"They left early. She was twenty-one and they wanted her to have a good time. The food was served all night as a buffet. The parents helped sing 'Happy Birthday' while she cut the cake. They gave Bree two presents—a twenty-thousand-dollar ruby-and-diamond pendant and a red Beemer convertible. Then the old folks left.

"About midnight, when the party was in full swing, Ana brought out a special treat, *chapulines*, for Bree and her inner circle. Ana said the snack was low-fat, low-carb and high-protein. The birthday girl scarfed them down like popcorn. So did her friends. Ana said they ate two big bowls of *chapulines* and begged for more. But she was out of grasshoppers."

"Grasshoppers? That was her special treat?" Helen said.

"Toasted and seasoned with salt and lime. It's a Mexican snack. And Ana wasn't lying. Grasshoppers are low-fat, low-carb and high-protein."

"Ick!" Helen said.

"Bree and her crowd were so out of it, they didn't know what they were eating."

"So Ana got her revenge," Helen said.

"And then some," Phil said. "At one o'clock, Bree was still wearing her ruby necklace. A server saw her go into a downstairs powder room—and in that crowd, it really was a powder room—with her boyfriend, Standiford W. Lohan the Third, known as Trey."

"Was Bree wearing the necklace when she left the powder room?"

"Ana doesn't know. But she's setting up a meeting with two servers from the party. Want to talk to them?"

"You bet," Helen said.

"How was the séance?" Phil asked. "Did you raise Flora Portland?"

"Flora's deader than disco, except to the true believers,

Lisa and Blair. Melisandra the medium went into a so-called trance and said exactly what I thought she would: The library must be saved at all costs."

"Any cold spots during the séance?" Phil asked.

"Only when the air-conditioning kicked on. But Lisa, the library board president who bopped the patron with a bookend, felt the cold when Flora appeared. Lisa also said the ghost touched her arm."

"Where were the medium's hands?" Phil asked.

"Firmly gripping the hands of both Blair and Lisa, keeping the magic circle. However, I did feel the edge of the tablecloth move."

"Melisandra used her foot," Phil said. "A fraudster's favorite. One creep pulled it on the Empress Eugénie, wife of Napoleon the Third. The medium slipped off his shoe and touched the empress's arm. She thought it was one of her dead children."

"How cruel," Helen said. "Melisandra could have easily slipped off her shoe under the table. You know the most surprising things."

"Yes, I do," Phil said. "Do you believe in ghosts?"

"Did I tell you about staying at Aunt Frankie's haunted house? I was about nine. While my little sister Kathy had her tonsils out, I stayed with my aunt Frankie, a big cheerful blonde. She was renovating a house in south St. Louis. Beautiful place, built in 1904. The neighbors said it was haunted by an old woman who'd died when she fell down the staircase. They claimed her ghost walked those stairs and hung around the guest room, reading over people's shoulders."

"Makes the afterlife sound pretty boring," Phil said.

"Maybe, but the neighborhood kids wanted to hold a séance there on Halloween. I wasn't used to old houses with creaky floors and dark wood," Helen said, "and I was scared to sleep in the haunted room. Aunt Frankie promised there was no ghost, and said if I kept the bedroom door open she'd be right down the hall.

"Late that night, there was a wild storm—lightning,

thunder, howling wind. My room had one of those old pocket doors that slide into the walls, and the door started closing all by itself. I was too scared to scream. Aunt Frankie ran in to check on me and saw me shaking and shivering. She hugged me and said the wind made the door move.

"*Everything in this old house is off-kilter,* she said. *It's drafty. That ghost is nothing but a breeze.* Sure enough, when Aunt Frankie got storm windows, the ghost went away."

Helen tried to hide a yawn.

"Is it the company?" he asked.

"It's the time," Helen said. "It's one o'clock. I have to go in early tomorrow and catch a ghost. A live one."

CHAPTER 15

. . . .

Alexa looks like a ghost this morning, Helen thought as the library director unlocked the staff entrance door.

Alexa managed a weak smile, but her tailored lavender suit was the same color as the circles under her eyes. She looked pale, and her dark hair was frizzy and lifeless.

"Helen," she said, and forced another smile. "Come in and let me introduce you to Seraphina Ormond, a good friend of Elizabeth Kingsley. She's in the reading room and she wants to meet you." Alexa toyed with that lock of white hair, another sign something was off.

"Uh, we already met," Helen said. "In the parking lot two days ago. And she wasn't very happy with me."

"I know," Alexa said. "But I think she wants to make amends. And I need her. Please, Helen? I've been working on her and I think I can bring her around so she'll head the fund-raiser if the board approves the building restoration."

"Okay," Helen said. "At least we'll be meeting in public here in the library."

"Thank you," Alexa said.

"You seem tired," Helen said.

"I am," Alexa said, "and worried about our library. How will last night's séance affect our already divided board? I want to save our library, too, but that séance will only make our problems worse."

The library director sighed. "Sorry, I shouldn't burden you with my problems. Mrs. Ormond is waiting. Follow me. After your chat, please come to my office. I need to talk to you."

About what? Helen wondered. There must be another problem. Alexa's been wrestling with the fate of the library for weeks now.

She saw Seraphina Ormond browsing large-print books in a corner near the entrance.

Your basic rich blonde, Helen thought. Tall, fit, obnoxiously thin, with hair the color of dry champagne.

Seraphina wore tennis whites and socks with little balls so they wouldn't slide into her tennis shoes. Her skin was tanned from hours on the tennis court.

"Helen Hawthorne, meet Seraphina Ormond," Alexa said. "Seraphina is one of our most generous donors."

Seraphina presented her hand as if it was an honor to shake it. Her grip was strong and firm, but her smile didn't quite reach her pale blue eyes.

"Helen," she said, with that upper-class bray straight from a fox hunt. Everyone in the reading room turned to stare at the women. Helen could see at least a dozen curious patrons. Gladys, the librarian at the checkout desk, edged closer.

"Now I know why you're here. Elizabeth said she hired you to find that missing million-dollar watercolor," Seraphina said. She was so loud, Helen was sure the patrons upstairs, as well as everyone in the back halls, could hear her. Worse, the woman had perfect enunciation.

"Who would have thought that dotty old Davis would stick anything that valuable in an old book? I told Elizabeth the family should hire someone to watch the old boy as soon as he started getting gaga. But she and her brother didn't want to hurt their father's feelings. Instead they waited until he was almost completely out of it before he had an attendant. And now look what's happened.

"I heard he hid family papers and property deeds in his books. Then that Scarlett"—she made a sour face—"gave every single book to the Friends. Who knows what else the old boy left in his collection."

Helen glanced at the reading room. Patrons were no longer cocooned in their comfortable chairs or pounding their computers. Now she saw the gleam of alert eyes, like watchful forest creatures. Even Mr. Ritter, the old man in the dark suit, had put down his precious *New York Times* editorial page to eavesdrop.

Gladys had drifted over to the history section, ten feet from Seraphina. Helen swore the librarian's ears were twitching.

"So did you find it yet?" Seraphina asked. "The million-dollar watercolor? No, I guess not, or you wouldn't be here."

Helen was relieved she didn't have to answer. Seraphina never stopped her monologue and didn't seem to expect a reply. But the PI was also dismayed. She'd hoped to conduct her search quietly, behind the scenes. Now everyone—library staff, patrons and volunteers—knew she was looking for the million-dollar watercolor.

Helen saw a small, white-haired woman quietly abandon her book on her chair and drift toward the Friends of the Library's used book shelves near the checkout desk. Ms. White gathered as many dollar hardcovers as her short arms could hold, and carried them to the checkout desk, where she politely tapped the bell. Gladys hurried over to ring up her purchases.

Seraphina was still talking. "Elizabeth is in financial distress," she said, "but she wouldn't be if she'd listened to me. I told her not to go with that broker in Miami."

She said the *M*-word as if the city were social Siberia, Helen thought. Maybe it is in her world.

"I warned her," Seraphina said. "Our kind doesn't go to brokers. But she wouldn't listen. She thought he was a hoot—until she lost everything. Well, who's laughing now? Elizabeth desperately needs an income and she's had to hire an outsider to look through scads of old books donated to the Friends."

Helen looked around wildly, hoping she could escape before Elizabeth's so-called friend broadcast any more information about Helen's search.

The forest animals in the reading room were stirring now, setting down their novels, closing their laptops and slipping toward the Friends of the Library sale shelves. There they grabbed armloads of sale books—fat diet guides, cracked-spine medical books, shabby bestsellers— and rushed to the checkout desk. The line was around the room, and Gladys looked harried as she rang up the purchases.

Seraphina finally paused long enough for Helen to ask, "Is there anything I can help you with?"

"No, I just wanted to see what a private eye looked like on the job," Seraphina said. "I thought you'd be more interesting."

"My trench coat is at the dry cleaner," Helen said. "If that's all, I have to work."

CHAPTER 16

Helen escaped down the hall and ducked into Alexa's office, where the director was signing papers. The room was flooded with sunlight and the tall orange and yellow canna flowers outside the window made it look like it was on fire.

Now it was Alexa's turn to ask, "Are you okay?"

"No," Helen said. "Seraphina announced that a million-dollar watercolor was left in the books Scarlett Kingsley donated to the Friends. It's caused a run on the sale rack."

"Good," Alexa said. "We'll get some benefit. Why are you upset?"

"I thought we were keeping this assignment quiet," Helen said.

"Don't worry," Alexa said. "The people who heard Seraphina talking don't know the whole story. Everyone connected with the library knows the Kingsley collection is locked away in a room and we've stopped selling it until the painting is found. Make sure you keep that room locked."

"I will," Helen said, "but I wish we had something more secure than a skeleton key. You wanted to see me?"

"Yes. I came in this morning and found more proof the ghost was active last night—and I'm not talking about Flora Portland. Water was splashed all over the women's restroom again, and there was heavy twine from the window latch to the stall door hinge. I think it was a makeshift clothesline."

"So our ghost is washing her clothes?" Helen asked.

"From the drip pattern, that's my guess. I wiped up the water because I don't want anyone here to know that the ghost is a homeless woman until we actually find her."

"Well, at least she's a clean ghost," Helen said.

"And a hungry one," Alexa said. "The Chinese food from last night's supper was missing from the staff fridge."

"The food Lisa ordered for everyone who stayed for the séance?" Helen asked.

"Yes, she ordered way too much. You and Jared didn't eat any. Gladys was the only one with any appetite. We decided to keep the leftovers for lunch today. I came in this morning and they were gone."

"Are you sure someone didn't take them home last night?" Helen said.

"No, we all left here at the same time. You know that."

"Were the empty cartons in the trash?" Helen asked.

"I searched the staff room and the public rooms," Alexa said. "Nothing. Not even a grain of rice."

"I need to step up my search now that Seraphina shot off her big mouth," Helen said. "I'll go back into the collection room and keep searching for the watercolor."

"Good," Alexa said. "But I need you to perform your volunteer work, too. We have to keep up appearances that you're a volunteer, even if Seraphina did out you. Report back here at eleven, please."

Before Helen could leave, Blair knocked on the door and blocked her escape. "Alexa, are you still going to have Helen search for the Sargent watercolor? When Seraphina Ormond mentioned—"

Shouted, Helen thought.

"—that a valuable painting was hidden in the Friends sale books, there was a stampede for the shelves," Blair said. "People bought everything, even old biofeedback books and recipes from the seventies. Fortunately, they didn't understand that the books with the watercolor were in a different room. We made more than five hundred dollars, but now we're short of books for our shelves."

Good heavens, Helen thought. Blair is really wearing a twinset. A beige twinset with a calf-length box-pleated skirt.

"It's not too late to stop the search," Blair said. "The Friends could go through those books for free. All our stock sold out this morning. If we find the painting, it will pay for the renovation of Flora's library. It's what she wants."

"The late Davis Kingsley wanted his daughter to have that painting," Alexa said.

"But Elizabeth's family donated those books to us," Blair said. "We should have that painting if it's in one of our books."

Helen wasn't sure if that "we" meant the library or the Friends of the Library.

"Elizabeth doesn't deserve to own a John Singer Sargent," Blair said. "She doesn't know a thing about his work. She wants to sell it for the money."

Is there any other reason to sell something? Helen wondered.

"Blair," Alexa warned, but the woman kept talking, desperate to make her case.

"Davis Kingsley paid more than a hundred and fifty thousand dollars for a LeRoy Neiman painting!" She said *LeRoy Neiman* as if it were an obscenity. "And it was a ballplayer!"

Somehow, Blair made that sound dirty, too.

"LeRoy Neiman's sports art is very popular," Alexa said.

"LeRoy Neiman's *paintings* are very popular," Blair said. "No one serious calls that junk art. You know he drew those disgusting Femlins for *Playboy* magazine."

Helen knew what those were—tiny, shapely women wearing high heels, black stockings, long black gloves and nothing else—who cavorted in the Party Jokes section of *Playboy.*

"Naked women are serious subjects for art," Alexa said, trying to get Blair to lighten up.

She failed. The head Friend was not amused. Her thin mouth was set in a hard line.

"Blair, I won't change my mind," Alexa said. "The Sargent watercolor is Elizabeth's inheritance. She's entitled to it legally and morally."

"But what about Flora Portland's life's work?" Blair said. "You have a moral duty to preserve this library."

"I've said all I'm going to say on the subject. I won't discuss this anymore," Alexa said.

A furious Blair stomped out. "I'd better get to work," Helen said. Alexa didn't seem to hear her awkward excuse.

Helen left Alexa's office with the enchanting view of the garden to search the moldering Kingsley collection. She was facing a day of dust, backaches and boredom. Helen's mood was nearly as gloomy as the windowless room that awaited her.

On her way there, in the poorly lit labyrinth at the back of the library, Helen saw the cat in the dark hall. She reached into her purse for a treat.

"Here, Paris," Helen said, and tossed the treat.

But instead of running to her, the calico twirled in the center of the hall and said, *Merr.* Helen saw the cat dancing around something dark.

"What is it, kitty?" she asked, hoping Paris hadn't left her a dead mouse, as a cat thank-you gift.

She approached the dark object carefully, then sighed with relief. It was a sock. An ordinary black sock.

Helen picked it up. The sock was damp.

Nobody wore damp socks at the library. Did the ghost wash it and drop it in the hall?

Once Helen picked up the sock, Paris ran off to fetch her treat. Helen stayed still and studied the closed doors that lined the hallway. No light came from under the doors or the glass transoms over them.

All the doors were shut.

But one door, narrower than the others—a storage closet?—had a bit of dark fabric shut between the door and the jamb. The closet was across from the damp sock.

Helen froze.

Silence. She heard the gurgle of a water pipe, the cat chomping on her treat and the rumble of a library cart on the other side of the hall.

Soundlessly, Helen reached over and threw open the closet door.

Crouched inside was a young woman in a business suit.

She shrieked.

So did Helen.

CHAPTER 17

. . . .

"Who are you?" Helen asked the woman cowering in the closet. "Why are you hiding?"

"I, uh . . ." the woman said.

"Hurry," Helen said. "The staff heard us. They'll be here in a moment. You're the library ghost."

"Yes, I'm Charlotte," she said, her brown eyes pleading. "It's a long story, but don't turn me in. I have something you want. Your watercolor. I found it."

Helen heard footsteps running down the hall. Alexa, the director; Blair, the not-so-friendly Friend of the Library; Jared the janitor; Lisa the board president; loud Seraphina; and hip Gladys were pounding down the hall toward them.

"Quiet!" Helen said, her voice a whispery hiss. "And maybe I won't turn you in."

She tossed the sock into the closet and slammed the door as Alexa said, "Helen! Why were you screaming?" In the low light, the director looked like a horror movie escapee. Her face was flour white.

"Sorry," Helen said. "Paris startled me. The cat jumped out in front of me, chasing a mouse."

When in doubt, blame the cat, she thought.

"See? That animal has no business here," Blair said, eager to attack her feline foe.

"Oh, yes, she does," Lisa said. "Flora herself told us that her calico's descendants still serve this library."

Blair looked trapped. Lisa was her ally, but the cat was her enemy.

Helen held her breath until Lisa said, "You startled us. We were worried. Things can happen in this big old building, and this hall is so isolated. Someone could be lurking in these rooms. Why did you slam the closet door?"

"It was open and the mouse was heading straight for it," Helen said. "When I shut it, Paris and the mouse ran that way down the hall." She pointed to where the shadows shifted. Lisa seemed to buy her explanation, along with everyone else.

"Sorry to disturb you," Helen said, and managed a shaky laugh. "I'm a little jumpy after last night."

"We all are," Alexa said. "I'm glad it's nothing serious. I'm going back to my office."

The others took that as a signal to disperse. When the library staff and volunteers were gone, Helen unlocked the Kingsley collection room. Now she heard Gladys talking to patrons at the checkout desk. Seraphina brayed good-bye to Alexa. Jared was hammering something, and Lisa and Blair had retreated to the staff break room.

Helen checked the hall again, then dashed over, opened the closet and put her finger to her lips. She dragged Charlotte to the collection room, and shoved the very solid ghost into a chair.

Charlotte was trembling, but only her pale skin was ghostly. She was short and slender, dressed professionally in black flats and a navy suit. Her dark hair was pulled into a snug bun. She wore pink lipstick and a little eyeliner.

"You're in trouble," Helen said. "You've stolen from the library, damaged property and terrorized the staff and patrons. A woman was bludgeoned because a frightened board member thought she was a ghost. Tell me why I shouldn't call the police."

"Please don't," Charlotte said, and Helen saw the fear in her eyes. "I'm homeless. But if my job interview goes well today, I won't be. I'll be out of here and making a good living.

"My name is Charlotte. Charlotte Ann Dams. I lost my job at a Fort Lauderdale medical supply company in February. I'd been living paycheck to paycheck, but I managed to hang on to my apartment until June. Then I ran out of money and put my furniture in storage. I got a good deal if I paid for a year up front. I tried to find a place to live, but there was no room for me in the homeless shelters."

Helen knew the overcrowded local shelters were a constant media topic.

"At first I lived out of my car," Charlotte said, "but I didn't get much sleep. There aren't many places where you can park a car overnight. People—men, mostly—would prowl around my car and I was afraid I'd be, you know, attacked."

"Don't you have any family?" Helen asked.

"Just my mother, and she doesn't live here. She wanted me to come back home to Titansville, Missouri."

"Where's that?" Helen asked.

"South of nowhere," Charlotte said, "at the corner of nothing to do. Mom didn't approve of me moving to Florida. Said it was a godless place. She'd only help if I returned to Titansville.

"I was determined to stay in Fort Lauderdale, no matter what. I like it here, even if I am having a hard time."

She'd relaxed enough that Helen could tell her age—early twenties. Her features were regular but plain. Now Charlotte settled in as if they were two friends gossiping.

"For a while I lived in my storage unit," Charlotte

said. "At night, I slept on my couch and used the storage facility's public restroom. But my unit didn't have air-conditioning or windows."

Helen couldn't imagine living in a flat-topped box with no air-conditioning in the Florida heat.

"Some nights, the temperature was over a hundred and ten degrees," Charlotte said. "I had to be up, washed, dressed and out before the manager showed up at six every morning. All of us did."

"How many homeless people were living there?" Helen asked.

"Three of us. Living in storage units happens more than you'd think.

"I kept checking the shelters, but there was still no place for me. I used the library computers to help find jobs. The Flora Park Library was the best. There wasn't a long wait to use the computers.

"Disaster struck about a month ago. The manager of the storage facility caught me sleeping there. I'd finally dozed off about four in the morning and I didn't wake up in time. The manager was real nice about it, but he said the storage units weren't designed to be lived in. If he caught me again, he'd call the police.

"I came back here to the library and wondered what I should do. Paris the cat came to see me—it's like she knew I was in trouble. I scratched her for a bit, and then she jumped off my lap and ran down the back hall. She looked over her shoulder at me, and I followed her.

"I saw those rows of doors and all but one was unlocked. Then I found the staff break room with the kitchen. I figured I could live here until I got a job."

"But how did you get away with it?" Helen asked.

"I'd come back to the library about closing time and go in the staff entrance. No one was around. I timed it when the staff was busy preparing for closing. I'd slip in and hide in a room in the hall. At night, I used the blankets in the hurricane kit."

"Alexa said a kit was missing," Helen said. "An expensive kit."

"I'm sorry," Charlotte said, and she did seem contrite. "But it really was an emergency.

"The library doesn't have an alarm system. I'd hide until Jared finished cleaning. Once he was gone, the library was mine."

"What do you do every night?" Helen asked.

"Most nights, I read by flashlight," Charlotte said. "I play with Paris. I watch the battery-operated TV from the hurricane kit, and eat the food and drink the water in it."

"You also spent the kit's five hundred dollars," Helen said.

"I needed gas for my car," she said. "I drive an old green 'eighty-seven Honda. Not much to look at, but at least it's reliable. I still have about two hundred left.

"Once a week I wash my hair and dry it with the hand dryers in the bathroom. If I let my hair air-dry, it looks frizzy.

"I usually wait until I have a job interview. Once, Alexa almost caught me. I checked my e-mail early in the morning and learned I had a job interview that same day. I was drying my hair when Alexa came in early and I ran for a closet."

"You ate the staff food, too," Helen said.

"Not much. I microwaved the leftover coffee, but I always cleaned the pot," Charlotte said. "The staff doesn't clean the coffeepot, so nobody complained. Sometimes I'd help myself—"

"You mean steal," Helen said.

"Okay, I'd steal tea bags. I took some food, but only if it had been in the break room at least two days."

"The Chinese food was gone overnight," Helen said. "You keep lying and I'll call the police now."

"I was hungry!" Charlotte said. "I'd been living on stale sandwiches and rock-hard pastries. When I smelled that moo shu pork last night, I couldn't resist."

"So where are the empty cartons?" Helen said.

"In my briefcase. I take out any trash I create when I leave for my job hunt."

"And nobody here at the library notices you?" Helen asked.

"Just Paris the cat. I wait until the library is busy and the staff is distracted. If anyone who works here sees me, they've never acknowledged me. It's like I'm . . . well, I'm a ghost."

"You almost got a woman killed," Helen said. "Lisa thought she saw a ghost and hit a patron with a bookend."

"I'm sorry about that," Charlotte said. "Lisa must have seen me running down the hall in my long lavender robe and thought I was Flora Portland's ghost. Lisa is very excitable."

"With good reason," Helen said.

"Look, I'll pay for everything," Charlotte said. "I'll return the five hundred dollars, with interest. I'll add another hundred for food and batteries. And I'll tell you where I hid the missing watercolor. Just let me go to this job interview.

"It's the third time Norton Management Associates has called me back. My starting salary will be forty thousand dollars. Please let me get this job and I'll clear out, pay back the library and never return."

She started for the door, but Helen blocked it. "Not so fast. Tell me about that Sargent watercolor. How did you hear about it?"

"I was next door when the Kingsley boxes were delivered to the Friends' intake room, and the volunteers opened them.

"The books that looked valuable were set aside and handled with white cotton gloves—like those elephant folios on the table there. The Friends decided there were ten boxes of potentially valuable books. A book dealer took the books to appraise. He's coming back for those elephant folios next week.

"The Friends put the first batch of bestsellers on the sale shelves. Shortly after that, the Kingsley papers—the birth certificate and the deed—were found and returned. You wouldn't believe the flap. Alexa called Elizabeth Kingsley and they had a discussion here in the hall."

"Why didn't they talk in Alexa's office?" Helen asked.

"Alexa thought Blair listened at her door—and she does. I've seen her. Alexa conducts her private conversations here in the hall.

"That night, I started searching the books. I'd open a box, go through the books and retape it. I found the watercolor last night, after the séance. It was in a huge photo book—sort of like an elephant folio, but it wasn't in with the rare books. It was called *Portraits from North American Indian Life* by Edward S. Curtis, with gorgeous sepia photos of Native Americans."

"Why didn't you say something to Alexa this morning?" Helen asked.

"I didn't get a chance," Charlotte said. "She nearly caught me when I was getting my laundry out of the women's john. I ran for the storage closet. I had to leave my clothesline up and then Paris was playing with a sock I'd dropped. That's when you showed up."

"Give me the watercolor," Helen said.

"It's worth a million dollars," Charlotte said, and her face looked feral. "I know you're getting a fee for finding it. Split your fee with me and it's yours."

"I'll think about it," Helen said.

"You don't have time. I have to leave for my job interview now. Yes or no, Detective?"

"How do I know you still have it?" Helen asked.

"Don't worry—it's still here. I hid it well. When I get back, I'll serve it to you on a platter. That's a clue."

And that was a taunt. Helen glared at the plain woman in the severe suit. She didn't like Charlotte, but she was saving Helen hours of work.

"Well?" Charlotte said.

"Yes," Helen said.

"My briefcase is in the other room," Charlotte said, standing up and smoothing her skirt. "I'll be back at the library by three at the latest and we'll draw up the contract."

"What contract?" Helen said.

"The one you're going to sign so I'll get half your fee," Charlotte said.

CHAPTER 18

"Wait!" Helen said, and put her ear to the door. "Now what?" Charlotte said. "I'm going to be late for my noon interview."

"Sh! I think I hear something," Helen said.

Was Blair listening at doors again? she wondered. Would the well-bred Lisa stoop to snooping? Does she even have the energy? Helen pressed her ear harder against the wooden door, but it was at least two inches thick.

Scritch, scritch. She thought she heard a small scratching sound. Paris the cat? Or someone's fingernails?

Charlotte moved restlessly. "I have to leave," she whined. "I can't miss my job interview."

"Just a second," Helen hissed. "Stand behind those books."

When Charlotte was out of sight, Helen flung open the door. She heard a scuffling sound, then feet—or maybe paws—pattering down the hall. Paris? Blair? Gladys, Lisa or Alexa? Surely not those four women, Helen decided. She could still hear Jared hammering. She couldn't see who—or what—was in the dreary hall.

No wonder people believe this library is haunted, Helen decided, looking up at the single bare bulb strangled by the gloom. Good lighting would lay the ghost to rest.

"Okay, Charlotte," Helen said. "Get your briefcase and go."

"How do I look?" Charlotte twirled so Helen could see her.

"Brush the dust off your right sleeve and I'd hire you in a heartbeat," Helen said. "Good luck. Make sure you're back by three o'clock, or you won't get your share of the reward."

"Don't worry," Charlotte said, ducking out of the Kingsley room. "I need that money."

Helen heard her reach into the closet across the hall for her briefcase, then carefully close the closet door. She watched Charlotte hurry down the hall until the shadows swallowed the intruder.

Then Helen checked her watch. Almost eleven o'clock, she thought. Charlotte has plenty of time to make her noon interview. When she returns, my work here is done.

Helen tidied up the dusty room as best she could, stacking the boxes she'd already opened, making sure the elephant folios were safely wrapped in acid-free paper, and the white cotton gloves rested on top of them.

I won't miss the dust or the depressing wallpaper, Helen thought, but I hate that Charlotte's claiming half of my reward.

Except the homeless woman did find the watercolor. Maybe I can find a better-paying job and make that money without being shut up in a windowless room.

But Helen was still annoyed, and she slammed a box down with extra force.

"Helen, it's me, Lisa." The library board president's knock on the door interrupted Helen's brooding. "May I come in?"

Lisa didn't wait for an answer. She walked in, looking

lean and rangy in a gray chalk-striped pantsuit. "So." She attempted a smile. "Did you find anything?"

"A lot of dust," Helen said, her thoughts scrambling wildly. Lisa's not supposed to know about the search for the watercolor. But thanks to Seraphina's big mouth, everyone connected to the library knows now.

"No sign of the missing million-dollar painting?" Lisa said.

"You would have heard the shrieks of joy throughout the library if I had," Helen said. "Be careful. Your white French cuff is dragging in the dust on the pile of boxes."

"Oh, yes, yes, it is," Lisa said. She brushed off the dust and it left an ugly black smear on her snowy cuff. Helen saw her dismay. Was the handsome white blouse a carefully preserved remnant from a happier time?

"I'd better get this dirt off in case it stains," Lisa said.

She was barely gone before Helen heard the rumble of a cart in the hall and another knock on the door.

"Yes?" Helen said.

Blair pushed her way inside the Kingsley collection room. "I'm here to help," she said.

"I'm doing fine, thank you," Helen said, her voice crisp with distrust.

"We didn't get off to a good start," Blair said, "but you came to the séance last night and treated it with respect. I'd like to start over." She held out her hand as if she were giving Helen a gift.

Helen shook it dutifully, and Blair said, "I thought if I helped you search these boxes, we could go through the Kingsley books faster. As I explained to Alexa, we need to put out more books."

Helen didn't like or trust Blair, but she figured she might as well get along with her while she worked at the library.

"You can take that stack by the door right now," Helen said. "The boxes numbered one through ten. That should get you started."

Blair propped open the door with the heavy, brass-trimmed wooden cart. She was taller than Helen, and had ropy muscles. Helen helped her load the boxes on the cart.

"There," Helen said. "That's the last one. It's eleven o'clock and I have an appointment with Alexa."

"Of course," Blair said, all smiles. Helen watched her trundle the cart toward the Friends' sorting room, then locked the Kingsley collection door and headed for the director's office.

"Helen!" Alexa said, and greeted her with a genuine smile. "How's progress?" The director looked more relaxed in her office, and she had more color.

Helen looked at the door. "Can we speak freely here?" she asked.

Alexa stepped into the hall and checked it. "It's empty," she said. "Did you find our ghost?"

"Yes," Helen said. "That's why I screamed this morning. I surprised her in the storage closet. As we guessed, she's homeless. She lost her job in February."

She quickly told Alexa the story. "Charlotte confessed to stealing the hurricane kit and eating the library food. And she found the watercolor."

"The search is over?" Alexa said.

"At last," Helen said.

"So where is the painting?"

"She hid it," Helen said.

"She *what*? And you let her out of the building?" Alexa asked.

"Charlotte has a job interview at Norton Management Associates at noon," Helen said. "It's the third time they've called her back and she's sure she'll get the job. I let her go because I thought it was better if Charlotte had a job. Now she'll be able to rent a home and pay back the money and goods she stole."

"What's she look like?" Alexa asked.

"Slender. Brunette. Rather plain, but dresses like a business professional," Helen said.

"I can't place her at all," Alexa said. "She's been slipping in and out of this building like a . . ."

She stopped.

"Ghost?" Helen said.

"What makes you think she'll return?" Alexa said.

Charlotte has five thousand reasons, Helen thought, but I'm not telling Alexa the woman demanded half of my fee. But the price of Charlotte's stolen goods is coming out of her share, not mine.

"All her clothes are still here in the library," Helen said. "She has to come back. Besides, where is a young woman from Titansville, Missouri, going to sell a valuable watercolor?"

Clunk! Patter, patter, patter.

"What's that?" Helen said. "I heard something in the hall." Alexa started to get up from behind her desk when Paris pranced into the room and rubbed against Helen's legs. Helen scratched the cat's tail and reached into her purse for more treats.

The calico sat up like a puppy and begged for them.

"Don't overfeed her, Helen," Alexa said. "She's our organic mouse catcher, remember. She's supposed to be a little bit hungry."

Hungry. Feed. Helen saw herself stumbling out of bed this morning, with only minutes to spare before she was due at the library. Phil was long gone. He'd left for his undercover landscaping job at five this morning. Phil always fed Thumbs.

"Oh, no," Helen said. "I forgot to feed my cat. Can I go home at lunch and give Thumbs some food?"

"Of course," Alexa said. "Take an early lunch and leave now. But I need you here this afternoon."

Helen hopped over the cat and ran out the staff door. She was back at the Coronado Tropic Apartments in fifteen minutes. As she slammed the door on the Igloo, she heard Thumbs howling.

She ran up the sidewalk past her landlady, who was

lunching at an umbrella table. "Finally," Margery said. "What's wrong with the furbag?"

"I forgot to feed him this morning," Helen called as she sprinted past Margery.

An irate Thumbs met Helen at the door and bawled her out all the way to the kitchen.

As she poured his dry food, he nudged the bag out of the way and stuck his head in the bowl. Helen waited for Thumbs to come up for air, then filled his bowl again.

"Sorry, buddy," she said.

He glared at her with golden green eyes, and she gave him a handful of treats from her purse. After she changed his water, Helen poured him yet another bowl. "Just in case I have to work late tonight," she said.

Thumbs bumped her hand, a sign that she was forgiven. Helen fixed herself a chicken sandwich, poured a glass of iced tea and wandered out to join Margery at the pool.

Her landlady was in purple clam diggers and a breezy lavender top, enjoying a post-lunch Marlboro.

"How's the case?" Margery asked.

"I found the ghost," Helen said. "She's a homeless woman, but not for much longer. She found the watercolor."

"So did you turn it in?" Margery asked.

"No, I let her go on a job interview. She's going to give it to me after she gets the job."

Once again, Helen didn't mention that Charlotte had claimed half of Helen's fee. She was ashamed and angry—too angry to discuss it with Margery.

"And you let her go to that job interview alone?" Margery said.

"She'll come back," Helen said.

"I hope so," Margery said. "I hope she's safe."

"Why wouldn't she be?" Helen said.

"Your ghost could be in danger," Margery said. "It's easy to kill a dead woman. Who's going to miss her?"

CHAPTER 19

. . . .

"Why is a book with the F-word in this library?" the woman demanded at the checkout desk. Jaw rigid, teeth clenched, her voice rose to a shriek as she said, "It's in the children's section!"

Dressed in full rich-lady rig, the woman wore a pink Chanel suit, ropes of pearls and gold, and heels. Her gray hair was sculpted into impossible waves.

Helen, back from lunch at the Coronado, was shelving novels nearby. She eased her massive mahogany-and-brass library cart closer to listen.

This was better than any fiction she was handling, especially with Gladys at the desk. The irate woman glared at Gladys as if she expected the librarian to crumple like a Kleenex.

"What word is that, Mrs. Sutherland?" Gladys asked. The tattooed librarian stood tall. She wasn't intimidated by a rich patron.

Helen edged closer. Now she could see the offending children's book, *Walter the Farting Dog*. She forced herself not to laugh. She'd read the series about the lovable gasbag hound when she'd worked at a bookstore.

"I can't bring myself to say it," Mrs. Sutherland said, and pointed to the F-word.

"Have you read the book?" Gladys asked.

"Of course not!" Mrs. Sutherland said. "As soon as I saw my grandson reading it, I tore it out of his hands and brought it straight back here. I want that book removed from this library. Now."

Gladys handed Mrs. Sutherland a white form. "You must read the book and write a report on why you find it offensive before we can consider your request," she said. "May I check it out for you?"

"Absolutely not! I want to speak to your supervisor. Immediately!"

Gladys looked around wildly for Alexa, but the director was nowhere in sight. The librarian wanted rid of this difficult woman. Helen caught her frantic look, stepped up to the desk and said, "May I find the director for you?"

"Yes, please."

Good for Gladys, Helen thought. She fearlessly withstood Mrs. Sutherland, who must be a force in this community.

Helen found Alexa at her office computer and filled her in on the crisis.

"We get this all the time," Alexa said, and sighed. "Requesting a report almost always takes care of the problem. People who want books banned rarely read the works they want removed."

Alexa marched to the checkout desk, where Mrs. Sutherland was lecturing Gladys on smut and America's moral fiber.

"You wished to see me, Mrs. Sutherland?" Alexa asked.

"I wish to see this book out of my library!" she said.

"After you read it and write a report, we'll consider your request," Alexa said.

"That's not acceptable," Mrs. Sutherland said. "It should be removed instantly."

"We have procedures," Alexa said. "You have the

right not to read any book in this library. You have the right to regulate your grandson's reading. But you do not have the right to ban books for the citizens of Flora Park without a hearing."

"Then this is the last you'll see of me and my family," Mrs. Sutherland said, and swept out of the reading room.

"She seems to think that's a threat," Helen said.

"Please continue to shelve books, then take your break, Helen," Alexa said, ignoring her remark. "I have another assignment for you at one thirty."

Helen rolled her cart over to the large-print books section and went back to work.

Alexa turned to Gladys, who was trying hard not to laugh, and gave her a warm smile. "Good work," she said. "You handled a difficult situation well. Would you like me to watch the desk while you have a cup of tea?"

"Tea! I'd like a stiff drink after dealing with that battle-ax," Gladys said.

"Not at the library," Alexa said, "but you deserve a long lunch. Be back by four."

"Thanks," Gladys said. "I'm outta here before you change your mind."

Helen reached for the next book, *Definitely Dead* by Charlaine Harris.

D, E, F, G, H, Helen thought. Harris, C, goes before Harris, T, and she slid the book before Thomas Harris's *Black Sunday*.

As she shelved books, she frequently recited sections of the alphabet. She found this never-ending library chore soothing. Helen liked putting the authors in their proper places, and straightening out literary jumbles, especially on the upper shelves.

She was pulling Nelson DeMille's mysteries out of a cluster of Jeffery Deaver's novels when she heard Alexa say, "You're perfect for this job, Helen."

"Really?" Helen said. "Is it my charm? My command of the alphabet?"

"Could be," Alexa said, and grinned. "But you're tall. It's hard to get help who can reach the top shelves."

Helen didn't mention the times she'd been tempted to leave bottom-shelf books on the cart for the shorter librarians, but she'd felt duty-bound to put those books away, even though her knees had sounded like popcorn when she kneeled down.

"It's one thirty," Alexa said. "I need you to go upstairs and supervise the library computers. Every single machine is taken, and an impatient man is waiting. You'll have to tell people their time is up and someone else needs their computer."

"How will I know their time is up?" Helen asked.

"Check the sign-in sheet on the clipboard," she said. "Each patron gets thirty minutes. Good luck."

Helen didn't like the sound of this. Once upstairs, she saw seven men and five women hunched protectively over their keyboards, while a fortysomething man with short grizzled hair and huge ears circled the table. The computer users ignored him, staring at their screens as if they'd disappear when they looked up.

The big-eared man headed straight for Helen. "Are you in charge? I'm David," he said. "I have as much right to a computer as anyone in this room. I've been waiting *forty minutes*. No one will leave. Someone's time has to be up by now."

"I'll help you, sir," Helen said. She scanned the sign-in sheet. Time was up for computer number two, being used by Violet, a young woman with straight brown hair and a pretty complexion.

"Violet," Helen said, "your time expired ten minutes ago."

"I'm almost done," Violet said. "I'm working on a paper."

Helen glanced at the screen. A kitten jumped at a shadow and slid down the wall.

"It's my turn," David said.

"What kind of paper involves cat videos, Violet?" Helen said.

"It's a sociology paper on the feline influence in societal memes," Violet said.

"Your time is up," Helen said again.

"One more minute," Violet said. "I'm almost done. I had to wait a long time to get on. I'd be done already if this thing wasn't so slow."

"You're finished now," Helen said, and handed Violet her notebook. "David, please take the seat."

Violet, her face pink with anger, slunk off, and David triumphantly took her seat.

Peace was restored. After the verbal tussle with Violet, the other patrons left quietly when their time was up. David used his computer for twenty minutes. During another rush, an older man complained his mouse was broken. Helen checked it and found the mouse was dead. She ran downstairs and found him a replacement, installed it, then found the right form and wrote a report about the defective equipment. Finally, two hours later, Helen was alone in the room, the computer screens blinking at her.

She read the browsing histories on computer six. The last patron had read an online magazine story headlined "Diane Keaton Says, 'I don't think Woody Allen molested Dylan Farrow.'" That same patron, or maybe the one before, had watched a YouTube video called "How to hot-wire a car." Helen wondered if the library could be blamed if the local car theft rate went up.

She moved on to computer five. Someone had been reading "One Hundred Most Popular Baby Names." Jackson and Sophia were the top names for boys and girls, Helen noticed.

The next story on the browser declared, "Egyptians used ferrets to guard their grain before they kept cats."

Did the Egyptians have library ferrets? she wondered. Why did this ancient civilization switch from ferrets to cats? Did they worship ferrets the way they did felines?

Before she could find out, she was interrupted by the library director.

"Helen!" Alexa said.

Helen jumped. She hadn't heard Alexa enter the room. "Please tell me you aren't violating our patrons' privacy by reading their browsing history," she said.

"Uh," Helen said.

"I'll excuse you this time, since you didn't know," Alexa said. "But we don't release information on what our patrons check out. We don't tell anyone their reference questions. Actually, we don't keep records on those, though some of our librarians keep lists of unusual questions.

"We also consider patrons' database searches, inter-library loans, any materials or equipment they use, even library fines and lost books, private information. Even law enforcement agencies can't have this information unless they get a subpoena.

"Now, are we clear on this policy?"

"Yes," Helen said. "A library is like Las Vegas. What happens here, stays here."

Alexa looked a little startled, then said, "Yes, that's correct. Unless a patron breaks the law in the library, and then we call the police. And where is your law-breaking homeless woman? Isn't she supposed to be here by now? It's three thirty."

"Three thirty! Charlotte said she'd be back by three o'clock at the latest," Helen said.

"Then call her cell phone."

"I don't know if she has one," Helen said. "If she does, I don't have her number."

But she has mine, Helen thought. She saw Charlotte in her mind's eye, dressed in that navy suit, reaching into the storage closet for her briefcase, then disappearing down the hall with the briefcase.

A briefcase big enough to hold a million-dollar watercolor.

And Helen hadn't checked it.

CHAPTER 20

. . . .

Helen fought the traffic on Broward Boulevard, but she was trapped in the concrete canyons of downtown Fort Lauderdale. Cars poured out of the nearby parking garages and clogged the streets. Her progress could be measured in inches. The rush hour was just beginning.

It was sticky-hot at three forty-five, and an over-heated black Mercedes died in the far-left lane, snarling traffic further.

Helen had to get to Norton Management Associates on the other side of I-95, but the whole town seemed to be heading for the interstate. She eased out of the middle lane and found herself behind a bus belching diesel fumes.

There's a reason why they call this the slow lane, she thought, and swung out in front of a pickup truck with inches to spare. The driver gave her the bird and a well-deserved horn blast.

Time's running out, Helen thought. I have to get to Norton before everyone leaves the office. I only hope information about job interviews isn't confidential.

If Charlotte's made off with the Kingsley watercolor,

I'm sunk. Why was I so trusting? She doesn't need this job. She just wanted to get away. Now she has a car, two hundred bucks and a million-dollar painting.

I can't believe I didn't check her briefcase. Some detective I am.

I was careless because Charlotte said she grew up in a small town. Well, plenty of people consider somebody like me from St. Louis a hick from the sticks. I assumed Charlotte couldn't sell the watercolor because she didn't have the contacts, but she's been living at the library. Surrounded by books and computers. Information's everywhere.

Everyone's connected these days, thanks to the Internet.

Traffic eased slightly once Helen crossed the railroad tracks. As long as she stayed in the middle lane on Broward, she kept moving. Now she was past the exits for I-95, a major traffic hurdle. The cars thinned to a manageable number. Not much longer now and she'd be at Norton.

What time was it?

She checked her dashboard clock. Three fifty-five. If she pushed the Igloo, she'd make it before the evening exodus. Then the traffic light turned yellow. She slammed on the brakes and waited. Another delay. Fort Lauderdale had such long traffic light waits, but she'd had enough tickets from the blasted red-light cameras.

Helen drummed her fingers on the steering wheel. In the distance, she could see the white Norton Management Associates sign on the top floor of a blue glass tower. Almost there.

Then she hit an unexpected jam: A line of cars was backed up to enter the Norton parking lot. The six-story blue-glass building shimmered like a mirage. So close, but still out of reach.

As she crawled forward, the cause of the slowdown became clearer. The Norton building was planted in a small parking lot, landscaped with palms and edged on the north side by a tall ficus hedge. There was a break midway down the hedge for another driveway.

Now Helen saw a carnival of flashing police lights and emergency vehicles clustered at that driveway break. Was there an accident in the Norton parking lot? Was someone sick? The victim of an assault?

At last she swung the Igloo into the Norton driveway. Now she had a clearer view. Gawkers were three deep, most in business dress, clustered at the gap in the hedge. Helen could see a chain across the gap to keep cars from entering the lot next door, but anyone could step over it.

The crime scene—or whatever it was—was on the other side of the hedge, but the view was blocked by a boiling mass of busybodies.

Shameless, Helen thought. The Norton building must have emptied out so the office workers could watch the commotion next door.

She caught a better glimpse of what was going on. Now she saw a vast, potholed asphalt parking lot that belonged to a boarded-up supermarket with a rusting sign. MONARCH MARKET: THE KING OF DEALS, it said, and was topped with a prophetically slipping crown.

Helen saw half a dozen cars parked on the Monarch Market lot, including a lizard green Honda with a dented passenger door. Helen felt her stomach lurch.

Didn't Charlotte say she drove a beat-up green '87 Honda?

Now Helen saw uniformed cops demanding that the crowd move, unceremoniously shooing them away from the scene, while CSI workers erected a screen. Something terrible had happened.

Helen was sweating, even though the Igloo's air-conditioning kept the car cool. She had a bad feeling.

Don't jump to conclusions, she told herself. There are a lot of old green cars and Honda is a popular brand.

She drove around the lot twice before she found a parking spot near the back of the Norton building, next to a smelly Dumpster enclosure. A knot of ghouls had gathered there at a break in the hedge, watching the scene with avid eyes. The police didn't seem to notice them.

Helen was ashamed to join the nosy rabble, but she had to know if something had happened to Charlotte.

She pushed her way through the morbidly curious crowd. "Excuse me," she said. "Sorry." She elbowed her way toward the front, earning angry hisses and glares, but Helen didn't care. They were watching someone else's pain, sucking in a stranger's agony for their entertainment. They didn't deserve courtesy. And she had to know if Charlotte was safe.

One last elbow in a fat man's side, and Helen could see a little more. A woman was sprawled on the sun-faded gray asphalt, a long plume of dark blood pooled under her head. The woman had dark hair, matted with blood.

No, she thought. Oh, please, no. She felt dizzy, and it wasn't the Dumpster stink or the late-afternoon heat.

That woman can't be Charlotte, she told herself. This building is filled with twentysomething brunettes.

"What happened?" she asked a tall, broad-shouldered black man next to her. She couldn't keep her voice from shaking, but he didn't seem to notice.

"Hit-and-run," he said in a rich baritone. "Our office manager left for lunch about an hour ago. She discovered the body and called the cops. Eleanor. That's her by the cop car, talking to a detective."

Body? Helen thought. That means the woman is dead.

The tall man pointed to a plump woman in a red suit straining at the seams, talking to a man in a rumpled beige suit. Eleanor kept shaking her head and wiping her eyes with a tissue.

"Never enough parking places in this lot, so we use the empty one next door," the tall man said. "That poor young lady had passed, God rest her soul, when Eleanor found her. They think she was out here awhile, all alone."

Helen had to see the dead woman. "Please excuse me," she said to the tall man. "I need to see if I know her."

He stepped aside—and by the sound of an angry screech—on the toes of someone, and Helen popped to the front, like a cork out of a bottle. The air was better here, slightly cooler.

Now Helen could see the hit-and-run victim wore a navy suit, hiked up her thighs and ripped at the shoulder. She couldn't bear to look closer at the dark head in the lake of blood. The woman's feet were bare, her dark shoes flung off. She had a briefcase at her side, the same color as Charlotte's, and it was open. Inside, Helen could see a black notebook, three pens, a wallet, lipstick and a hairbrush. A set of keys was tossed about two feet from the woman's outstretched hand.

Charlotte. Helen had no doubt now.

She remembered Margery's warning: *Your ghost could be in danger. It's easy to kill a dead person. Who's going to miss her?*

Was it only this afternoon that she and Margery had been sitting by the Coronado pool, talking about the library ghost? It seemed like weeks ago.

From the way Charlotte's body was positioned, Helen guessed she'd been walking toward the building on her way to her job interview. She'd never made it. She never got her job or her chance for a new life. Now Charlotte really was a ghost.

Helen felt queasy. She had to get out of here. She pushed her way out of the crowd, but this time people let her pass without comment.

Once she was free, Helen ran toward her car. She needed to sit down before she passed out. As her feet pounded the pavement, she heard this message in her head: Charlotte's dead. She's dead. Dead.

Who did this? Who ran down Charlotte and left her to die?

Was she killed to keep from revealing where she hid the million-dollar watercolor?

Is her killer back at the library now, searching for it?

Or did the killer take the painting?

CHAPTER 21

"**P**hil," Helen said, "the ghost is dead." Her voice shook and her fingers trembled as she tried to hold on to her cell phone. The cool air in the Igloo had calmed her a little, but she was relieved when Phil answered.

"You're not making sense, Helen," he said. "What ghost? Where?"

"Oh," she said, "I didn't get to tell you what happened this morning. I found the library ghost. Her name is Charlotte and she's homeless. She found the Kingsley watercolor and said she hid it at the library."

She told her disjointed tale several times, until Phil figured out what had happened.

"So Charlotte, who may or may not have walked off with the million-dollar watercolor, was killed by a hit-and-run driver," he said.

"Right," Helen said. "She told me she'd hidden the watercolor at the library. We need to search for the painting now."

"How do you know she was telling the truth?" Phil asked.

"I don't," Helen said. "But if she wanted to skip town, she could have. Instead, she went for the job interview."

"When does the library close tonight?" he asked.

"Early. Five o'clock," she said. "I'll ask Alexa to help us search."

"Make sure she sends everyone else home," Phil said. "Charlotte's killer has to be someone connected with the library."

"I thought someone was listening at the Kingsley collection door," Helen said, "but I didn't see anyone. They might have heard me talking to Alexa, the director, too. You don't think Charlotte's death was a real hit-and-run accident, do you?"

"That would be an amazing coincidence," he said. "Too amazing. I'll leave for the library now and wait for you in the lot."

She felt a little calmer when she called Alexa. Helen needed only two tries to make the library director understand that Charlotte was dead.

"That poor young woman," Alexa said, "living from hand to mouth for months, then killed before she could start a new life. Of course I'll help, Helen. The library closes in fifteen minutes. I'll meet you and Phil at the staff entrance."

Half an hour later, Helen was at the Flora Park Library. The late-afternoon sun painted the old stucco building a creamy pink, and the gardens looked cool and inviting.

She saw Phil waiting in his black Jeep, and parked next to it. He folded her into his arms. "You look white and shocked," he said.

"I am shocked," Helen said. "Oh, Phil, if you could have seen that poor woman. Her death was so terrible—and so unfair."

He held her tight and she felt the comfort of his strong arms. Then Helen looked up and winced when she saw his burned face.

"Ouch. You're peeling," she said.

"You mean ap-pealing, don't you?" he said, and held her close.

"Seriously, how do you feel?" she asked, and kissed his red, flaky nose. They walked hand in hand toward the staff entrance.

"I was so busy edging the drive and walkways at the Coakley house," he said, "I barely noticed the sunburn. Ana fixed us another spectacular lunch. She loves cooking for an appreciative audience."

"Learn anything else about Bree's stolen necklace and the missing golf cart?" Helen asked.

"No, but Ana's set up a meeting with the two servers from Bree's birthday party. One o'clock tomorrow in her kitchen. Can you make it?"

"Definitely," Helen said.

"Be prepared for a treat," Phil said. "Ana's cooking lunch again. Both servers have to leave for work at three o'clock."

"I'll bring my appetite," Helen said. But she wondered if she'd be able to eat tomorrow. She felt numb now.

Alexa met them at the library door. Helen could see the long day—or the news of Charlotte's murder—had taken its toll on the library director. Fresh lipstick didn't disguise how worn she looked. Even her hair seemed tired.

"I had a hard time getting Lisa to leave," Alexa said. "The only reason she finally went home was she got a call from her mother's caregiver. Some problem with a prescription. Now everyone's gone but Blair."

"What's she doing here this late?" Helen asked.

"She took an extra-long lunch and now she insists on staying and sorting books for the Friends' sale shelves."

Or snooping, Helen thought. Did Blair overhear Charlotte? Is she conducting her own search for the missing watercolor?

"I know how to get Blair out of the library," Helen said. "Take me with you this time."

Blair was in the Friends' intake room, sorting through tattered paperbacks. "More worthless donations!" she said, holding up a paperback with the cover stripped off. "We can't resell bookstore returns. The stores strip the covers off unsold paperbacks and send them back to the publishers. We still need more books for our Friends' shelves."

"I appreciate your dedication," Alexa said, "but I need to lock up and leave. Please."

Here goes, Helen thought. "I'll help you tomorrow, Blair," she said. "I'll come in at ten and sort until lunchtime."

"Well," Blair said.

Alexa took that as a yes. "Super!" she said, steering Blair toward the staff door. "Here's your purse. Thank you so much." One more polite shove and Blair was out the door. Alexa double-locked it, then began dousing the library lights.

A few minutes later, Helen, Phil and Alexa heard a car engine start in the parking lot. "I think it's safe now," Alexa said. "Helen, where should we start?"

"I surprised Charlotte hiding in the storage closet in this hall," Helen said.

Alexa flicked on the single bulb, but it barely made a difference, it was so dark in the windowless hall. "We'll need flashlights for the search," she said. "We keep two in the break room."

Alexa was back shortly. She handed a big yellow flashlight to Helen and kept the other.

Now twin pools of light danced off the hall's dark woodwork and faded wallpaper. The rows of closed doors seemed to be hiding secrets.

"How did Charlotte stand it, living alone in this gloom?" Helen asked.

She felt uneasy. Helen swore she saw Charlotte in the shifting shadows. Paris capered at her feet, but even the playful calico couldn't lighten her mood.

Helen jumped when she saw Charlotte's sad brown eyes staring at her.

"What's wrong?" Phil said.

"Nothing," Helen said, relieved it really was nothing. The mournful brown eyes were simply the wood grain in an old door.

She pointed her flashlight at a narrow door. "This is the storage closet where I found her. I'll search if you two will hold the flashlights."

The closet held a janitor's rolling bucket, mops, brooms and shelves of cleaning supplies. Helen picked a black sock off the floor and felt herself tear up. The sock was still damp, but the woman who'd washed it was dead. This morning, Charlotte had been conniving to take half of my money, she thought. Now she's a murder victim.

She wiped her eyes.

"Are you sure you're okay?" Phil asked. She could see his concern in the dim light.

"Tired," she said. "Like everyone else."

They searched each room on that side of the hall and found broken chairs, three-legged tables, dusty bookshelves, a broken book cart—the usual library odds and ends.

The trio crossed the hall to open the other row of doors. Helen shined her light on the Kingsley collection door and saw a flat, dusty handprint on the wood, fairly high up.

"Look at that," she said. "Someone was definitely listening. Someone tall."

Blair? The head Friend of the Library was known for listening at doors, Helen thought. Lisa the board president? She was tall and skinny, but was she also a snoop? Seraphina, Elizabeth's snarky friend? Gladys the leggy librarian? Jared, the bitter janitor? His closet was across the hall. What sweet revenge if he could steal the Kingsley watercolor. But I heard him hammering. Except I didn't check to see if it was him. Just like I didn't check Charlotte's briefcase.

"Let's take a look," Alexa said. She opened the Kingsley collection room with her skeleton key. Helen saw the stacks of numbered book boxes, the table with the elephant folios protected by their acid free paper, the pair of white cotton gloves resting on top of the folios, the scissors and tape.

"This looks the way I left it," Helen said.

The search was numbingly dull. Only Paris, chasing shadows and flashlight beams, relieved the boredom.

"What time is it?" Helen asked.

"Ten thirty," Alexa said, and yawned. "I'm ready to fold. Only the library supply room and the Friends' intake room are left."

"Did Charlotte say anything that might give us a clue?" Phil asked.

Did she? Helen was so shocked by Charlotte's death, she hadn't thought about their conversation. She'd raced back to the library before the killer found the painting. But now she remembered Charlotte's taunt, just before she left.

"She may have," Helen said. "She told me, *Don't worry—it's still here. I hid it well. When I get back, I'll serve it to you on a platter. That's a clue.*"

"It is?" Alexa said.

"That's what Charlotte told me," Helen said. "Didn't sound like a clue to me. I'd rather check the supply room first. It's cleaner."

The supply room was under what used to be Flora Portland's lavish dining room. The long, narrow room was painted a fresh white. Four gray metal shelves were arranged in a U that took up half the cramped space. Behind the shelves Helen saw four tall wooden bookcases.

"Gladys does an excellent job of organizing our library supplies," Alexa said. The shelves were stocked with library secrets: bar code labels, liquid plastic glue for book repairs, date-due cards, book jacket covers and more.

"Everything in order here," Alexa said.

"What's behind those metal shelves?" Helen asked.

"Old oak bookcases," Alexa said. "They haven't been touched in years."

"I want to check," Helen said. She and Phil carefully pushed a metal supply shelf aside, and Helen squeezed past. The oak bookshelves had been rearranged to form a room. One shelf was left at an angle, and Helen slid through it. Little Paris followed her.

Helen found a makeshift bed of old cushions and new blankets. The empty shelves had been dusted and held a few sweaters, blouses, underwear, jeans and socks, all neatly folded. She saw a flashlight, half a bottle of shampoo, three energy bars and a stack of paperbacks. The battery-operated TV sat on a box.

A small wooden box held a photo of a smiling, brown-haired woman in a pink dress, and a few papers, including a birth certificate for Charlotte Ann Dams, born May 6, 1993. She was twenty-two.

"I've found Charlotte's hideaway," Helen said.

Phil and Alexa crowded into the tiny space. "Do you think she hid the watercolor in here?" Helen asked.

"I hope so," Alexa said. "I don't want to tackle the Friends' intake room tonight."

They checked behind three of the heavy bookcases, but found nothing except an old globe. "Boy, is this map of Europe outdated," Helen said. "It still has East and West Germany."

"I'm exhausted," Alexa said. "Let's sit for a minute."

The three searchers plopped down on Charlotte's bed. Helen noticed the director had a smudge on her cheek. She kicked off her heels and sighed. Phil looked like he was molting.

"There's nothing else to search," Helen said, "except behind that bookcase against the back wall."

"Do we really want to move it?" Alexa said.

"No," Helen said. "But it's either that or the bug-infested Friends' intake room."

Alexa groaned, but she stood up and dusted off her suit. "Let's go," she said.

Paris the cat ran in front of them and squeezed her

small furry body behind the heavy bookcase. "Now we have to get Paris," Helen said. "We can't shut her up in here overnight. Come on, kitty. Come on out."

Merp! Paris said, but the cat refused to budge.

"We can't leave her," Helen said.

Phil pulled on the massive bookcase, and it rolled out easily from the wall.

"It's on castors," Alexa said.

"There's a small door in the wall behind it," Helen said.

"That's an old dumbwaiter," Alexa said. "It must have taken food to the dining room upstairs."

"The dumbwaiter!" Helen said. "That's what Charlotte meant when she said she'd serve it to me on a platter."

"I should have figured that out," Alexa said.

"How could you?" Helen said. "You couldn't see it, hidden behind the bookcase. Let's see if it still works."

She pressed a red Bakelite button set into the wall and the dumbwaiter rumbled to life, then stopped at the door.

On the platform was a giant book of sepia photos: *Portraits from North American Indian Life* by Edward S. Curtis.

"The watercolor," Helen said. "Charlotte said she hid it in this book."

• •

CHAPTER 22

"**O**pen it, Helen!" Phil said. "Don't just stand there holding the book. Is the watercolor inside? Quit admiring the cover and find out."

"I can't help it," Helen said. "The photo is stunning. This procession of Native Americans on horseback is straight from a John Ford Western."

"Admire it quickly, please," Alexa said. "It's past eleven."

Curtis's *Portraits from North American Indian Life* was a big book—Helen guessed it was about a foot and a half wide and fifteen inches long—and a heavy one, weighing four or five pounds.

She set the massive photo book on the closest shelf, and Paris the cat hopped up next to it. The calico sat down, fluffed her fur and gave a warbly purr, as if congratulating herself.

"You did good, girl," Helen said, and opened the giant book.

No watercolor was pressed between the cover and title page. Nothing was in the two introductions, or the descriptions of the photos.

When she came to the first sepia photo, Helen said,

"Look at these Piegan people with their horse-drawn travois."

"Helen!" Phil said. She heard the warning in his voice, and began thumbing through the photos faster. She'd been paralyzed when she first held the book. Now she was almost afraid to keep going.

If I don't find the watercolor, I've screwed up twice, she thought. Charlotte has lost her life and I've lost our client's future. Well, I can't stay in here all night.

She turned the pages as quickly as she could without tearing them. The book was more than forty years old and the paper was fragile. The photos were eerie windows into the past. She caught a glimpse of Princess Angeline, her serene, aged face etched with wrinkles, on page seventeen. She paged past photos of a Cheyenne girl with solemn dark eyes, a Makah tribe whaler and a happy Apache baby. Page after page of photos, but no sign of the watercolor.

I'll come back and linger over them another time, she told herself. She could feel Alexa's and Phil's impatience. It was almost a physical force in the small airless space. They were so impatient she thought they might take the book away.

Keep turning the pages, she told herself. If you've made a mistake, then you'll have to live with it. And so will Elizabeth. Charlotte doesn't get that luxury.

Helen felt cold, even though sweat ran down her forehead. She wiped it off.

Now there were fewer than ten pages left. As Helen neared the end of the book, she felt the dread pressing on her, sucking the oxygen out of Charlotte's makeshift bedroom. I'm a poor excuse for a private eye, she thought.

Then, when she came to page 173, she said, "Geronimo!"

"His photo's in there, too?" Phil asked.

"Yes," Helen said, "and Geronimo has our alligators." There, on top of the Apache warrior, was the John

Singer Sargent watercolor. Alexa and Phil moved closer to examine it. Helen could feel Phil's breath on her sweaty neck. The colors were mostly muddy brown, blue-gray, red-brown, and green.

The watercolor sat perfectly still on the page, but it seemed to move. The six sun-drenched, mud-caked gators were a menacing mass. The ridge-tailed reptiles slithered and pulsed with primeval life. A small gator crawled to the front of the watercolor, teeth bared. The alligators' slitty eyes were small and mean.

"This is not Grandma's sweet daisies watercolor," Helen whispered. "It has power."

"I read about the Sargent watercolor," Alexa said, "once I heard it might be in our library. This one is slightly smaller than his other alligator watercolors. It fits neatly into this book."

"The technique is incredible," Phil said.

"You can see where Sargent scratched the thick paper to make the alligators' teeth seem sharper," Alexa said. "If you hold it up to the light, you'll see where he applied wax to give the alligators their rough texture."

"Really?" Helen said, and reached for the drawing.

"Don't touch it!" Alexa said. She ran to the supply shelf and tossed Helen a pair of white cotton gloves.

"I want to see if Clark Gable signed the back," Helen said.

She slipped on the soft gloves, then carefully turned over the painting. "There's the writing, with what looks like a black fountain pen," she said, and read the inscription out loud. "'I lost this fair and square to Woodrow Kingsley—W. C. Gable, 1924.'"

"Looks like a man's handwriting," Phil said.

"The loops on the lowercase *F*s are thin," Alexa said. "The *T*s are looped and crossed with straight lines, and the uppercase *G* is classic Palmer method. It looks like Gable's writing."

"How do you know about Gable's handwriting?" Helen asked.

"I've seen samples online," Alexa said. "Elizabeth will have to have it authenticated by a handwriting expert, of course, along with the watercolor."

"You're amazing," Helen said.

"Not for a librarian," Alexa said. "We find out things."

"It's heading toward midnight," Helen said. "Should we call Elizabeth with the news?"

"Would you want to wake up and hear you had a million dollars?" Alexa said. "Let's call her from my office."

Helen held the book like a trophy. She'd never carried a million dollars before. Phil and Alexa followed her down the dim hall, Paris padding at their feet.

When the book was safely on Alexa's desk, the library director sat behind her desk, and the private eyes settled themselves in the barrel chairs. Helen put her phone on speaker and called Elizabeth.

"What's wrong?" the groggy Elizabeth said. Helen imagined her in a sensible cotton nightgown with a high collar and long sleeves, her gray hair in a plait for the night.

"Nothing," Helen said. "Everything is fine. Extra fine. I'm calling from Alexa's office at the library. We've found your watercolor."

"You did?" Now Elizabeth was fully alert. "At this hour?"

Helen told her the whole story—well, almost—she left out her own careless mistakes and Charlotte's demand for half of her fee.

Elizabeth interrupted only once. "Charlotte? Was she the young woman who was killed in the accident at Broward and Bettencourt? I saw the story on the evening news, but the reporter didn't give the victim's name."

"That's her," Helen said. "But her death was no accident."

"We think she was murdered," Phil said.

"Dreadful," Elizabeth said. "Who do you think killed her?"

"We believe the murderer has to be connected with

the library," Phil said. "The killer heard that Charlotte found the watercolor and killed her before she could come back and claim it."

Helen heard a gasp.

"What if someone kills me?" Elizabeth said. "Can't we keep this quiet?"

"The killer will tear the library apart, looking for the watercolor," Phil said.

"Better to make it public knowledge," Alexa said. "And safer for you. I'll mention that the painting has been found tomorrow."

Today, Helen thought.

"And have a courier take it to your lawyer's office," Alexa said, "where it will be safe until it's appraised and sold."

"Is it safe to keep a million-dollar painting in the library tonight?" Elizabeth asked.

"I'll lock it in our safe," Alexa said.

Helen hoped Elizabeth didn't ask how many people knew the combination to the library safe.

"It will be fine," Alexa soothed. "This is the best way to handle it."

"I suppose," Elizabeth said. "I hope I live long enough to enjoy the money."

CHAPTER 23

. . . .

"The body of a twenty-two-year-old Fort Lauderdale woman was found in this abandoned supermarket lot at three thirty yesterday afternoon," investigative reporter Valerie Cannata said, "the victim of an apparent hit-and-run."

The TV camera panned the desolate parking lot under a watery lemon sun. No cars were in the lot at seven in the morning. Even at this early hour, Valerie was poised and stylish in a lime green sleeveless dress that bared her well-toned arms and showed off her red hair.

Helen knew the glamorous Channel 77 reporter, and hit Record on the DVR so Phil could see the broadcast after work.

"Authorities are not releasing the dead woman's name pending notification of her family," the reporter said. "Channel Seventy-seven broke the story yesterday. This morning, we're talking to the detective assigned to the case. Micah Doben is a Bettencourt crimes-against-persons detective."

The plump detective had a face like a potato, a monk's fringe of white hair and raisin eyes behind rimless glasses. Doben wore a baggy gray suit with a lavender shirt and dark purple tie that looked like something his wife had picked out. Helen guessed his age as mid-fifties.

"Detective Doben, what can you tell us about this accident?" Valerie asked.

"The victim was apparently struck and killed between eleven thirty a.m. and three thirty p.m.," he said, reciting the facts in a flat voice. "We believe the fatal accident most likely occurred between eleven thirty and noon. The victim had a twelve o'clock appointment for a job interview at Norton Management in the building next door. It was a callback; and the victim was going to be hired. The company's customer service manager said the victim did not report as expected."

"Was the victim taken to the hospital?" Valerie asked.

"No, she was pronounced dead at the scene," Detective Doben said. "The medical examiner believes she was killed instantly."

"Was this accident caught on camera?" Valerie asked. "Are there any witnesses?"

"No," the detective said. "There are no witnesses and no video. However, at a preliminary autopsy, the medical examiner did find chips of white vehicle paint on the victim's body."

"Do you know the vehicle's make and model?" Valerie asked.

"We will need more time to determine that," the detective said. "This is the third fatal hit-and-run accident at the corner of Broward Boulevard and Bettencourt Street in three months. It's a very dangerous intersection, and we are asking pedestrians and drivers to exercise caution.

"A sixteen-year-old high school student was killed August sixth at three p.m. and a thirty-four-year-old man was fatally injured September ninth at seven ten in the evening. Now this woman was killed yesterday."

"But Charlotte's accident isn't close to that corner," Helen said to the TV set.

Valerie's next question echoed Helen's objection. "This parking lot is more than two blocks north of that intersection," the TV reporter said, "but you're saying this fatality happened at Broward and Bettencourt."

Good for you, Helen thought. You're thinking on your feet.

"It's in the same vicinity," the detective said, "and we will be investigating it as a vehicular homicide."

Helen, who'd encountered smart cops and dumb ones, now had doubts about Detective Doben. Bettencourt was a small, tightly knit community in west Broward County, best known for the exclusive Bettencourt Country Club. The police force was mostly older, white, male, and respectful to the residents. Detective Doben had already dismissed Charlotte's death as a hit-and-run, which gave the town the quick, easy answer it wanted.

"Bettencourt police are looking for information about this hit-and-run accident," Valerie said. "If you saw the accident, noticed a white car or truck speeding away from the scene, or know of a white vehicle that has recently been in an accident, please call this number."

Helen found a pen and wrote down the number. She'd probably have to tell the detective what she knew about Charlotte. But not without some legal advice first.

She poured herself a cup of coffee and called attorney Nancie Hays. Coronado Investigations was the lawyer's in-house private-eye firm. Helen knew the little lawyer would already be at her desk, dressed in a sensible suit. Nancie was an early riser.

Helen winced at Nancie's blast of good-morning cheer. "Helen," she said. "How are my favorite newlyweds? Not in any trouble, I hope."

"That's why I'm calling you," Helen said. "Did you see the story about the hit-and-run death on Broward Boulevard yesterday?"

"Yes. Was the victim a client of yours?"

"Not exactly," Helen said, and told her how she knew Charlotte.

"You should go to the police," Nancie said. "Definitely. But before you can disclose any information to the cops, you'll need permission from your two clients, the library director and Elizabeth Kingsley."

"Both?" Helen said.

"In writing," Nancie said. "You know the law, Helen. Private eyes can't disclose anything without their clients' permission, and you have a duty to report what you know. Also, I should be present during any police questioning."

Helen groaned. "Do you have to be?"

"No, not if you want a repeat of what happened last time."

"Okay, okay," Helen said. Nancie would save her hours wasted in a claustrophobic room at a police station.

"Start calling," Nancie ordered.

Helen reached Alexa at home. "Do we really have to do this, Helen?" the library director said.

Helen caught the hint of a whine. Maybe she hadn't had her coffee yet.

"The police need the information about Charlotte," Helen said, "and I can't give it to them without your permission."

"This is going to cause problems," Alexa said. "Our homeless man, Ted, has always been well behaved, but if word gets out that someone was actually living here, the Flora Park Library will become a mecca for homeless people. They like to congregate at libraries: We're quiet, free and safe. The homeless are a nationwide problem."

"Where else can they go?" Helen said. "And what if Charlotte's death wasn't a simple hit-and-run? What if she was murdered because of that watercolor?"

"That's what you believe?" Alexa said.

"Yes," Helen said. She held her breath. She could feel Alexa edging closer to consenting.

"Well, we've talked about starting a community outreach program for the homeless," Alexa said.

Helen kept still. Alexa inched closer to agreement.

"And it is the ethical thing to do. So I say yes. I'll write a letter giving you permission. Can I fax it to your office and give you the original?"

"Thank you so much," Helen said. She felt weak with relief. One tough call down, one to go.

Elizabeth was awake at eight o'clock, alert and delighted to hear from Helen—until the private eye explained why she was calling.

"I'd prefer not to have my private business made public," Elizabeth said.

"I understand," Helen said. "But a young woman was murdered."

"A woman living illegally at the Flora Park Library," Elizabeth said. The last traces of friendliness were gone. Helen could feel ice on her cell phone, freezing her fingers.

"Charlotte was twenty-two and homeless, through no fault of her own," Helen said. "She was out of work and would have had a new job, if she hadn't been killed. Surely, you of all people understand what it's like to need money."

"I don't parade my financial difficulties before the world," Elizabeth said.

The ice burned Helen's fingers. I'm liking my client a little less with each sentence she says, she thought.

"Elizabeth, you do realize that Charlotte may have been killed because she knew about your watercolor."

"Yes, but catching the killer won't bring her back. I don't like having my privacy invaded."

Did she really say *priv*-acy, like an actor on *Downton Abbey*? Helen wondered. And why am I defending Charlotte, a crafty woman who'd tried to take half my fee? Because I only had to open thirty or forty boxes, thanks to her, instead of three hundred. Nice work for five grand.

"Elizabeth, last night you were concerned about your safety. So concerned that Alexa is getting an armed guard to deliver the watercolor to your lawyer."

"I'll be safe once it's with my attorney," she said.

Helen wanted to scream. Elizabeth was maddening. I need to think like a rich person, she decided.

"Elizabeth," Helen said. "I understand why you don't want this story public. But you do know part of the painting's value is its association—the story behind that Clark Gable signature."

"So?"

"More publicity may increase the painting's value," Helen said.

"You're right," Elizabeth said. "It is my civic duty. I'll give you the authorization."

Finally, Helen thought. I've learned to think like a rich person. Now if I only had the money to go with the mind-set.

She thought talking to Detective Doben would be the easy part. She was wrong again.

Doben agreed to meet Helen and Nancie Hays at the Bettencourt police headquarters, which turned out to be next to the first tee at the famous country club. The cop shop lawn looked like an extension of the golf greens, and a small neat sign warned people parking their cars that the police were not responsible for any damage due to golf balls. Helen parked the Igloo on the far side of the lot, and Nancie joined her moments later in her practical Toyota.

Detective Doben was not pleased when he met Helen and Nancie. In fact, he was hostile. Nancie had a reputation for tenacity and had ruined more than one incompetent detective's career.

He recognized the notorious lawyer and showed the two women into a small cluttered room with a coffee-ringed table and bulletin boards papered with Wanted posters and yellowing memos. Doben carried a foam cup of coffee but did not offer them any.

"Why do you need to drag in a lawyer?" he said, his face nearly the same shade of purple as his tie.

He glared at Nancie while she explained why she'd

accompanied Helen. Detective Doben seemed bored by Helen's story, though he did take notes.

"So I believe there may be a connection between Charlotte's death and the million-dollar watercolor," Helen said, finishing her story with a flourish.

"You do, huh? You know what I believe, Ms. Hawthorne? I believe you have a vivid imagination. How many hit-and-runs have you investigated?"

"None," Helen said.

"I thought so. I've seen more hit-and-run accidents than you've had birthdays. I know what they look like. Miss Dams's death is a straightforward hit-and-run. No fancy theories. Some driver in a hurry hit that poor girl and killed her. It's my job to find that person.

"Now, if you'll excuse me, ladies, I have a killer to catch."

CHAPTER 24

· ·

Helen read the praise on Morris Mosselman's science-fiction bestseller, *Foundation of Doom*. "A meaty novel . . . a must-read."

A meaty novel maybe, she thought. But spoiled meat?

Helen was helping Blair sort books in the Friends of the Library intake room, and this seven-hundred-page novel was in her four-foot stack of donations. She was glad she was wearing latex gloves. So far this morning, she'd encountered used tissues, wriggling silverfish and a squashed spider stuck to a back cover. Now she had to deal with this smelly novel.

Foundation of Doom fell open to page 457 and Helen saw the source of the stink.

"Ick." She tossed the fat book in the trash can for infested books and slammed down the lid, as if it could crawl out.

"What's wrong?" Blair asked, looking over the top of her equally tall stack. Today, her brown hair was twisted into a tight knot and her long, lean body encased in a dirt-colored pantsuit.

"Someone used a strip of bacon for a bookmark," Helen said.

"It could go with the fried egg I once found in a book," Blair said. The head Friend was in a chatty mood this morning. She didn't seem to mind that Helen had showed up fifteen minutes late, and Helen didn't mention she'd talked to the Bettencourt detective. Blair was too full of her own news.

"You missed the excitement," she said. "Alexa called us together and said that a homeless woman had been living in the library. Can you imagine?"

"Must have been uncomfortable," Helen said.

"I would think so," Blair said. "Homelessness is an issue for libraries. Did you know that Washington, DC, even has rules about homeless people? I read that they cannot have bare feet, drink alcohol or have an odor that can be smelled six feet away."

"Amazing," Helen said.

"Fortunately, our homeless man, Ted, is no trouble at all."

She makes the man sound like a pet dog, Helen thought.

"What's going to happen to the woman who lived in the library?" Helen asked. "Will the library prosecute her?"

"Oh, no," Blair said. "Alexa said she was killed in a car accident last night. It was on the TV news, but the story didn't give her name."

"I saw the news at seven this morning," Helen said. "The accident happened at the corner of Broward and Bettencourt." She gave the wrong location to see if Blair knew where the accident really happened.

"Actually, the accident took place in the old Monarch supermarket lot," Blair said, "almost two blocks away."

And how did you know that? Helen wondered. "Valerie Cannata interviewed the detective for the case early this morning on Channel Seventy-seven," she said. "Is that the story you watched?"

"No, I saw it on the ten o'clock news last night," Blair

said. "Valerie Cannata is such a good reporter, isn't she? She always looks so chic."

What Valerie's wardrobe had to do with her reporting, Helen had no idea, but she agreed as she thumbed through a David Ellis mystery. That hardcover was safe to sell and she put it in the "keep" pile.

"Oh, I forgot to tell you the other news," Blair said. "The John Singer Sargent watercolor has been found. Alexa had an armed guard take it to Elizabeth Kingsley's lawyer's office."

Good for Alexa, Helen thought. She handled the transfer of the watercolor quickly and sensibly. I'm glad she didn't mention my name.

"That's exciting," Helen said. "Did you see it?"

"No, I wish I could have. I've never seen a million-dollar painting before, except in a museum," Blair said, "but it was already wrapped in protective acid-free paper.

"Alexa said now that the watercolor's been found, the Friends can sort and sell the Kingsley collection."

"You'll find those books are in much better shape than these," Helen said.

"I know," Blair said. "We went through a few boxes before Alexa made us stop. I wanted to sort through the last of these donations before we go to work in the Kingsley collection room."

She opened a Leslie Glass mystery and found a recipe card. "Look at this," Blair said. "A recipe card for mango curry chicken. No name on it, but the recipe looks tasty. Think I'll keep that."

Blair was so delighted that the Friends could start selling the Kingsley collection again, she never asked Helen if she'd found the watercolor. To keep her distracted, Helen asked, "What else have you found in books besides bugs and recipes?"

"Oh, the usual," she said. "Shopping and to-do lists, airline boarding passes, birthday and sympathy cards. You expect to find those, along with people's mail. I've found brochures on treatment options for cancer, leukemia and Parkinson's disease in books. I hope those books weren't part of the sick person's estate.

"Once, I found a dirty gym sock that had been used as a bookmark. Banana peels are fairly common. And sand. Lots of sand."

"Real beach books," Helen said.

"The sand is annoying, but it doesn't have six legs," Blair said. "You should ask the librarians. They love talking about the strange things they find in books."

"Ever find any money?" Helen asked.

"Oh, yes. I found seven dollars once. Of course, I donated it to the Friends. We have one library patron who uses a dollar bill as a bookmark. Sometimes he leaves the dollar in the book when he returns it. The librarians at the checkout desk always give it back to him the next time he comes in. He says it's cheaper to use a dollar than to buy a bookmark."

Helen wondered about that. Her bookmarks were either free or to-do lists and airline boarding passes.

"I've found some lovely pressed flowers and leaves," Blair said. "I could talk all day about what turns up in books."

Instead, Helen let her talk until twelve noon, when Blair wanted her lunch break. She thanked Helen somewhat formally.

I have an hour before I meet Phil at the Coakley mansion to interview the servers from Bree's wild birthday bash, she thought. Might as well say good-bye to Alexa now.

Helen stopped by Alexa's office and found the library director having tea with Elizabeth Kingsley. The two women sat on a pale yellow sofa on the far side of the room. Alexa presided over a Blue Willow tea set and a tiered plate of iced cakes and crustless sandwiches.

"Helen, I'm glad you stopped by. Would you care to join us?" Alexa asked. The library director looked rested and relaxed today. Her dark hair was perfect, and that unusual white lock was accented by her cool cream suit. Elizabeth was the picture of a well-bred lady in Minton blue.

"Just a quick cup," Helen said. "I have to leave at twelve thirty. I wanted to say good-bye, since my work here is done."

"That's one of the things we wanted to discuss with you," Alexa said.

One? Helen thought as she took the delicate blue-and-white cup from Alexa.

"Elizabeth and I have your permission letters," Alexa said. "How did the interview with the police detective go?"

"He wasn't interested in my information," Helen said, and sipped her tea. "He believes Charlotte's death is a hit-and-run accident."

"That's a relief," Elizabeth said. "Maybe we won't be in the paper after all."

"I don't believe your work here is finished," Alexa said. "Both Elizabeth and I agree that we need you to find Charlotte's killer. Do you still think the killer has a connection to this library?"

"Absolutely," Helen said. "It's no coincidence that Charlotte was killed right after she told me she'd found the watercolor. Someone here at the library overheard her talking to me. I think that person was listening at the door. I thought I heard something, but when I opened the door, I didn't see anyone. Charlotte left for her job interview and was run down before she could return and tell me where she hid the painting."

Helen mentally ticked off the people who'd been in the library at that time: Elizabeth's jealous friend, Seraphina. Blair, the annoying head Friend who listened at doors and wanted the watercolor to restore the library. Jared, the bitter janitor who was mopping floors instead of enjoying a comfortable old age. Gladys the librarian babe in debt down to her designer shoes. Lisa Hamilton, the tall, thin library board president who'd enlisted a medium to call up the ghost of Flora Portland and save her beloved library.

"I think the killer wanted Charlotte out of the way to look for the Sargent artwork," Helen said.

"We cannot have an unsolved murder here, no matter how tenuous the connection to our library," Alexa said.

"And I won't feel safe until the killer is caught," Elizabeth said.

"That's why we'd like you to find Charlotte's killer," Alexa said.

"I can't quit this job no matter how hard I try," Helen said, but she smiled. "I'll draw up a new contract and bring it in tomorrow."

"Yoo-hoo." Seraphina stuck her head in the door. "Come out and see my super new Mercedes."

Elizabeth's towering, horse-faced friend wore a striped navy top and white linen pants, with a sweater tied around her neck. Why do rich people drape their sweaters like capes? Helen wondered.

Elizabeth raised one eyebrow in surprise. "I thought you liked Beemers, Seraphina," she said, sipping her tea.

"Time to move up," Seraphina said. "Naughty of me, I know, but I bought an S-Class—the S65 AMG."

She'd just spent more than 220,000 bucks for a car, Helen thought. Phil, who had a keen interest in cars, had been talking about the S-Class recently. Not that he would—or could—trade in his beat-up Jeep for one. The Jeep was good for surveillance, and blended in to most neighborhoods.

"Come for a test drive," Seraphina said, flashing a pearly row of white teeth. "You won't believe the ride."

"This is sudden," Elizabeth said. "I thought your Beemer was pretty."

"I'm tired of white cars," Seraphina said. "Old ladies drive them."

"Don't tell Lisa that," Alexa said. "She loves her white Jaguar."

"Well, Jaguars are different," Seraphina said, though Helen wasn't sure why.

"I gave my white Beemer to my son, Ozzie. He needed a car for school. He demanded a black Beemer, but I put my foot down. *You can have a free Beemer that's white or you can buy yourself one in a color you like. If you really want a black Beemer, you can pay to have it repainted.* He complained, but he couldn't afford to turn it down. That boy is so spoiled." She said that as if she was proud of his faults.

"I bought myself this coal black Mercedes," Seraphina said, and smiled. "I've moved to the dark side."

CHAPTER 25

Someone driving a white car killed our ghost, Helen thought. Ran down Charlotte Ann Dams in a grim, potholed parking lot before she could begin her new life. Now it's my job to find her killer.

Helen didn't stay to admire Seraphina's overpriced car. Instead, she fired up the Igloo in the library parking lot, and headed for the Coakley mansion to interview the servers from Bree's birthday party.

As she followed the twisty, tree-shaded streets in Flora Park, Helen thought about the strange, elusive woman who'd lived in the library.

Charlotte was a survivor. Homelessness breaks most people: They're defeated by drugs, alcohol, illness, loneliness, heat, hunger and hatred. But Charlotte made a safe haven for herself in the library, and escaped detection for more than a month.

Charlotte was proud. She could have gone home and lived with her mother in a place she didn't like, but she preferred to fight to live where she wanted—in Florida.

Charlotte was ambitious. She left her comfortable

library berth every morning to look for a new job and a better life. She struggled to keep herself and her clothes clean and dress professionally for her job interviews.

Charlotte had an eye for the main chance. She heard about the lost Sargent watercolor. At night, when the library was closed, she searched for the missing painting in an airless, dusty room, and found it.

When Helen surprised her, Charlotte quickly leveraged her find into a promise of cash. Five thousand dollars would be a sizable nest egg for her.

Charlotte was honest. Yes, she connived to take half of Helen's fee, but she could have made off with the painting and brokered her own deal with Elizabeth Kingsley. Getting that job was more important than cashing in on a quick sale.

Now Helen steered the Igloo onto busy Federal Highway in Fort Lauderdale, lined with look-alike franchises and struggling businesses, and wondered: How did Charlotte come to grief? Why was she killed right before she claimed her long-awaited prize—the coveted job?

She died for that watercolor. Someone else wanted that million-dollar painting. Someone with easy access to the Flora Park Library. Someone who thought she—or he— could outsmart the homeless woman, find Charlotte's nest inside the library and take the painting.

A killer with a white car.

Except Helen, Alexa and Phil had found the watercolor first.

A white Lexus cut Helen off in traffic, and a waddling creamy Lincoln hogged the fast lane.

White was a common color in South Florida. Snowbirds avoided white vehicles in the cold north because they're harder to see in the snow. Once northerners moved down to Florida, they rushed out and bought white. Longtime Floridians were also partial to that color.

Why did Seraphina, Elizabeth's snotty friend, suddenly give her white Beemer to her son and buy a black Mercedes? Everyone knows black cars show the dust and dirt, especially during South Florida's rainy season.

I guess if you can afford to spend nearly a quarter of a million dollars on a car, Helen thought, you don't worry about car-wash costs. Maybe Seraphina has staff who clean her car.

Or maybe she was telling the truth: She really did go to the dark side—and kill Charlotte.

Lisa Hamilton, the library board president, drives a white Jaguar. Did she need money?

What color car does Blair, the cat-hating Friend of the Library, have? Helen wondered. I never noticed.

What about Gladys, the librarian who longed for a Ferrari? Was Gladys tired of living on a librarian's salary and ready to splash out? If she sold that million-dollar painting, she could live in style.

Helen couldn't see it. But then, Helen had trouble seeing the real Gladys beyond the stereotypes that plagued her profession.

What did Jared, the disappointed janitor, drive? A pickup truck? A van? An old clunker?

I never noticed, Helen thought. But people don't notice the help, do they? That was what ruined Jared's chance for retirement.

The great Davis Kingsley had made a princely promise to his faithful servant, but never bothered to find out what Jared would need for a decent pension. Stealing the dotty old man's watercolor would be the ultimate revenge.

Helen turned the Igloo off Federal Highway into the charmed circle of Peerless Point, a wealthy bougainvillea-draped enclave where the royal palms whispered secrets and the residents kept them.

The Coakley mansion was on the right, an extravagant sugar cookie of a building with lacy arches and delicate French windows, neatly whitewashed and set amid emerald lawns. Lawns that my husband mows and waters with his sweat, while he tries to learn who stole twenty-one-year-old Bree's ruby pendant.

Helen pulled into the Coakleys' circular drive, parked next to the family's white Range Rover and locked the door of her own white car.

CHAPTER 26

. . . .

"It feels good to have someone wait on me for a change," Mercedes said. The server patted her flat stomach.

"My pleasure," Ana said as she set another huge platter in the center of the round oak table. "You've only started eating. Here's more."

The motherly cook smiled at the hungry people crowded around her table in the back of the Coakley mansion.

We must look like cats begging for dinner, Helen thought. She sat next to a sweaty, sunburned Phil, who was tearing into his lunch like it was his last meal.

John and Charlee, the two full-time gardeners, ate with equal gusto, all the while stealing sideways glances at the pretty Latina servers from Bree's party, Mercedes and Rosita.

Brown-skinned Rosita was strong and chunky with a flat face, soft brown eyes and gold highlights in her brown hair. Mercedes was slender and short, her long dark hair pulled into a high ponytail. Helen guessed both servers were in their early twenties. Their English was good, but Rosita spoke with a trace of an accent and seemed less worldly than Mercedes.

Ana sat next to Helen and began heaping her own plate with food. "Cooks like people with hearty appetites," she said. "It's discouraging when I cook all day and they leave it untouched because it's fattening."

Helen was sure "they" were the Coakleys, probably the mother, Ashler ("I'm not Ashley"), and her daughters, Bree and Chloe.

"But your food is low-cal, isn't it?" Helen said. She was savoring her salmon tacos with chipotle lime yogurt. "What's healthier than grilled salmon? The spicy yogurt dressing isn't as fattening as sour cream, and the cabbage salad is good for you."

"Doesn't taste healthy," Phil said, helping himself to more. That was his idea of a compliment.

"This crab and guacamole salad is amazing," Rosita said.

"What's wrong with Mexican steak and homemade refried beans?" John asked. Helen thought the gardener was dishing himself a third helping.

"It's red meat," Ana said. "And refried beans are fattening. They don't like either one." Helen heard the cook's disgust.

"Their loss," Charlee said. Sun-browned and stocky with short, dark hair, he and John could have been fraternal twins, except Charlee was maybe ten pounds heavier.

"Charlee, do you and John eat this much food every day and then go back to work?" Helen said.

"We work it off fast in the heat," Charlee said. "Today I mowed the St. Augustine, and John was Weedwacking. We gave Phil the coolest job—cleaning the koi pond. He got to play in the water."

"And the muck," Phil said, reaching for the dish of steak and refried beans.

"Where I come from, we look at food differently," Ana said. "We work around our eating schedule. In the US, people eat around their work schedule. They hurry, hurry, hurry. They want a quick bite. That can't be healthy. No time to relax, to talk."

"About that talking," Phil said as he cleaned his plate with a warm tortilla, "can we ask Rosita and Mercedes about Bree's party now?"

"Absolutely," Ana said, and stood up to gather their now-empty plates. Helen rose to help her, but Ana said, "Sit! You're working and I know where everything should go." Helen sat.

"We need you and Phil to find the missing necklace and stolen golf cart," Ana said. "We're all under suspicion until it's cleared up."

John and Charlee nodded agreement.

"These people always blame the help," Mercedes said. "They never think their own kind do anything wrong."

"Not even when Missy Bree has an unsuitable, uh . . . *novio*?" Rosita looked doubtful, as if searching for the right word.

Novio, Helen thought, could mean groom or boyfriend in Spanish.

"Boyfriend," Mercedes said. "From the way Trey and Bree behaved at the party, he should be her husband. They were going at it on a chaise by the pool when I brought them another round of drinks. I wanted to pour it on them. I left the drinks on a nearby table and they never even noticed I was there."

"Disgusting," Ana said. "That party was a Roman orgy." She set a plate of little almond cookies dusted with powdered sugar on the table, and circled the table pouring everyone strong hot coffee.

The rich black coffee tasted of cinnamon and the snow-dusted cookies melted in Helen's mouth.

"I don't know why Bree's parents let her date a young man like that," Ana said.

"Like what?" Helen asked. "Is he into drugs?"

"Of course," Ana said, as if Helen had asked, Does

he have two arms? "But Mr. Coakley is a big-deal lawyer. He took his cell phone into the kitchen one night—
the show kitchen—and I heard him talking to Trey's
father. The mister said he didn't handle criminal cases
but he could refer him to a lawyer who did. Trey was at
the police station for a DUI. Trey also tried to borrow
money from Bree. I overheard that, too. She gave him
some, and he got angry and said it wasn't enough."

"Why did he need money?" Helen asked. "Isn't his
family rich?"

"He's a gambler," Ana said. "Bets big money on
sports teams. Lost his allowance and then some."

"Did Trey know you heard him ask Bree for money?"

"I wasn't listening at doors or anything sneaky," the
cook said. "I'm just a fat, old lady, as far as Trey's concerned. He said it right in front of me, like he'd talk
around a lamp or a table."

"I understand someone saw Bree and her boyfriend
go into the powder room about one thirty the night of
the party," Helen said.

"That was me," Mercedes said. "Those two don't mind
fornicating in the open, but they do their drugs in private.
They went into the bathroom near the downstairs hall
and stayed locked in there about ten minutes."

"Was Bree wearing the ruby necklace when she
came out?" Helen asked.

"Yes," Mercedes said. "She was so out of it, she could
hardly walk. He half carried her into the living room and
I lost track of her."

"I was passing around glasses of champagne in the living room," Rosita said. "Bree had her necklace tangled
in her hair. She has long blond hair and she said it hurt
and asked Trey to help pull it out of her hair. He was
drunk, too, and his hands weren't working so well. It took
him a long time to free the necklace. But he wasn't helping with the necklace the whole time."

"What was he doing?" Helen asked.

Rosita blushed. "First he had both hands down the front of her dress and squeezed her . . . you know. Then he unzipped the back. He said he needed to reach the necklace."

"That boy has some smooth moves," Phil said.

"I was glad I didn't have to watch them," Rosita said. "I was still passing around the champagne. By the time I got back to that part of the room, Bree's dress was off, and she wasn't wearing anything. She'd fallen asleep on top of him. Then she laid—lay—I can never remember which word is correct."

"Probably both," Phil said, and Helen glared at him.

"She stayed there on the couch with him," Rosita said, blushing furiously. "Then a guest took my last glass of champagne and his girlfriend wanted one, too.

"By that time I left to get more glasses of champagne, and when I came back, Bree had passed out or fallen asleep on top of Trey. He looked like he was almost asleep.

"That's when Chloe staggered over and said to her sister, *You are such a slut*. I don't think Bree heard her, she was so far gone."

"Why was Chloe staggering?" Phil asked.

"Because she was drunk," Rosita said. "I didn't want to serve her champagne, but her parents said it was their house and she could have a drink to celebrate her sister's birthday. A drink! She had a bottle, at least. And Chloe wasn't celebrating. She was pouting. She was there with her boyfriend, Snake Boy, but she hardly talked to him the whole night."

"Who's Snake Boy?" Helen asked.

"I don't know his name, but he goes to college to study snakes. He wants to be a herpes-something."

"Herpetologist?" Helen guessed.

"That's the word," Rosita said.

"He's short and stocky with a dark beard?" Helen asked. How many budding snake specialists could there be in Fort Lauderdale? "Is his name Ozzie Ormond?"

"That's him," Rosita said. "He collects snakes and keeps them at his house."

"He's always asking us if we've found any snakes," Charlee said. "He gave me ten dollars for a little baby rattlesnake."

"A pygmy rattlesnake?" Helen asked.

"Yes," Charlee said. "It had a little rattle on its tail. I usually kill them, but I sold it to him. I tried to get twenty for it, but he said he already had one."

So did Aunt Blair get the rattlesnake from Snake Boy? Helen wondered. Ozzie had slithered into the library carrying a cardboard box that morning while I was talking to Gladys. When I came back from lunch, I found the snake in the book box.

"He bought one I found, too," John said. "A red rat snake, but he only gave me five dollars because it's harmless. He pays more for the poison ones."

"He's a snake for real," Ana said. "Chloe was upset that her sister got such a beautiful necklace. She said big jewels were for 'tacky old ladies.' Snake Boy tried to put his arm around her and kiss her, but she shook him off and sat in a corner all night, staring at her sister. She couldn't take her eyes off that necklace.

"Snake Boy couldn't, either—or maybe he was drooling over Bree. He started hitting on her, and Trey, Bree's boyfriend, finally said, *Cool it. Bree's mine.*"

"Was he mad?" Helen asked.

"More like playful mad," she said. "But Bree was really mad. She said, *I'm not your property*, and went off with Snake Boy. I don't know what they did or where they went, but when she came back later, she and Trey were all lovey-dovey."

"So Chloe didn't party much at Bree's birthday bash?" Helen asked.

"She sulked all night," Ana said. "That girl is so jealous. She talks in riddles and plays stupid games. When I first came here, I asked what she wanted for breakfast and she said, *Boneless chicken.*

"I thought she was on some kind of diet, so I grilled her a boneless chicken breast and put some nice fresh fruit on the plate so it didn't look so plain. She laughed at me and called me a stupid beaner. She said boneless chicken was a hard-boiled egg. Why didn't she just say so?"

"She's rude," Helen said. "Chloe and Snake Boy are running some kind of scam. I think she—or he—stole the necklace."

"Like that movie *The Bling Ring*, where a bunch of rich kids broke in to celebrities' houses, like Paris Hilton's and Orlando Bloom's, and stole designer clothes and jewelry," Mercedes said.

"Exactly," Helen said. "Did you and Rosita see anything else? Did Trey or Snake Boy slip the necklace into their shirt pocket?"

"I didn't see anyone take it," Mercedes said.

"Me, either," Rosita said. "When I came back, people were grabbing for the champagne and I was trying not to spill it.

"Next time I looked, Bree and Trey were snoring on the couch together."

"This is nothing like the story Bree told me," Phil said.

"I'm not making it up!" Rosita said, her face flushed with anger.

"No, I think she may have misremembered," Phil said. "Did you see any other guests near Bree when she was sleeping on the couch?"

"No," Rosita said. "Just her boyfriend, Trey, and her sister, Chloe. But I wasn't there the whole time."

"When did Bree notice her necklace was missing?"

"Not until the next afternoon," Ana said. "I don't know when Trey left the party, but Bree spent the night sleeping on the couch. At least, she was still there when I went back to my room at four thirty in the morning. Chloe had gone up to her room about four o'clock. I covered Bree with a blanket. The last guests were gone by then."

"Where were her parents?" Helen asked.

"They stayed at the Riverside Hotel downtown so the party could be fun," Ana said. "The mister went to work from there and the missus came home about eleven the next morning. The cleaning crew had been working since six and they were just finishing."

"We're still fixing the damage to the grass and plants," Charlee said. "The flower beds were trampled."

"From being used as beds," John said.

"When Missus got home, Bree was in the breakfast nook nursing a hangover," Ana said. "She didn't really wake up until about one o'clock. That's when she noticed her necklace was gone. We spent the rest of the day tearing the house apart looking for it. Oh, the tears! The drama!"

"Where was Chloe?" Helen asked.

"She said she didn't care. If Bree was stupid enough to lose her necklace, it was her fault. She left.

"Then Missus wanted to use the golf cart to go play bridge and we couldn't find that, either. John and Charlee searched the grounds while we searched near the house. When the mister came home at seven, the family finally concluded both were stolen."

"And the Coakleys didn't call the police," Phil said.

"Instead they hired you," Ana said. "And suspect us."

. . . .

CHAPTER 27

"Bree's ruby-and-diamond pendant could have been stolen by anyone at her party," Helen said. She and Phil were standing by Helen's car in the Coakley mansion driveway after Ana's sumptuous lunch. Phil's Jeep was banished to the back of the house with the junkers driven by the staff.

"It could have," Phil said, "but we know for sure that her boyfriend, Trey, definitely had access to the necklace. If he has major gambling debts, he needs money in a hurry."

"Then there's Bree's jealous little sister, Chloe, and her boyfriend, Ozzie," Helen said. "Either one could have stolen it."

"Or both," Phil said. "From what you said, those two work as a team. Maybe they really are running a bling ring and boosting jewelry at parties."

"Did you say 'boost,' shamus?" Helen said. Phil got a little carried away with his vintage PI slang.

"Okay, steal," he said. "Chloe bragged that she has a lot of money, and it's not from her allowance. She says she and Snake Boy work together."

"Plus Snake Boy wants money to paint his white Beemer black," Helen said.

"And he has all those snakes to feed," Phil said. "I say we start checking my list of Lauderdale pawnshops."

Helen groaned. "There has to be a pawnshop on every major road."

"Sometimes two," Phil said. "We have about two hundred and eighty in Lauderdale alone."

"We'll be looking all year," Helen said.

"You forgot. I updated my list of the dicey ones known to accept stolen goods. There are about forty. We can each take twenty." He handed Helen a copy of a list.

"I'll take the first twenty," she said. "They're clustered fairly close together. I can start now."

"Me, too," Phil said.

"You're not working in the yard this afternoon?" Helen asked.

"I've learned all I can working with Charlee and John. The gardeners will happily spray for mealy bugs and spider mites and trim coconuts, if I get their coconuts out of this vise."

"Are they that worried?" Helen asked.

"Amis Coakley told me to search their pickup—twice—and follow them home after work. John and Charlee live down the street from each other and travel together to this job. Every night, they've either gone straight home, or stopped for beer on Dixie Highway or at a Mexican grocery. They never go near pawnshops. They don't throw money around, as if they made a big score.

"Charlee and John told me they have an offer for a higher-paying job in Boca, but they're afraid Amis may give them a bad reference if they take it."

"Then we'd better hurry," Helen said. "We know what Trey and the missing necklace look like. You've got the party photo of Trey and Bree on your iPhone. The one where she's wearing her birthday necklace."

"And her boyfriend," Phil said. "He's draped around her like a cape. Tell me, do women find him attractive?"

"Bree does," Helen said. "I don't. He's got a hot body, gym muscles and thick blond hair, but I don't like his sneery pout. He smacks of entitlement, and I want to smack that look off his overprivileged face."

"But how do you really feel?" Phil said, and grinned at her. "I'll see you back at the Coronado in time for the sunset salute. Ana's letting me clean up in her rooms and I brought a fresh shirt and pants."

Helen prepared for her role inside the Igloo. She put on heavier makeup, unbuttoned the top two buttons on her blouse, then tied the tails around her midriff. She finger-combed her dark hair so she looked like she'd just gotten out of bed.

The first pawnshop on Dixie Highway was the prototype for the others. Inside, the shop bristled with security cameras. Helen saw two men with bodies like melting ice cream, one with a receding hairline and the other with a ratty gray ponytail, behind a scarred Plexiglas shield with a pass-through slot.

Their clientele must be as dodgy as their goods, Helen thought.

The long, dingy shop's shelves were piled with cameras, construction tools, saxophones and electric guitars. The dark carpet needed vacuuming and the windows were dirty. Glass display counters were crammed with watches and iPads. Expensive rolling luggage was lined up on the floor, the suitcases two and three deep.

I guess if your life's going downhill, you don't need luggage, Helen thought.

After the two men sized up Helen, Ponytail lumbered out and gave Helen a pre-owned smile straight off a used car lot.

"My boyfriend said I can treat myself to nice jewelry," she said, smiling stupidly and hating the ditzy pretext she was using. "Really nice. And I get to pick it out all by myself. I want a necklace. A dangly kind."

"You mean a pendant?" Ponytail asked.

"Yeah. One of those," Helen said.

Ponytail rubbed his plump hands together. "We have all kinds. Gold, platinum, silver, diamonds . . ."

"Diamonds," Helen said. "And a ruby. A great big ruby."

Ponytail rapped on the Plexiglas, and his partner rattled around in the back room, then slid a velvet box through the pass-through.

"We have this beautiful ruby pendant," Ponytail said, opening the velvet box with a flourish.

Helen shook her head. "No," she said. "I want something bigger. I'm sorry."

Really sorry, she thought. Because I'll have to go through this charade at another pawnshop. Bree's daddy had shelled out twenty thousand bucks for her pendant necklace with two fancy-cut rubies weighing more than three carats, surrounded by marquis-cut diamonds. That pawnshop pendant is probably only worth two or three thousand.

Variations on this scene were repeated six more times before Helen pointed the Igloo toward the Coronado Tropic Apartments. She had just enough time to change before the sunset salute.

Phil whistled when Helen walked into her apartment. "Nice outfit," he said. "But a little too much makeup."

"I wanted to look like my sugar daddy was buying me an expensive ruby necklace," she said.

"You look expensive to me," he said, pulling her down to him on the couch. "We haven't done much of this lately." He unbuttoned the rest of her blouse. They made quick, urgent love on the couch, and then had a slower session in the bedroom.

"I needed that," Helen said. She kissed his red nose, now flaky and peeling. "I'm glad you're not doing yard work anymore."

"So am I," Phil said. "But I did get a cool hat. I gather you didn't have any luck at the pawnshops."

"Nope. I went to seven this afternoon. I'll stop by a few more tomorrow after I spend some time at the library."

"We should wander over to the sunset salute," Phil said.

"You feed the cat while I shower," Helen said.

Phil brought a six-pack of cold Heineken and Helen carried a bottle of wine out to the evening gathering. Margery, Markos and Peggy were already out by the pool. Markos's white T-shirt was stretched to the limit on his muscular chest. Margery wore gauzy purple accessorized with cigarette smoke. Peggy looked chic in a little black dress and heels. Her shoulder seemed bare without her parrot, Pete.

"Save your wine for next time, Helen," Peggy said. "I brought merlot and a cheese platter tonight. We're celebrating my thousand-dollar lottery win. I've figured out how to spend it."

"Since Peggy brought wine, I didn't make mojitos," Markos said. "But I did bring more healthy snacks. This is vegetable satay made with broccoli and cauliflower." The skewers were artfully arranged sculptures.

Helen watched Phil struggle not to show his disgust.

"And I have roasted beet crostini," Markos said.

"Beef and beer are an unbeatable combination," Phil said, raising his bottle.

"Not beef," Markos said. "*Beet.* I use the entire beet plant—the root, stems and greens. The beet roots are roasted and pureed with goat cheese, then topped with the sautéed greens and stems."

Helen had to turn away so Markos wouldn't see her grin. Margery winked at her behind a veil of cigarette smoke.

"Sounds healthy," Phil said. Helen knew that was not a compliment.

Markos did not. "And it's low-cal," he said with a happy smile.

"Cheers!" Phil said, and toasted Markos with his beer. Phil cut himself a healthy slab of Peggy's aged cheddar and politely took a beet crostini. Helen knew it would end up abandoned on his plate.

"Where's Pete?" she asked Peggy.

"Inside. Daniel's picking me up for dinner in a few minutes."

"The romance is still going strong?" Helen said.

"Oh, yes," Peggy said, eyes shining. "That's why I decided to spend my lottery money on a mate for Pete and a new cage for the happy couple. Pete shouldn't be alone, either."

"Money can buy love," Helen said.

The back gate creaked, and brown-haired Daniel hurried up the sidewalk toward them, his eyes on Peggy. The lawyer's well-tailored suit made his thick body seem solid and slimmer. *Solid* was the right word for him, Helen thought. In the best sense of the word.

Daniel gave Peggy a kiss and declined a drink. The lovebirds were anxious to be on their way. "I'll put away the cheese and wine, Peggy," Helen said. "You two run along."

After the couple left, Markos said, "Have you found the missing ruby necklace yet?"

"We're checking pawnshops now," Phil said. "Our client didn't report the necklace stolen, so that makes our job harder."

"Why didn't they call the police?" Markos asked. "Are they illegal?"

"Nothing like that," Phil said. "They're the kind of people who don't want the cops in their enchanted circle. Especially if there's a chance someone in that circle is a thief."

"They'd rather lose an expensive necklace?" he said.

"They can afford it," Phil said.

"I want to ask you about stolen goods," Markos said. "My restaurant, Fresh and Cool, is in Sweet Grass Plaza, the little shopping center on Federal Highway."

"I know it," Phil said. "One-story tan stucco buildings. Striped awnings. Upscale businesses."

"Right. My restaurant is on one end. I like to stop for a drink at Light Up the Night, at the other end."

"The martini and cigar bar?" Helen said.

"That's the one," Markos said. "I think people are selling stolen goods in there. Two guys show up about eleven o'clock one or two nights a week. One night last week they were selling watches. Another night, it was speakers. It's like a bazaar between eleven and midnight."

"If you see them selling jewelry," Phil said, "especially a rather large ruby-and-diamond pendant, give us a call." Helen, Phil and Markos swapped cell phone numbers.

"What do the thieves look like?" Helen asked.

"Mid-twenties," Markos said. "One has dark hair and a beard. The other is blond. They dress to blend in with the upscale crowd. I'll keep an eye out for them. I'm working nights the rest of the week."

"There's a reward for you if we catch them selling the pendant," Phil said.

"I would have told you anyway," Markos said. "But I won't turn down money."

Margery had been quietly sipping wine and smoking while she listened to the conversation. "It's eight thirty," she said. "I'm going to turn in."

Helen, Phil and Markos helped Margery clear away the party debris. Markos's appetizers were gone, thanks to Helen and Margery, and Phil had eaten most of Peggy's cheese plate.

"You might as well take those last two slices, Phil," Margery said. "Unless Markos wants them."

"No, thanks," Markos said. "Night, all."

After Markos was in his apartment, Margery said to Helen, "Your ghost was that young woman killed in the hit-and-run on Broward, wasn't she?"

"Yes," Helen said. "You predicted it, too. I talked with the detective in charge. He didn't see any connection between Charlotte's murder and the watercolor. Now it's my job to find her killer. The library hired me."

"That's good," Margery said.

Was it? Helen thought. Charlotte planned to help herself to half my fee, and I resented her. Instead, she was murdered and I got to keep all the money. Plus, I got credit for finding the million-dollar watercolor she discovered, even though I only opened about forty boxes. Now I'm making more money investigating her murder.

I feel like a fraud. A guilty fraud.

CHAPTER 28

. . . .

Rrrrrrrrrrrrrrrrrrrrrrrrrrrrrrrrrrrrrrrrrrrr!
Helen saw a streak of red, heard a sound like a
Harley crossed with a lawn mower, and slammed
on the Igloo's brakes just in time.

What the heck?

Gladys pulled up into the parking spot next to Helen's
on a fire red Vespa scooter, and revved the engine. She
wore a short denim jacket, sedate white blouse, flirty
red pleated skirt and those black buckled boots.

"Morning, Biker Babe," Helen said as she climbed
out of her car. "Cool ride. What happened to the mom
mobile?"

Gladys pulled off her red helmet and shook out her
long black hair. "Fender bender on my way home from
work the day before yesterday," she said.

"I'm sorry," Helen said.

"I'm not," Gladys said. "The mom mobile is probably
history, but the dude who did it in is smokin' hot. Nick's
a professional diver and plays in an alternative band."

"Hey," Helen said.

"Even better, he actually reads. We exchanged information."

"It's required by law," Helen said, solemnly.

"And we wouldn't want to break the law," Gladys said. "We ran into each other—well, he ran into me—on Federal Highway near a Vespa dealer. After the police came and the mashed mom mobile was towed, we walked over to the Vespa place and I fell in love."

"With the red scooter?" Helen said.

"Of course."

"Do you have a motorcycle license?"

"Thanks to an old boyfriend who was a cell's angel— a lawyer who rode his Harley on weekends," she said. "We took a motorcycle safety course together and I got my license."

"You're amazing," Helen said.

"A scooter doesn't have the same feel as an eight-hundred-pound Harley, but I adjusted to it fairly quick. I'm renting this one until the insurance mess is sorted out. Then I may buy it."

"This will smash the boring librarian stereotypes," Helen said as she admired the scooter's sleek shape and shiny chrome mirrors. "Love the color."

"Dragon Red," Gladys said as she pulled her purse out of a surprisingly roomy compartment behind her seat.

"Lots of room," Helen said.

"That's called a top case," Gladys said. "It's like a trunk for a scooter." She stashed her bright red helmet inside and locked it. "My little dragon gets sixty-five miles a gallon."

"Better than a Ferrari," Helen said.

"Nobody buys a Ferrari for good gas mileage," Gladys said. "But this will be fun to drive until I get mine."

"Where was this accident?" Helen said.

"Fort Lauderdale," Gladys said.

Miles away from Charlotte's fatal hit-and-run, Helen thought.

"I was on my way to the grocery store to pick up something for dinner when Nick ran into me," Gladys said. "He felt so bad, he offered to buy me dinner.

"I wasn't all that upset. I never cared much for the mom mobile, and if the insurance totals it, I'll have a polite way to get rid of it without hurting my mother's feelings.

"Nick's car was dented but drivable, so I followed him on my new scooter to his favorite restaurant, Hot and Soul."

Helen whistled. "The man has good taste. That's the international soul food restaurant tucked away in a little shopping center at Federal and Oakland Park. I've heard good things about that place."

"They're all true," Gladys said. Helen saw that the blush on the librarian's cheeks was natural and her eyes were dreamy. "I had the Louisiana gumbo and Nick had the oxtail gnocchi. Amazing craft beer, too, but I only had one. I didn't want to be too wobbly when I went home on my new scooter."

"I bet Phil would like that place," Helen said. "You didn't ride your scooter to work yesterday."

"No, I wanted to get used to it on the back streets before I rode it in rush-hour traffic," Gladys said.

They were at the staff door of the mellow, sun-splashed library. Jasmine drifted on the sultry air and palm trees whispered like conspirators.

"Good talking to you," Gladys said. "I'd better hurry. I don't want to be late."

Inside the library, Gladys clocked in with a minute to spare, then ran for the circulation desk. Helen stashed her purse in the sunny staff break room. Blair looked like she'd stepped out of a fifties sitcom in a styleless beige shirtwaist and a string of pearls. She gave Helen a nod, poured herself a cup of coffee, then disappeared into the grim, bug-infested Friends' intake room. Jared was trundling his rolling mop bucket down the hall. Lisa and Alexa were nowhere to be seen.

The coffeepot had a half inch of tar at the bottom. How could Blair drink that sludge? Helen wondered as she cleaned the pot. Before she could make more coffee, she heard raised voices at the checkout desk.

Blair hurried out to the front of the library, Helen following. She saw a short man, his broad shoulders visible under his plaid shirt, pounding on the desk so hard his thick white hair fell into his eyes. Helen pegged him at a strong seventysomething. His tanned, weathered face was crisscrossed with wrinkles like a cracked, drying mud puddle.

"Tuck in your shirt!" he said, like a drill sergeant.

The regulars in their wicker wing chairs were already settled in their usual places in the popular library. Several well-coifed women looked up and frowned at the disturbance. Mr. Ritter shook his *New York Times* until it crackled. Helen guessed he was impatient at the interruption.

"My shirt is supposed to be out, Mr. Atkins," Gladys said.

"It's longer than your jacket," he said.

"That's the style," Gladys said.

Helen was amazed at her mild tone.

Blair edged closer to hear the controversy better. Mr. Ritter cleared his throat. Helen took that as a warning signal.

Mr. Atkins ignored it. "You're wearing biker boots," he said. "Why don't you dress like a librarian?"

"I do," Gladys said. Helen admired her patience with the rude man.

"You're a disgrace," he said, then pointed to Blair. "Why don't you dress like her? She looks like a librarian."

"Ms. Hoagland is not a librarian," Gladys said quietly. "She's the head of our Friends of the Library. Now, do you wish to file a complaint with the library director about my clothes, or may I check out your books?" She slid his library card off the stack of fat Tom Clancy thrillers and began scanning the books.

"I filed a complaint last time," he said. "It didn't do any good. Some people have no respect."

"These are due in two weeks, Mr. Atkins. Have a good day," Gladys said, and pushed his books toward him. The angry man gathered them and stomped off, ignoring the glares of the library's wing-chair readers.

"He's right, you know," Blair said to Gladys. "Proper dress is important."

"Feel free to discuss it with Alexa," she said.

"Hmpf!" Blair said. She marched back to the Friends' intake room.

"Brava," Helen said softly. "I thought you would have ripped Mr. Atkins a new one."

"No point," Gladys said. "We go through this every two weeks, when he comes in for his books. It's a ritual, like a Japanese kabuki drama, without the white makeup. This is the first time Blair's come out to watch. She usually complains about my clothes behind my back. Alexa lets her complaints go in one ear and out the other.

"Hey, let me show you what I found in a novel when I was scanning the returned books," she said, her eyes dancing.

She pulled out several sheets of paper. Helen read the first one, a formal request and explanation for four days of sick leave from the Baxtrix Corporation. The request had been granted, but Gladys had put a small bit of paper over the name to protect the patron's privacy.

"Now look at what was next to it in the same book," she said.

Helen saw a four-page bill from the luxurious Ritz-Carlton hotel in Sarasota, Florida, for those same days. Again, Gladys made sure Helen couldn't see the name.

"Think this person was truly ill?" Helen asked.

"Working a job for that computer company would make me sick with boredom," Gladys said, "but I don't think our patron was too terribly ill."

"What are you going to do with these?" Helen asked.

"Put them in a sealed envelope and give them to the patron next time that person comes in—which should be soon."

"I'm impressed how you protected his privacy," Helen said.

"Or hers," Gladys said.

"Time for me to start shelving," Helen said.

And find out who killed Charlotte, she thought.

CHAPTER 29

· ·

Helen was peacefully shelving and snooping at the Flora Park Library, hoping to find a clue to Charlotte's murder. She enjoyed mornings in the mellow reading room, when the sun gilded the airy arched windows and patrons quietly enjoyed their books and worked on their laptops.

Until she heard a screech like an angry peacock. "No—you got the last new large-print book, Roberta! I'm entitled to this one."

Helen turned to see who the old bird was. Two snowy-haired women were fighting over a book.

"Then you should have reserved it, Lily," Roberta said. "I saw it first."

Roberta was a bony five feet seven or so, and her pale blue pantsuit flapped on her scarecrow frame. She clutched the book with skeleton fingers, protecting it from a small, round woman in an elegant black pantsuit. She must be Lily, Helen thought. Her black cane was painted with flames.

"I saw it before you did," Lily said. "But when you saw me heading toward the new releases, you raced over and took it. I can't move as fast as you with this cane."

"If you hadn't drunk three martinis at lunch, Lily, you wouldn't have twisted your ankle."

Gladys the librarian came bustling over from the checkout desk. "Ladies, ladies, is there a problem?" Her voice was as soothing as a kindergarten teacher's.

"That old bag stole my book," Lily said. The flames on her cane seemed to run up her arm and out her mouth.

"Old!" Roberta said. "You're two years older than me." Her chin trembled.

Gladys interrupted. "I believe you were discussing a problem with a new release?"

Gladys is definitely cool, Helen thought.

"I was taking this novel off the shelf when Lily said she was entitled to it," Roberta said, and held up the title: *Fifty Shades of Grey.*

Helen ducked behind her book cart so they wouldn't notice her giggling.

"She got the last new large-print," Lily said. "I should have this one."

"Let's go over to the checkout desk and discuss this issue quietly," Gladys said. Helen abandoned her book cart and slid behind a bookcase to listen.

"My book club is reading *Fifty Shades* next month," Roberta said. "I need to read it."

"I was reaching for it when she stampeded past me and grabbed it," Lily said.

Gladys was clicking on the computer. "Roberta," she said, "you owe more than six dollars in overdue fines. Six dollars is our limit. You must pay the fines before you can check out another book. You may pay your fines now and take the book or give it to Lily and I'll put your name on the reserve list. It will be yours as soon as you pay your fines."

"Never mind," Roberta said. "I'll buy a used copy for a dollar."

"Cheapskate," Lily said.

"The only time you've seen handcuffs, Lily, was when the feds took your husband away," Roberta said. She tossed *Fifty Shades* on the checkout counter and stomped toward the door.

"He was indicted," Lily shouted after her, "but he wasn't convicted."

Helen went back to shelving. The other patrons, who'd been watching the altercation as if it were a BBC drama, returned to their books and computers.

This is why I love libraries, Helen thought. They attract smart, funny people. Even the arguments are fun to watch.

She picked Nancy Pickard's mystery *The Scent of Rain and Lightning* off the shelving cart and recited to herself L, M, N, O . . . P for Pickard. Helen slid *Rain and Lightning* onto the shelf right before Pickard's *Ring of Truth*.

The Flora Park Library wants its fiction alphabetized, Helen thought, which makes sense. But I don't get why series novels have to be alphabetized, too. I think Pickard's *Ring of Truth* should be shelved with the other two books in the Marie Lightfoot series. Except . . . I'm a volunteer. I'm not going to be here much longer. Get back to work.

Gladys cleared her throat, and Helen realized the tall, leggy librarian was standing beside her, in a skirt that was barely there and a demure white blouse.

"Was that a hoot and a half? Two old ladies fighting over *Fifty Shades*," Gladys said.

"Now you're stereotyping again," Helen said. "Those women are old, not dead. You should meet my seventy-six-year-old landlady. You'd think she was younger than me."

Gladys looked fifty shades of embarrassed and switched the subject. "I'm glad you're helping here," she said. "Shelving is an endless chore."

"I enjoy it," Helen said. "I like putting things back in order."

"I thought you'd quit once you found the missing watercolor," Gladys said.

"I'm sticking around for a little longer," Helen said. "What did you think of the séance?"

Gladys shrugged. "It was interesting, but I didn't believe it. Melisandra, the medium, was definitely faking it, but Lisa really thinks she saw the ghost of Flora Portland wandering the halls here. Blair does, too."

"What about you?" Helen asked. "Do you believe in ghosts?"

"Me? Definitely not. Flora Portland's long gone. Lisa may believe she saw her ghost, but she also saw an opportunity to get her way here at the library. She's determined to save this historic building and get it fixed. Lisa will go to the cemetery and dig up Flora Portland herself if it will help her get what she wants."

"Has the séance changed the library board vote?" Helen asked.

"From what I can figure out, there's one other believer on the board who thinks Flora's ghost was at the séance. The four other board members want to preserve Flora Park's heritage and history. If Lisa can find a way to fund the restoration, they'll all vote to save the library.

"Blair, the head Friend of the Library, is not on the board, but she's using all her influence to get the necessary votes," Gladys said.

"Blair has that much influence?" Helen said.

"Don't be fooled by her ragbag wardrobe. Blair could be a DC lobbyist. She's been working. Thanks to Blair, four members are now in favor of the renovation. Lisa, as board president, will make the vote unanimous. But everything depends on getting the money. Blair and Lisa are determined to save and restore the library."

"Where will they get the money?" Helen asked.

"If the board has any sense, they'll ask Seraphina. She's the library's primo fund-raiser. That woman can talk the balls off . . ."

Helen raised an eyebrow.

Gladys grinned. ". . . a pool table."

Helen burst out laughing.

"Personally, I think Blair missed a major lobbying opportunity," Gladys said. "She took her stodgy white Chrysler in for a major overhaul when she went to lunch the other day. The shop offered her a loaner, a sporty black convertible."

"That sounds like fun," Helen said.

"I thought so, too," Gladys said. "Blair could have shown off that black convertible to the whole board. She would have had a captive audience. But she wouldn't drive it. Said convertibles weren't safe. Instead, Blair took a boring gray sedan."

"I don't think I saw it in the lot," Helen said.

"Even if you saw it, you wouldn't have noticed it," Gladys said.

"I did see a white Chevy Impala," Helen said. "I thought it was yours."

"No, that's probably Lisa's rental," Gladys said. "Actually, her second rental. She came back from lunch the other day all upset because she hit a dog."

Helen winced. "Did she kill it?" she asked.

"Yes. She was crying. Lisa's not my favorite person, but I admire the way she takes care of her mother, and she felt terrible about that poor dog.

"Alexa took her into her office and gave Lisa tea and sympathy. She tried to convince her to go home and rest, but Lisa wanted to stay. Then Lisa got a call from her mother's caregiver. Some minor emergency, and she left."

"What's the story on our library director, Alexa?" Helen said. "I admire her, but I don't know her very well."

"Join the club," Gladys said. "She's good. She gets

along with some difficult personalities, but she's a private person. She and her husband are both from old-line Flora Park families. I met him at a Christmas party. He's a perfect match for Alexa: dark-haired, handsome, stylish without being stuffy."

"What's he do?" Helen asked.

"He's a big-deal architect."

"Alexa says she didn't care if the library is renovated or a new building is built," Helen said.

"That's what she tells everyone," Gladys said. "But if the library can't find the money to save this old building, the contract to build the new one will go to Alexa's husband. I hear his family is lobbying quietly for his firm to get the job, and they'll put up the seed money.

"Oh, did I tell you? You may be seeing my white Impala in two weeks. I'm getting the mom mobile fixed," Gladys said. "I decided I'll need it for the rainy season. Meanwhile, I'm zipping around on my red Vespa. I'm buying it. It's too much fun."

More debt, Helen thought, then quickly told herself, It's none of your business. Unless Gladys's debts drove her to murder.

"I'll be glad when Lisa's Jaguar is fixed," Gladys said.

"Lisa always seems tired," Helen said.

"I'm tired of listening to her complain that it's a comedown to drive a Chevy when she's used to a Jaguar. She has a vintage white Jag, a 1997, I think. That Jag didn't have a dent or a ding—at least until two days ago, when a judge in a Mercedes hit it."

"This was before Lisa ran over the dog?" Helen asked.

"Right. She's not having a good week. Lisa wasn't injured, but you would have thought the judge ran over her, the way she carried on. I know this is a difficult time for her, but the judge is picking up the whole cost. He even towed her Jag to a special body shop up in Boca. That Jag will look better than new when it's fixed, and I'm losing sympathy for her."

"Why is it a difficult time for Lisa?" Helen asked.

"Her mother has to go into a nursing home and money is tight," Gladys said.

"I thought Lisa had money," Helen said.

"She used to," Gladys said. "She married her dream lover, some kind of stockbroker. Her family disapproved. They said he was a huckster, but Lisa was wildly in love. She thought she was following in Flora's romantic footsteps. They were newlyweds when she inherited her grandmother's Flora Park home, and she put the house in both their names. Lisa and her husband spent her trust fund remodeling and redecorating the place until it was a showcase. They'd been married about ten years when he left her for another woman. Since the house was joint property, they had to sell it—at the bottom of the market. They practically gave it away."

"Too bad," Helen said.

"Florida real estate is tricky," Gladys said. "Lisa was fortysomething when she divorced and she'd reconciled with her mother. Her father was dead and bad investments took the family fortune. Lisa moved in with her mother and got a job as a medical billing specialist so she could work at home. She takes care of her mother, who has Alzheimer's, with a part-time caregiver. Now her mother's become too difficult for Lisa to care for, even with help. Lisa's worried sick about finding a good place for her mother. She's desperate for money."

"Is Mom's house worth anything?"

"It's too far gone. Any remaining money has already been spent on her mother's care. Lisa will have to sell the house as a fixer-upper. She clings to that Jaguar as the last remnant of her good life."

A small, round woman at the checkout desk tapped the bell and glared at Helen and Gladys.

"I'll let you go back to work," Gladys said. "I have a patron at the desk."

Helen shelved adult fiction for the next half hour.

She noticed many of the books seemed well-read. They weren't falling apart, but they'd clearly been enjoyed. Occasionally, a page had a coffee ring or tea splash.

Helen could picture the readers curled up in comfortable chairs, enjoying a favorite book and a beverage. The new releases with their pristine pages didn't seem as attractive to her. They hadn't felt the book lovers' benedictions yet.

Helen pushed her heavy, creaking cart over to the humor section for a trip back in time. She wanted to see if her favorite book was still in the library.

There it was, a slim blue volume. Will Cuppy's *The Decline and Fall of Practically Everybody*.

The section on Alexander the Great was one of the few quotes she remembered more than thirty years after she'd first read it: "Alexander's empire fell to pieces at once, and nothing remained of his work except that the people he had killed were still dead."

As far as Helen was concerned, Will Cuppy was the last word on territorial wars. She picked the book off the shelf and paged through it reverently. She was pleased to see that the patrons of Flora Park loved it as much as she did.

When Helen was growing up, the St. Louis County Library was her refuge. Her parents never argued, but Helen's father was unfaithful. Even a naive teenage Helen figured that out when she met one of Daddy's special friends, a brightly painted redhead who reeked of perfume and beer at three o'clock on a Saturday afternoon. The fact that she was wrapped around Helen's father was another clue.

Dolores, Helen's hyper-religious mother, believed divorce was a mortal sin. Each time Helen's father found a new girlfriend, he'd have to work late. Dolores wasn't fooled, but she never confronted her husband. Instead, she conducted a cold war, keeping an eerie, icy silence at home, banging pots and pans and aggressively vacuuming the carpet.

Helen fled to the library, and found comfort in Will Cuppy and other books.

Poor Daddy died in the saddle in a hot-sheet hotel. And my long-suffering mother died of a stroke more than a year ago. I hope she's finally at peace. Helen put Will Cuppy's history book back on the shelf and wished she could put her own ghosts away as easily.

Quit wandering down Memory Lane, she told herself. You have a killer to catch.

CHAPTER 30

I need a break, Helen thought, after her trip back into the past. A walk will clear the cobwebs. The library garden was a cool, green cathedral lit by slanting golden rays of sun. The scent of something sweet drifted on the afternoon breeze.

Helen wandered past the tropical flowers until their outrageous colors brightened her mood.

She heard a car door slam and saw Jared getting out of a black Ford pickup, wearing khakis and a disreputable ball cap. The janitor unlocked the truck bed compartment for his toolbox.

Helen met him near the staff entrance. "New truck?" she asked.

"It's a loaner," he said. "Some asshole—pardon my French—sideswiped my pickup."

"The blue one?" Helen asked.

"Mine's white," he said. "Took it to my brother Jeremiah's shop and he let me borrow this one. Good thing I'm getting a family discount because my truck will be in the shop at least a week."

There it was again, Helen thought, Jared's deep well of acid eating his insides. She wondered if the janitor ever had a day when he wasn't reminded that Davis Kingsley's neglect had forced him into a life of hard labor.

"What's the name of your brother's repair shop?" Helen asked.

"Kobek's Kwik Auto Repair," Jared said. "On Federal near Commercial. Jeremiah does good work, even if he is my brother."

"Thanks," Helen said. "My car's due for an oil change."

"You should call now," Jared said. "Oil is the lifeblood of a car, and you got yourself a nice little Cruiser. Tell Jeremiah I sent you. But whatever you do, don't call him Jerry. He hates that nickname."

Jared recited the shop number. Helen punched it into her iPhone, and Jeremiah answered. "If you bring in your car now, I'll take a look at it," he said.

It was two o'clock when Helen reached Kobek's auto repair, and she was glad she'd decided to take in the Igloo. The Cruiser's brakes didn't feel quite right. She saw a white pickup in the yard with a badly dented fender on the passenger side.

Jeremiah was as tall and thin as his brother, and wore a grimy cap, but he had an Old Testament beard to go with his name. Helen couldn't tell if he was older or younger than Jared.

"I work with your brother at the library," Helen said. "Is that Jared's truck by the fence?"

"Yeah, I'm waiting for parts," Jeremiah said.

"I need an oil change," Helen said. "And would you look at the brakes? They feel mushy."

Jeremiah checked the maintenance sticker on her car windshield and said, "You're overdue. You know, oil is the lifeblood of a car."

"That's what I heard," Helen said. She popped the hood latch and handed the mechanic her car keys.

He poked around in the Igloo's innards and said, "You got a leak somewhere in a brake line. I'll have to keep your car overnight."

"I'll call my husband for a ride," Helen said. Phil answered his cell phone and Helen told him why the Igloo was in the shop.

"I'll be right over," he said. "Give me twenty minutes."

Jeremiah had his head in her car engine, so Helen examined Jared's dented pickup while she waited. The truck was surprisingly clean. The front bumper was loose, and there were scrapes on the paint, but that was all she could see.

I don't know what damage from a fatal hit-and-run looks like, Helen thought.

The repair shop lot was chalky white gravel with patches of oil. Helen was wearing a white blouse and jeans. She decided to risk a look under Jared's pickup.

She made sure Jeremiah was still deep in her car's guts, then pulled out her key-chain flashlight and crawled under Jared's pickup. The sharp gravel stuck in her back and neck. Helen's two-inch flashlight's beam was a weak, yellow gleam. She didn't see any dark hair or blood on the undercarriage, but the underside looked like it had been hosed off.

Did Jeremiah clean the undercarriage so he could work on the truck? she wondered. Or did Jared try to hide Charlotte's murder by washing his truck before he took it to his brother's shop?

The sharp gravel was digging into her neck, head and back. Helen heard tires crunching and hastily pulled herself out from under the truck. Phil's black Jeep was idling in the lot. She dusted off her pants, climbed inside and waved good-bye to Jeremiah.

"Hurry, Phil," she said.

"You moonlighting as a mechanic?" Phil asked.

"That white pickup belongs to the Flora Park janitor," Helen said. "It was in an accident about the time Charlotte was killed. I was checking underneath for blood or hair. I didn't find anything. Looks like someone washed it off."

"He can't wash it all off," Phil said. "If he killed

Charlotte, a forensics exam will turn up blood and tissue."

Phil's Jeep wasn't air-conditioned. While he drove, Helen tried to brush the white gravel dust off her clothes. The wind whipped her hair, taking more dust with it.

"How's the pawnshop search?" she asked.

"I'm burning down the list," he said. "I'll take the rest tomorrow. This afternoon, I'm trying a new tactic to flush out the thief. Want to go with me?"

"Sure. Where?"

"To catch a cart rustler, pardner," he said. "We're going to look at shops selling used golf carts. Those are good places to find stolen carts."

"Don't used golf carts all look alike?" Helen asked. "Old white carts driven by old white men?"

"Not true," he said. "They come in colors now. They're transportation in rich, private communities, and people like to pimp out their golf carts. I've seen some tricked up like Rolls-Royces, 'fifty-seven Thunderbirds, even Ferraris.

"The Coakleys own a white golf cart, but they had the upholstery custom-made to match their lawn furniture. The color is Resort Stripe Hampton—that's medium blue with wide white and blue stripes. Check out the photo on my cell phone."

"I sat on that furniture when I talked to Chloe," she said.

He handed Helen his iPhone at the next red light and she found the golf cart photo, Bree's father behind the wheel.

"Classy," Helen said. "But any cart can have blue-striped upholstery."

"But not every cart has this serial number," he said. "The Coakleys' cart is a 2014 Club Car Precedent i2 Excel Electric with its own serial number. I e-mailed the number to your phone."

Helen looked up the e-mail. "Got it," she said. "Where do I find the number on the cart?"

"It's on a bar code decal mounted on a plaque at the lower edge of the dashboard," he said. "Glad the Coakleys had their owners' manual."

"How are we playing this?" Helen asked. "As private eyes or private citizens?

"How about if we go in as a suburban couple?" she said. "If I see a cart that looks like it's the Coakleys', I'll go all girlie, jump in the cart and pretend to take photos while I look for the serial number. If I find it, I'll say, *This is the one*."

"That should work," Phil said. "If the cart's here, we'll turn into private eyes. I'm starting at this place here on Powerline Road, because it has lots of new and used golf carts and ATVs."

He parked in front of the Fore! Sale showroom, located next to a golf course. Window signs proclaimed NEW MODELS JUST IN!!! GOOD DEALS ON PRE-OWNED CARTS!!! OPEN 7 DAYS A WEEK!!!

Six shiny red carts were lined up in front, next to a black golf cart that looked like a BMW with a sign on the leather seats: LET US CUSTOMIZE YOUR CART!!!

"Fore! Sale sure does like exclamation points," Helen said as she combed her windblown hair and added lipstick. "Any gravel dust on the back of my shirt and pants?"

Phil dusted off her shirt and spent way too much time patting her rump.

"That's enough," she said.

"It's just so luscious," he said.

Helen brushed him off and opened the showroom door. It was a car dealership in miniature, complete with a bald thirtysomething salesman in a plaid sports coat with a red pocket square. He was so short Helen wondered if he made the golf carts look bigger.

"Hi. Dave here," he said, hurrying over. "I'm the owner. How may I help you folks?"

"My wife and I are looking for a good used golf cart," Phil said.

"Are you golfers, or do you need the cart for transportation?" Dave asked.

"Transportation," Phil said. "We'd like a white one with blue seats, if you have something like that."

"Traditionalists," Dave said. "We have several pre-owned vehicles that fit your description. They're in our back showroom."

The showroom was a cinder-block warehouse with a golf course painted on the walls. Helen wondered if it was windowless so the carts' former owners couldn't see them from the road.

"These four here might work," Dave said.

One cart was a baby blue Yamaha, another was a white E-Z-GO with navy leather seats, the third was a Club Cart with turquoise canvas seats, but the fourth looked like the Coakleys' cart.

"Oooh," Helen said. "I love these blue-striped seats." She started snapping photos of the cart.

"This is a 2014," Dave said. "Almost new. It seats two and goes nineteen miles an hour, which is top speed."

"Is it street legal?" Phil asked.

"No," Dave said. "But there's not a mark on it. You're looking at a cart that cost seventy-five hundred dollars new, including the custom upholstery."

There! Helen found the serial number, checked it against the serial number on her cell, then photographed it.

"This is the one," Helen said.

Dave broke out in a smile. "I knew you'd find one you like, and I can make you a hell of a deal."

"Actually, Dave, we can make you a deal," Phil said. "We're private eyes and this cart was stolen from the Coakley family last weekend."

Phil called up the photo on his iPhone. "Recognize it?"

The color drained from Dave's face. "I didn't know. It's not my fault. There's no way I could be blamed. There are no titles for golf carts, just bills of sale. I took the dude's word for it, but I was a little naive."

"Not true, Dave," Phil said. "Golf carts have serial numbers. Here's the number for the Coakley cart."

"It matches this cart's," Helen said.

"And where's this cart's charger?" Phil asked.

"Dude said it was broken," Dave said. "That's why he let me have this cart for only two thousand."

"Right," Phil said. "Broken. That cart's worth more than seven thousand dollars. Where's the bill of sale?"

"In my office," Dave said, stammering. "But I'll have to look for it."

"We'll wait," Phil said. "In fact, we'll go to your office right now. Unless you'd like us to call 911."

"I'll get it," Dave said, and Helen and Phil followed him to a closet-sized office decorated with plaques from civic organizations. A pressed sawdust desk was buried under an avalanche of paper.

Dave burrowed into the papers and retrieved a pink receipt. "It's this one here," he said. The sale was dated the day after Bree's party.

"You write this name and address?" Phil asked.

"No, he did." Dave was sweating. "The man who sold it."

"And you didn't think there was something odd about a man named Dicque Hardonne?" Phil asked.

"He said his parents were French," Dave said. He mopped his forehead with the red pocket square.

"The name's fake and you know it," Phil said. "So is the address: Sixty-nine Commode Circle. But you're going to be in the toilet if you can't describe the man who brought in that cart."

"I'm not sure," Dave said. "We get so many."

"So many stolen carts?" Helen asked.

"No!" Dave jumped and wiped his forehead again. "We get so many people here. In the showroom. We're next to the golf course and down the street from a gated community."

"Show us your security camera footage," Phil said.

"I'm not sure," Dave began, but Helen cut him off.

"I'm very sure I can call the police right now," she said, holding up her phone.

"All right, all right," Dave said. "The security footage is in the computer room next door."

They followed him into an unpainted cinder-block room with computer monitors and keyboards. He tapped some keys and called up the footage for the date on the receipt, then fast-forwarded through it. They watched the quick, jerky movements of people looking at carts, testing carts, and finally a pickup truck delivering a cart.

"Stop!" Phil said.

Two muscular men in their twenties were unloading a cart that had striped seats like the Coakleys' cart. The footage was gray and grainy, but both men wore jams and T-shirts. One was short and stocky with a beard. The other was tall and blond with gym muscles and the entitled sneer that irritated Helen.

"That's him!" she said. "Trey. The birthday girl's boyfriend. And the guy with the beard is Snake Boy, Ozzie Ormond. We got them."

CHAPTER 31

"What's that stuff that looks like dandelion greens on your pizza?" Phil asked. He was tucking into veal and pecorino cheese meatballs.

"It's arugula," Helen said. "That way you don't have to order a salad."

"Who says I have to order a salad?" Phil said.

"Wait and see," Helen said. "You'll have some on your beef carpaccio."

"The shaved Reggiano will counteract it," Phil said. "Raw meat is a manly dish."

"I guess so, if the cheese has to shave," Helen said.

After their visit to the Fore! Sale golf cart showroom, the PI pair stopped at D'Angelo's Pizza in Fort Lauderdale, an upscale tapas restaurant. Phil's dusty black Jeep was the most disreputable vehicle in the valet lot.

They took a table in the restaurant's cool, spare interior. Helen thought the sleek Italian chairs were surprisingly comfortable for fashionable furniture.

Helen's white pizza with arugula had arrived along with Phil's meatball tapas.

"So what's the next step?" she said, between bites of salad and white cheese pizza. "Can we arrest Bree's boyfriend, Standiford W. Lohan the Third, and Ozzie Ormond, Chloe's boyfriend? The Coakley daughters sure know how to pick 'em."

"We don't have enough to arrest yet. Not on the basis of that grainy security footage and fraudulent bill of sale," Phil said. "Dave, the showroom owner, claims he can't remember if that was Trey and Ozzie who sold him the Coakley cart."

Helen made a small noise of protest through a mouthful of pizza, and Phil said, "I know he's lying, and Dave knows we know, but we'll get them both.

"We've got two things going for us. In the security video, I saw what looks like a sign on the driver's side door of the pickup that delivered the cart. Dave made us a DVD and I'm going to work with it on my computer and see if I can pull anything off it."

Phil's plate of carpaccio arrived, the thin slices of red meat artistically arranged and, as Helen predicted, topped with arugula. He poked at the greens with his fork like a boy poking a snake with a stick until Helen said, "I'll take them."

She helped herself to his pile of arugula and he looked relieved once it was off his plate. "Really," he said, "I feel healthier having seen it."

"Right," Helen said as she took a bite of his salad topped with the salty Reggiano cheese. She wasn't sure truffle oil tasted different from any other, but the name sounded cool.

"Back to the stolen golf cart," she said. "We also got the truck's license plate off the security video."

"But we don't know if that's Trey's truck," Phil said.

"Too bad we can't have a friendly cop check the plate for us, like in the movies," Helen said.

"Cops don't want to go to jail for helping a PI," Phil said.

"I thought they just lost their jobs," Helen said. She

decided pizza and arugula was a good combination. The slightly bitter greens went well with the bland cheese.

"Oh, no, the punishment is much worse," Phil said. "A cop looking through a computer database leaves footprints. And a TAR report—that stands for Transaction Analysis Report, I think—can put lying cops in jail. Remember the flap over the deputy who said he stopped a woman for an expired temp tag? Then he just happened to see an unlabeled drug bottle in her purse and arrested her?"

"Vaguely," Helen said.

"It was an awful story," Phil said. "A Fort Lauderdale woman was heading home after dropping her son off at summer school when she was stopped by a Broward County sheriff's deputy for an expired tag. While she was looking for her license in her purse, the deputy spotted a prescription bottle with no label. She said it was medicine for her son and her ex-husband had given it to her. The deputy called her ex, who did not back up her story. She was arrested and strip-searched.

"Turns out she was set up by her ex, through the deputy. A TAR report showed the deputy had run a check on her a week *before* that surprise arrest. That's probably how the deputy knew about the expired tag.

"The woman's charges were dropped. Better yet, she got to see the deputy sent to federal prison."

"I can see why a cop wouldn't want to risk poking around in the TAR," Helen said. Most of her pizza was gone, along with all of Phil's salad. She was bursting with good health. "But a TAR report showing who owns the truck that delivered the cart would have made our life easier."

"Oh, we can still get a TAR report," he said. "Anyone can submit a public records request, and that's what I'll do when we get home."

"A letter takes forever," Helen said.

The waiter appeared and Helen and Phil ordered black coffee. Helen wanted homemade chocolate gelato.

"We can do it by e-mail," Phil said. "The request will take about a week. Some personal info is redacted, but we'll know who owns the truck, and that's what's important."

"What if Dave sells the Coakleys' golf cart out from under us? This gelato is amazing. Want some?"

Phil took a big spoonful, then said, "Dave won't dare. He could lose his showroom and go to jail if we report him. We documented our find with photos. There are two of us as witnesses, and he knows he accepted stolen goods.

"He'll keep the cart in storage and deliver it back to the Coakleys when we tell him to."

The waiter was back with more coffee. Helen ordered a second chocolate gelato. "To combat the effect of all that salad," she told Phil.

"So Dave's out the two thousand dollars he paid Trey for that cart," Phil said.

"Serves him right," Helen said. "What do we do in the meantime, while we wait for the TAR report?"

She finished her second gelato without Phil's help while he paid the check.

"I'll keep visiting pawnshops to look for the stolen necklace," he said, "and you'll go back to the library and catch Charlotte's killer."

"Wish it was as simple as you make it sound," Helen said.

CHAPTER 32

•••••••••••••••••••••••

Back in the Coronado Investigations office, Phil worked at his computer under Sam Spade's world-weary supervision, while Helen did their accounts. She watched the six o'clock news on Channel 77, wearing headphones so she wouldn't disturb her partner.

Instead, he disturbed her. "I got it!" he yelled.

"Huh?" she said.

"Take off your headphones. Look what's on the door of Trey's truck." Phil dragged Helen over to his computer, where the pickup truck door was enlarged and enhanced on the screen. Helen could see a stylized LCC and, under the letters, LOHAN CONSTRUCTION CORP.— FORT LAUDERDALE.

"This is going to be fun," Phil said. "Trey used a truck owned by his father's company."

"What does LCC do?" Helen said.

"The company Web site says it has 'affordable, furnished rental property in urban locations.' That's code for high-rent property in low-rent parts of town. I've seen those apartments. They have rickety, pressed-sawdust furniture, substandard appliances and a million code violations, including no screens and flimsy hollow-core front doors."

"So Trey with the fancy name is the son of a slum-lord," Helen said.

"And he's dragged Daddy's business into his theft," Phil said. "I expect Mr. Coakley to hit the roof. It's one thing for Trey to have his way with Coakley's daughter, but rustling a man's golf cart crosses the line."

"Now I can't wait for that TAR report," Helen said.

"I'll work on the request now," he said. "We can't move on the Coakley case until the pickup's ownership is confirmed."

"I'm looking forward to seeing Snake Boy arrested as an accessory," Helen said. "I wonder which one stole the necklace—Trey, Ozzie or Chloe?"

"Could be all three," Phil said, "but I doubt that Chloe will wind up in trouble with the law, no matter how guilty she is. What's going on with our accounts?"

"It's either good news or bad, depending on how you look at it," Helen said. "Thanks to my two library cases plus the Kingsley job, we'll have to make a bigger quarterly payment to the IRS. I'm figuring it out now."

Helen put her headphones back on and was playing her calculator like a virtuoso when she heard the voice of Valerie Cannata on the TV.

The reporter said, "A stolen white 1991 Toyota Camry was returned to the same strip mall from which it was taken." Valerie was on-screen, sleek and professional in a chestnut brown suit that made her red hair glow.

Helen tore off her headphones and turned up the sound. "Look at this, Phil," she said. "A stolen white car."

"So?" he said. "More than a thousand cars are stolen in Florida every year. Some of them are bound to be white."

"But our ghost, Charlotte, was killed by a white car," Helen said. "Listen!"

Valerie was in a landscaped parking lot next to a white Toyota. The woman with her was a perfect match for the car: Neither fat nor thin, old nor young, she was pleasantly average. So was her name: Mary Smith.

"The car, which the owner said she left parked in the lot three days ago," Valerie said, "was covered with dust and dirt when it was taken. Now it's been returned sparkling clean. Channel Seventy-seven talked with the car's owner today."

"I was coming into work at Julie's Smoothies," Ms. Smith said. "You could have knocked me down with a feather when I saw my car again. I thought it was gone for good. But it was back in the lot and back in the same spot where I'd left it. I haven't washed my car in six months. But it was returned to me waxed and gleaming. Even the seats were cleaned. But it's been in an accident.

"You know the strange thing?" Ms. Smith said. "Left inside my car was a pair of white cotton gloves. Who wears cotton gloves in Florida?"

"What kind of gloves?" Valerie asked.

"Cheap, flimsy cotton gloves," Ms. Smith said. "I don't know who would wear them, or why."

"I do," Helen said to Phil. "Librarians and bibliophiles wear cheap cotton gloves to examine valuable books."

He shushed her so they could listen to Valerie's story. Mary Smith was still talking about her clean car. "That car is a workhorse," she said. "It's not used to the white glove treatment."

Valerie smiled at the small joke, then turned serious. "Unfortunately," she said, "Mary Smith was not able to take possession of her shiny car. So far, police have found a fingerprint on the steering column, and they're looking for a match in the databases."

"Phil," Helen said, "that strip mall is about a mile from the Flora Park Library."

"Which means?" Phil said.

"I don't know," Helen said. "I need to think on it."

"You need a break," he said. "And so do I. It's time for the sunset salute. Let's go have a drink by the pool. I'll make the popcorn if you feed Thumbs."

Thumbs demanded extra scratches with his dinner, and it was a good ten minutes before Helen and Phil carried out their drinks and a big bowl of popcorn.

Margery was the only one out by the pool that night. She wore ombre purple palazzo pants, a necklace of hot-pink and purple beads, and matching mules. Phil kissed her cheek and said, "As usual, you class up the joint."

"Thank you," Margery said, batting her eyelashes. Their landlady was an outrageous flirt. Phil lit her Marlboro. She inhaled and breathed out a long stream of smoke, like a friendly dragon.

"I made popcorn," he said, stretching out in a chaise next to Margery. "I like your new renter, Markos, but I can't take any more health food."

"Then I won't tell you popcorn is high in fiber," Margery said, and grinned wickedly.

Helen piled popcorn on a plate and sat next to Phil. They sat quietly by the pool for several minutes, listening to the breeze ripple the turquoise water. This was Helen's favorite time of day. Purple bougainvillea flowers floated on the surface. The setting sun gave the white apartment building a soft, pink glow. The only sound was the crunch of popcorn.

Phil finally broke the silence. "Where is everyone?" he asked.

"Markos is working nights, remember?" Margery said. "Peggy and Daniel are out to dinner again, so it's just us on a Friday night."

Margery raised her wineglass, then said, "Helen, how's the search going for your ghost killer?"

"More questions than answers," Helen said. "So far, Seraphina, our client's good friend, suddenly gave her white Beemer to her son in college and bought herself a black Mercedes. Lisa the board president has had two accidents—and two rentals this week. The janitor's white pickup and a white Chevy Impala owned by a librarian have both been in accidents, and so was a dirty white car. It was stolen, then returned all clean and shiny, with a pair of white gloves on the seat."

"What kind of white gloves?" Margery asked. "Like the ones women used to wear in the fifties?"

"No, cheap, flimsy white cotton gloves," Helen said. "The kind librarians wear when they examine rare books."

"Other people wear gloves for work, too," Margery said. "People who handle documents, mail, negatives. Event staff, inspection staff, even waiters wear white cotton gloves. Kids in the local high school band wear them for parades. The car could have been stolen by a kid after school."

"I'm not convinced," Helen said. "I think there's a connection between those gloves and the library ghost's murder, but I can't get it to fit together.

"What I don't understand is why there are so many accidents involving white cars."

"There are a lot of accidents, period," Margery said. "Florida's one of the ten most dangerous states for drivers.

"South Florida is known for aggressive drivers who follow too close, make risky lane changes and speed like crazy. Even more dangerous are the road ragers—the angry morons who flash their lights if they think you're driving too slow. Road ragers tailgate, flip off drivers, yell at them, even throw stuff."

"Sounds like Saturday night on I-95," Helen said. "But why am I encountering so many white cars?"

"People down here love them," Margery said. "You have a white car. And by the way, where is it? I don't see it in the parking lot. You came home with Phil." Margery didn't miss much in her domain.

"It's in the shop," Helen said. "The brakes weren't working right."

"Well, you may have prevented one accident involving a white car," Margery said. "How are you getting to work tomorrow?"

"I can drive Helen to the library," Phil said.

"Why don't you borrow my car?" Margery said. "It's white."

CHAPTER 33

· · · · · · · · · · · · · · · · · · · ·

"Phil, if we can figure out Chloe's riddle, we may be able to close the stolen ruby necklace case tonight," Helen said. "I think she and her boyfriend, Ozzie, are running a bling ring to fence stolen goods. If we catch them, I'll never have to deal with the Coakleys again."

After the sunset salute, the two private eyes had strolled over to Phil's apartment, where he whipped up omelets with sharp cheddar. Thumbs, their six-toed cat, begged for a taste.

"Beat it, dude," Helen told the big-pawed Thumbs as she scratched his ear. "You're a cat. You're supposed to eat cat food."

Thumbs went back to his bowl and resentfully crunched his dry food.

"Chloe's sly," Phil said. "What were her exact words?"

"She said she couldn't tell me what she and her partner—I'm pretty sure that's Ozzie—were doing without his permission."

"Ozzie is Snake Boy?" Phil said.

"Right. Seraphina Ormond's son, who's going to college to be a herpetologist. Chloe said her partner wasn't doing anything illegal. She worded it very carefully."

"Which means she's doing something illegal?" Phil said.

"That's my guess," Helen said. "Then Chloe said, *I'll give you three clues: Rex, Crown, Jewel. Meet us there at nine o'clock any weekend night and you'll know.*"

"Rex, Crown, Jewel," Phil said. "They all have to do with kings and jewelry."

"Maybe someone named Rex is buying stolen jewels," Helen said.

"Where?" Phil said. "Is the address in those clues?"

"I don't know. I was just brainstorming," Helen said. "Chloe's tricky."

"She's got a mean streak, too," Phil said, "telling Ana the cook that she wanted boneless chicken when she really wanted a boiled egg."

"She called a Mexican woman a beaner," Helen said. "I'm surprised Ana didn't quit on the spot."

"Poor people with families don't have that luxury," Phil said. "You know better."

"I do," Helen said, and felt ashamed. How many low-paying jobs had she had when she was on the run from her ex-husband? She'd endured insults, long hours and low pay because she was desperate.

"Chloe has everything," she said. "She's pretty, her family's rich and her parents are indulgent."

"Maybe too indulgent. We'd better get working," Phil said, checking his phone. "It's eight ten and Chloe and her partner in crime start working at nine o'clock. Back to Chloe's clues—Rex, Crown and Jewel. Jewel could be a woman's name."

"Rex could be a dog—or a dude," Helen said. "Rex could be their fence."

"Where?" Phil said. "He can't stand on a street corner buying stolen goods—not in any neighborhood where those two white-bread suburbanites would hang out. They're not street-smart enough to sell in a tough area. They'd be skinned like bunny rabbits."

"Jewel, Crown, Rex," Helen repeated. "Rex. It could be a business name. Is there a pawnshop named Rex's?"

Phil Googled the name on his iPhone. "Yes!" he said. "There's a Rex's Best Price Pawn in Peerless Point, and it's on Jewell Road."

"Is that near the Publix store off Federal Highway?" Helen said. "Next door to a Walgreens and a Starbucks?"

"Everything in South Florida is next to a Walgreens," Phil said. "But that's it. It's eight forty-five. Let's go."

"Wait!" she said. "We figured out two clues, Jewel and Rex, but what about the third—Crown?"

"We'll work on that tomorrow night if we're wrong," he said, and they hurried out to Phil's Jeep. The sky was velvety black, but the night air was like being slapped with a warm, wet towel. There was no breeze to rustle the palm trees.

Helen was grateful the trip in the un-air-conditioned Jeep was short. Phil parked in the Walgreens' lot next door to the L-shaped, pale green stucco mall, prettily landscaped with feathery palms and bright red flowering impatiens. Rex's Best Price Pawn, Starbucks and a Chipotle Grill were straight ahead. Around the corner, Helen caught a glimpse of a liquor store, a designer consignment shop and, at the other end, Crowning Glory Hair Salon.

"Think the hair salon is Chloe's Crown clue?" Helen asked.

"Could be," Phil said. "What about the Regal Designer Consignment?"

"I could see Chloe selling stolen designer purses or clothes on consignment," Helen said. "But do resale shops take jewelry? And why would she need her boyfriend? Besides, consignment sales take time. She'd have to wait for the money."

"Chloe strikes me as someone who wants instant gratification," Phil said.

Time seemed trapped in the thick, sticky night air. Helen checked her cell phone clock, but the minutes refused to move. Finally, at 9:08, she said, "Look! A silver Acura's pulling into the lot. Now it's parking in front of the pawnshop."

"Why is that important?"

"Chloe said she got her mother's old silver Acura."

"I see two people inside," Phil said. "The driver looks like a cute blonde."

"I think that's Chloe," Helen said.

"A bearded twentysomething male is sitting next to her."

"Ozzie," Helen said. "Snake Boy. I'll start recording video on my cell phone as soon as one gets out."

Helen and Phil sat in the Jeep for three more sweaty minutes until Chloe hopped out, definitely dressed for a date in a short black sundress and ankle-strap sandals. She waved to Snake Boy, then flashed a lot of tanned leg as she strolled into Starbucks. Ten minutes later, she tripped out with an iced coffee and sat at an empty table.

"At least the light's good here," Helen said.

A small sun-faded red Nissan slammed into the lot, bass speakers vibrating. The car parked one row down from the Acura.

A blond-banged boy slouched over to Chloe, his thin, pale face splotched with acne, his board shorts flapping around his skinny white legs.

"He looks younger than Chloe, maybe sixteen or seventeen," Helen said.

"He'd have to be sixteen to have a driver's license," Phil said.

The pimpled stripling sat down next to Chloe and said something. She giggled and touched his arm with her pink manicured hand, then leaned forward to give him a better view of her nearly bare chest.

The boy turned red, but he also looked.

"Why is Chloe flirting with him?" Helen said. "Her boyfriend is in the car watching."

"You said she has a mean streak," Phil said. "That poor dude is definitely not in her league."

"He's also not on her radar," Helen said. "There has to be a reason she's turning up the heat."

"There it is!" Phil said. "He just handed her a fat roll of bills."

"Why's he paying her?" Helen said. "Is she hooking?"

"Why would she need Snake Boy?" Phil said.

"Because he's her pimp?" Helen guessed.

"No way I can see Chloe as a hooker," Phil said. "Not with a high school kid. An older man with money, maybe. But she doesn't have the patience to deal with awkward boys. Wait! She's going back to the Acura."

Now the pimpled boy was alone at the table with Chloe's iced coffee, watching her legs as she climbed into the car. She handed Ozzie the bills. Helen and Phil watched Snake Boy count the money and shove it in his wallet. Then Ozzie got out and strolled around the corner. Chloe went back to her table and continued flirting with the nervous, fidgeting boy.

"Ozzie's going to the liquor store," Helen said. She craned her neck to see the liquor store's name on the side. "Corona Liquor and Beer," she said. "That's the clue. Corona is a crown."

"And a beer," Phil said. "A double clue. Let's see what happens next."

After ten minutes, Ozzie came out with a case of Bud Light longnecks. He walked past Chloe and the pimpled boy and put the beer in the unlocked trunk of the red Nissan.

"I think Chloe and her boyfriend are buying beer for underage high school kids," Phil said.

"That would make sense," Helen said. "Chloe told me she and her mysterious partner didn't have 'a *job* job,' and said, *Last Friday we made two hundred dollars.* She also said, *We can make a couple hundred every weekend. More during spring break and in the summer when school's out.*"

"The scam is starting to come clear," Phil said. "Let's watch a little longer."

By ten o'clock, Chloe had flirted with three more young men, who ranged from painfully shy to pathetically awkward. Each one handed her a wad of cash. Each time, she took it to Ozzie, and each time he bought a case of beer and stashed it in the awkward dude's car. Then the freshly beered boys drove off and Chloe stayed at her table.

"Here comes another mark," Phil said. "Let's interrupt it when Ozzie comes out with the beer."

Helen winced when the young man shambled up to Chloe. He was all knees and elbows, with an acne-pitted complexion and buzzed dark hair.

She crossed her legs, fluttered her eyelashes and threw out her chest.

The discombobulated boy blushed and dropped his wad of money on the ground, then scrambled to pick it up and bumped his head on the table. When he finally handed Chloe the cash, she rewarded him with a seductive smile, patted his shoulder and rushed off to the silver Acura, where Ozzie counted the bills, then headed for the liquor store. She joined the latest mark at the table again and resumed her flirtation.

"Oh, good," Phil said. "Looks like Ozzie is buying a case of Heineken this time. My favorite. Let's go."

Helen and Phil stood at Chloe's table. "Hello, Chloe," Helen said. "You remember Phil."

Chloe's face went white.

"We figured out your clues," Helen said. "Who's your friend?"

"Uh, I'm Justin," said the acne-pitted mark. His voice started low and turned into a squeak.

"Nice to meet you, Justin," Phil said, introducing himself. "My partner, Helen, and I are private detectives. Are you old enough to drink?"

Justin's eyes darted like a flock of sunset birds. "No," he mumbled.

"How old are you?" Helen asked.

"Sixteen."

"How much did you give Chloe for that case of Heineken?"

"Forty-five dollars," Justin said, looking at his feet.

Ozzie was nearing the table with the beer when he stopped. "Hey, Ozzie," Phil said. "Come on over and join the party."

Ozzie looked like he might bolt, but Phil walked up and put his arm around Snake Boy's shoulders. It looked friendly, but he was actually forcing him to come to the table.

"You don't want to run, Ozzie," he said, his voice low. "My partner and I have been taping your underage beer-buying scam for about an hour. We recorded times, faces and license plate numbers. And what we didn't catch, the shopping center security cameras did." He pointed to one over Chloe's table.

"Now, Helen can use her cell phone to call the cops, or we can talk this out."

"I didn't do anything illegal," Ozzie said. "I'm just buying beer."

"For people too young to drink. And using another minor as an accessory. You're looking at criminal charges and a five-hundred-dollar fine—minimum. You can both be charged."

Chloe went a shade paler.

"Give Justin back his forty-five dollars, Ozzie."

"What? I just bought the beer."

"And you're not selling it to a minor. Give Justin his forty-five dollars. Now."

Ozzie peeled two twenties and a five off the bills in his wallet and dropped them on the table.

"Take the money, Justin," Phil said. "You've got a few years before you can buy beer legally."

Justin didn't argue. He grabbed the forty-five dollars, ran to his clunker and roared out of the parking lot, tires screeching.

"Nice scam there," Helen said. "That case of Heineken is twenty-four dollars, so you pocket about twenty bucks on that sale. More if they want cheap beer."

"I only ask forty for the cheap beer," Ozzie said.

"You're all heart," Phil said.

"Are you gonna tell my mom and dad?" Chloe asked in a small voice.

She doesn't fear the police, Helen thought, but she is worried about her parents.

"Not if you shut it down," Phil said. "Cops aren't stupid. If we figured it out in an hour, they will, too. If I catch you selling to minors again, you won't get a warning. I'll call 911."

"And give them this video," Helen said, tapping her cell.

Chloe and Ozzie started for the Acura, but Phil grabbed the beer away from Snake Boy. "The Heineken stays with me," he said. "It's my fee for taking up my Friday night."

When they were back in the Jeep, Helen said, "Tomorrow, we have to start over, looking for the stolen necklace again. This was a total waste."

"Not entirely," Phil said. "I got a case of beer."

CHAPTER 34

. . . .

Phil's cell phone rang at eleven twenty-three that
night.

"This can't be good," he said, reaching for his
phone on the nightstand.

He answered it, and Helen watched her husband's
face go from puzzlement to smiling recognition. "Markos," he said. "You called. What's going on? What? A
dude's selling a ruby necklace in Light Up the Night?"

Phil put his phone on speaker so Helen could hear
the conversation—and the bar sounds.

"Yes," Markos said. It sounded like "jess." As he
grew more excited, his slight Cuban accent thickened.
"It's big and there are diamonds on it. He wants five
thousand dollars."

"For a twenty-thousand-dollar necklace," Phil said.
"That's a real bargain. How much cash do you have
with you?"

"About five hundred in tips," Markos said.

"Give him everything you have," Phil said. "I'll pay
you back. Tell him you want the necklace for your girlfriend and your friend is bringing the rest of the cash."

"Will do," Markos said.

"Is he anywhere near you right now?" Phil asked.

"Dude's at the bar," Markos said.

"Is he short and brown-haired?" Phil said.

"Tall, with muscles and blond hair," Markos said.

"And a sneer?" Helen asked.

Phil frowned at her, but Markos said, "He looks down at me, and I'm not that much shorter."

"That's our man," Phil said. "Helen and I will be there in twenty minutes. I'll call you when we get there.

"Helen," he said, "run and get the whole five thousand out of the office safe while I track down a Peerless Point crimes-against-property detective I know. It may take a minute."

Helen slipped on her shoes, raced upstairs and opened the Coronado safe, where they kept five thousand in cash for emergencies. She bundled forty-five hundred dollars into a big manila envelope, then put five hundred in her purse.

When she returned to Phil's apartment, he was still on his phone. She heard him say, "Hey, Broker, sorry to wake you."

Broker must have made some smart remark. Phil grinned and said, "You can bitch now, Detective, but you'll owe me a beer for this. A college kid named Standiford W. Lohan the Third—goes by Trey—is selling a hot diamond-and-ruby necklace at Light Up the Night, the cigar and martini bar on Federal. Yeah, right now. He's about six feet, blond hair, one-seventy. He wants five thousand cash. It's worth twenty. The necklace belongs to my client.

"I've got an operative on the scene who's giving Trey five hundred dollars until I can get there with the rest of the money. When I make the buy, want to arrest him? I thought so. Backup is a good idea. I don't think he has a weapon, but he might run. Helen and I are leaving now."

Phil wore a black shirt and Helen had changed into a black blouse and pants to blend in with the bar crowd. "We look like a pair of gunfighters," she said.

They slipped out into the cool, quiet night. All the lights were off at the Coronado, even Margery's. They tiptoed through the moon-drenched yard to Phil's Jeep.

For once, Helen was glad his Jeep didn't have air-conditioning. The temperature had dropped since their beer-scam bust. Now the night air felt cool and smelled of the sea. When they were on Federal Highway, Helen said, "I'm looking forward to this. I've wanted to wipe that sneer off Trey's face since I first saw his picture. Looks like the cops will do it for me."

"If Trey is still there," Phil said. "If he took Markos's down payment. If Trey believes I'll show up with the rest of the cash, and if he lets Markos make the buy."

"That's a lot of *if*s," Helen said.

"Here's one more," Phil said. "If Broker arrives in time to make the bust."

"His name is Broker?" Helen asked.

"No," he said. "It's Stanley Morgan. Like Morgan Stanley, the brokerage house."

"Oh, right," Helen said. "I'm not the sharpest knife in the drawer at this hour."

The shopping center was on the left. Phil turned in and circled twice before he found a parking spot. Light Up the Night was living up to its name, its striped awnings overshadowed by a bright neon martini glass and a cigar with a swiggle of smoke. Young men and pretty women were clustered around the entrance, posing like models in a magazine shoot. The men—and some women—were smoking cigars.

Helen whistled. "They're wearing some expensive clothes," she said.

"They are? I don't see any designer logos," Phil said.

"The truly chic don't brand themselves like cattle," Helen said. "They expect anyone who counts to know."

"If you say so," Phil said.

One cigar smoker stood alone under a palm tree, away from the others, observing the crowd. "Broker,"

Phil said, waving to him. "This is my wife and partner, Helen Hawthorne."

"Your partner is a hell of a lot better-looking than any I ever had," Broker said. He was thirtysomething, and dressed as stylishly as the customers. Helen recognized his well-cut outfit as Hugo Boss.

"I got here ten minutes ago," he said. "Lots of blondes, but all girls. The only men had brown hair or were bald."

"Not him," Phil said, thumbing through his iPhone. "Here's a picture of Trey and the necklace."

"I'll remember him," Broker said. "The blond girl your client?"

"Her father is," Phil said. "Our client wanted to keep this out of the papers. He never filed a police report, but he has the sales receipt."

Broker nodded.

"Your backup in place?" Phil asked.

"Two uniforms at the entrance in back," Broker said. "A car is parked in the next lot if we need it."

"I'll call Markos, our operative, and tell him I'm here," Phil said. "I'll meet Markos and the seller at the bar. I have the cash." He held up the manila envelope.

Markos answered on the first ring. "I'm here," Phil said. "I've got the money in a manila envelope."

"He's waiting," Markos said, "but he's impatient."

"Order me a Bombay martini, straight up, lemon peel," Phil said, "and I'll meet you at the bar right away."

"I'm borrowing your partner when I go in," Broker said. "Maybe she'll make me look less like a cop."

Helen and Broker walked quickly to the bar door. "You nervous?" he said.

"I don't get nervous," Helen said, and hoped he didn't notice she was only pretending to be cool. Her heart was thumping so loud she could hardly hear him.

"I'll stand at the front entrance in case he runs," Broker said. "As soon as he takes the money, I'll move in."

"I'll hang out near Phil and signal when he makes the buy," Helen said. "If you see me raise my hand, come running."

Inside, Sinatra oozed from the speakers. There was very little smoke, but Helen definitely smelled the cigars. She rather liked the smell—it reminded her of her grandfather. But she was quite sure the fashionistas perched on the midcentury modern chairs wouldn't want to hear that. Every table was taken and people stood three deep at the bar, drinking birdbath-sized martinis.

Helen spotted Phil's silver hair. He was standing at the bar next to Markos, who looked so sweaty and shifty-eyed he could have been the thief. Trey, with his blond bangs, looked like he was doing Phil a favor by talking to him.

Helen watched Trey pull the necklace out of his shirt pocket. In the dimly lit room, it was a fiery beacon, but the smokers and drinkers didn't seem to notice. Helen carefully elbowed her way past a couple drinking dirty martinis. Now she was closer to the action, close enough to see Phil's martini in an icy glass, alone and abandoned on the bar. She wished she could drink it.

Focus, she told herself. You've got a crook to catch.

Trey was counting the cash now, and still nobody nearby noticed the deal going down. Then Trey smiled, the only attractive expression she'd seen on his face, and handed Phil the necklace.

Helen looked for Broker. The detective was near the door, trying—and failing—to look casual. He nodded, she raised her hand, and he pushed his way through the crowd.

Helen heard cries of "Hey!" "Watch where you're going!" and "You spilled my drink, asshat!"

Trey turned his head, and Helen saw the stunned look on his face as Broker clamped his hand on the thief's arm.

"Hey, what are you doing?" Trey said, giving a good impersonation of an innocent man.

"Detective Stanley Morgan, Peerless Point Property Crimes," he said. "Do you have a receipt to prove you own that necklace?"

"Do you have a receipt for those clothes?" Trey said.

"Let's step outside, sir, where we can discuss this," Broker said, and guided Trey toward the door. Two uniforms materialized and walked beside them through the trendy crowd.

Markos grabbed Phil's martini and drank it down. "Is it over?" he said. He looked frazzled, his thick, black hair standing up in spikes, his white waiter's shirt soaked through with sweat.

"It's over," Phil said, "and you did great."

Helen pulled a small envelope out of her purse. "This is yours," she said. "You won't have to wait for the police to give you your tip money back."

"I'll return this as soon as they do," Markos said.

"No," Helen said. "It's your payment. You were our freelance operative."

Markos straightened his shoulders and smiled. "I'm an operative? Like in the movies?"

"Exactly," Helen said. "We couldn't have closed this case without you."

CHAPTER 35

· ·

B ut the case wasn't closed, not yet.
  Trey tried to brazen it out, as if his supercil-
ious sneer and privileged blond-boy haircut were
protection. "Bree gave me that necklace to sell for her,"
he said. "Her old man's a tightwad and she needs money.
She likes to party, if you know what I mean." He made
sniffing sounds.

"Then let's ask him," Broker said. "Phil, will you
call Mr. Coakley? And put your cell phone on speaker
so we can all hear."

Amis Coakley was not happy that Phil woke him up
at twelve thirty a.m.

"Couldn't this wait until a more civilized hour?" he
asked.

"No," Phil said. "I've recovered Bree's ruby necklace."

"I still don't see why that news can't wait until morning," Amis Coakley said.

"Because the necklace was stolen by Trey, your daughter's boyfriend," Phil said.

"What!"

Helen could feel Amis's anger boiling through the

phone, like a controlled explosion that demolished whole buildings.

"He says Bree gave him the necklace to sell," Phil said.

"She did nothing of the kind," Amis said. Helen expected Phil's cell phone to burst into bits of plastic, metal and melted chips.

"Trey says you're a tightwad and she gave him the necklace to sell so she could have the cash." Phil was grinning now.

Helen gave him a warning look. It isn't smart to tease an angry client, she thought. Not when he hasn't paid our final bill.

Amis gave a low, guttural growl, a predator ready to rip out a throat.

"If you can prove that you bought the necklace and if Bree will say he's lying—" Phil began.

Amis cut him off. "Of course he's lying! I'm extremely generous to my daughter."

"The detective needs you to show him the necklace receipt," Phil said.

"My word isn't enough?"

"Sorry, but we need paper, sir, if the police are going to arrest him," Phil said. "And could you bring Bree so she can swear out an affidavit that she did not give Trey her necklace to fence?"

"I'll see if she's home," Amis said. "Hold on."

Home? Helen wondered. Oh, wait—she's twenty-one, it's Friday night, and we're in Florida, not the Midwest.

They waited. A curious crowd of martini guzzlers and cigar smokers had gathered in the parking lot, until the uniforms started asking the beautiful people if they knew anything about stolen goods being sold at the bar. Then they melted away like . . . well, like smoke.

Amis was back on the line. "Bree is here. Where should we see you?"

"We're in the parking lot of Light Up the Night, the cigar and martini bar," Phil said.

"I prefer not to conduct my personal business in public," Amis said.

Broker took the phone. "This is Detective Stanley Morgan, Mr. Coakley," he said. "We can come to your home with Mr. Lohan, or you can meet us at the Peerless Point police headquarters."

"I don't want that scum in my house again. I want you to take him straight to jail after we leave. We'll meet you at the police headquarters." Amis Coakley clicked off his phone.

"Let's roll," Broker said.

"What about my car?" Trey said, and pointed to a red Ferrari still in the lot.

"Son, that's the least of your worries right now," Broker said.

"But what if it's—"

"Stolen?" Broker interrupted. "I hope not, for your sake. I hear this place is crawling with thieves."

They had a parade to the Peerless Point police station. Trey was loaded into a patrol car that followed Broker's unmarked Dodge Charger. Helen and Phil brought up the rear.

Like many police stations in upscale communities, it was hard to tell that the Peerless Point building was a cop shop. Outside, it was prettily painted and landscaped. But inside were the same Wanted posters, depressing decor and lowlifes.

Trey was left in a drab interview room like a piece of luggage, while the private eyes and Broker waited for the Coakleys.

"Trey did more than steal Bree's necklace," Phil said. "He also took the family's golf cart. Hauled it off in his father's pickup truck. At least I think it was his father's truck. I've got a TAR request in for the license plate."

"You got the license number with you?" Broker asked. "I can look it up in the line of duty."

"Yep."

They followed him to a computer at a paper-piled desk, and Broker typed in the plate number and quickly had the information. "Black 2012 F-150 Ford pickup," he said. "Registered to LCC, Lohan Construction Corp."

"That's him," Phil said.

"Lohan," Broker said. "He the one who builds those insta-slums with the hollow-core doors?"

"That's Trey's dad," Phil said. "How'd you know about the flimsy apartment doors?"

"I've put my foot through more than one in the pursuit of justice," he said. "LCC apartments are magnets for stolen goods. Where's the golf cart?"

"Trey sold it for two thousand cash to a shop called Fore! Sale. The owner, Dave, took it out of the showroom and promised to deliver it once I was ready to return it. Trey's on the store security footage, delivering the stolen golf cart."

"This just gets better," Broker said. "You two realize that if Trey really did steal that necklace, you'll have to be witnesses for the state."

"Fine with us," Helen said.

"I'll get a warrant for the Lohan home and see if Sonny Boy's been stockpiling other stolen goods. There's a shoplifting ring that's been driving us crazy. I'd be tickled pink to finally make an arrest."

"You'd look good in pink," Phil said. He gave Broker the ruby-and-diamond necklace. Helen was hypnotized by its glitter.

That was when a grumpy Amis Coakley showed up with a sleepy Bree. Amis looked like he kicked puppies for fun. Bree was posing as a model citizen in a pink polo shirt and white clam diggers. Helen saw a delicate rose-gold Tiffany T wire bracelet on her wrist.

They crowded into the interview room, Helen and Phil against a wall, Amis and Bree facing Trey. He'd been handcuffed to the scarred table.

The thief didn't flinch when Amis glared at him— or when Broker read Trey his rights.

Broker produced the necklace. "Mr. Coakley, did you purchase this necklace?"

"I did," he said. "For my daughter's twenty-first birthday. Here's the receipt from the jeweler."

Trey's sneer stayed steady.

"Ms. Coakley," Broker said, "did you give Mr. Lohan permission to sell your necklace because you wanted more money?"

Broker didn't mention Trey's charge that Bree wanted drug money, Helen thought. Maybe he doesn't want to damage his witness.

"I did not!" Bree said. "And I never, ever said Daddy was cheap. He's the most generous daddy in the world." She was crying now, but Helen couldn't tell if she'd cleverly turned on the waterworks or those were real tears. She did notice Bree had the gift of crying prettily. Her eyes didn't redden and there was no unattractive sniffling. Her father put his arm protectively around her shoulders.

"You liar," Trey said, suddenly flushed with anger. "I had to listen to you bitch for weeks because your father would only give you one party—in Fort Lauderdale yet—and he wouldn't pay for any A-listers."

"That's not true," Bree screeched. She shook off Daddy's arm, then pulled the rose-gold Tiffany bracelet off her wrist and held it up. "Did you steal this, too? Did you steal my birthday present? Answer me!"

"I want a lawyer," Trey said.

"You did steal it," she said. She threw the bracelet at Trey, then punched him in the head.

Helen saw that Broker didn't move. She thought the detective enjoyed watching Bree beat Trey, but it was hard to tell. She did know that Bree packed quite a wallop. By the time Broker and her father stopped her, little Bree had not only knocked the sneer off Trey's face, but had also given her ex-boyfriend a bloody nose and a split lip. Her punch must have dazed Trey. He covered his face with his hands, but didn't fight back.

"The four of you will give me your statements while I wait for Mr. Lohan's lawyer," Broker said.

"Yes, Detective," Amis Coakley said. Bree nodded.

"We will," Helen said. "And we'll testify that you did not hit Trey Lohan, Detective."

Bree tried to retrieve her bracelet from the floor, but Broker said, "Sorry, miss. I have reason to believe that's stolen property. It stays with me."

"I'll buy you a new one, sweetheart," Amis Coakley said.

Helen was tired and groggy. She needed sleep. She wanted to go home. As she left the room, she looked back at Trey.

He was alone. His bloody nose dripped on the table and his right eye was swelling and turning into a rainbow. His air of entitlement was gone, along with his smirk.

Well, she thought. This might be more rewarding than a fat check.

· ·

CHAPTER 36

What's Lisa doing walking down Federal Highway with a Julie's Smoothie? Helen wondered.

It was ten thirty Monday morning, and Helen had slept in. After their wild weekend, she was so hopped up on adrenaline she had trouble sleeping, so when the alarm rang, she slapped it until it shut up, then fell back asleep. She knew she wouldn't be in any shape to investigate the library ghost's murder if she didn't get some sleep.

When she woke up at nine thirty, Phil was gone and Thumbs had been fed. She borrowed Margery's Lincoln Town Car. In the big square white car, Helen felt like she was driving a living room—a cigarette-smoke-filled living room. She rolled down Federal at a stately pace, terrified she'd ding one of the car's fenders.

About a mile from the Flora Park Library, she saw the board president trudging along the side of the highway, carrying a clear plastic smoothie cup filled with something pink. Tall, thin Lisa looked hot and uncomfortable. Her colorless hair was wilted. Damp patches of sweat bloomed on her faded blue blouse.

Helen pulled over and got out. "Lisa," she said, "may I give you a ride back to the library?"

"Thank you," Lisa said, and sank gratefully into the Lincoln's plush seats. "It's hotter than I thought it would be."

"Aren't you worried about walking along Federal?" Helen said. "There are no sidewalks here."

"Most of the walk's through Flora Park," Lisa said, sipping her smoothie, "and that part's pretty. Nobody ever has any problems. The library staffers and patrons walk over to the smoothie shop all the time. The drinks are probably full of sugar, but I feel so virtuous walking there. The heat and humidity got me today. I'm glad you stopped."

"Are Julie's Smoothies good?" Helen asked.

"The best. I like the mango-strawberry with a scoop of protein powder," Lisa said. "I feel guilty indulging, but I couldn't stand any more break-room coffee. The staff never cleans the pot. The coffee tastes like tar."

That's what Charlotte told me, Helen thought. The late Charlotte Dams.

"Are the smoothies that expensive?" Helen asked.

"I guess not," she said. "But Mother has Alzheimer's and I can no longer care for her myself. I've had to hire someone to be with her while I'm at the library, but one person isn't enough. Mother really needs full-time professional care and I have to move her into a home very soon. I need every dollar to get her in the best possible place."

"I'm sorry," Helen said.

"I am, too," Lisa said, twisting a lock of her sad colored hair. "She's such a good mother. Alzheimer's is a doubly cruel disease. First it took Mother's personality, and now it's taking her life. She barely knows who I am anymore."

"I am so sorry," Helen repeated, and felt guilty for even suspecting Lisa. But a million dollars would defi-

nitely solve her problems. And if a mother would do anything for her child, wouldn't a child—a devoted daughter
like Lisa—kill to keep her beloved mother in comfort?

Lisa's straw made that sucking noise that said her
smoothie was over. She stared silently out the window.

They were under Flora Park's cool tree canopy now.
Helen wondered if Lisa's personal revelation had
embarrassed her.

"Well, I didn't mean to go on about my problems,"
Lisa said. "Here's the library. Thank you so much."

Helen had barely parked the car when Lisa bolted
and ran for the staff door.

Helen sat in Margery's smoke-cured car, and noticed
that Lisa had left her smoothie cup. She could see her
fingerprints on the plastic surface.

White car. Fingerprints. Smoothie shop. Julie's Smoothies was in the strip mall where the white car had been
stolen and returned shiny clean. A car that had been in an
unknown accident. A car . . . that could have been used to
kill Charlotte.

I've been searching wrong, Helen thought. I've been
looking for white cars that have been in accidents. But
what if Charlotte's killer didn't use his—or her—own
car? What if the killer stole the car?

Charlotte's killer could have run—or driven—to the
smoothie shop, hot-wired a car, then gone to the building where Charlotte had her job interview. The killer
knew where Charlotte was going and her interview
time. Helen had heard someone listening outside the
Kingsley collection room door. The killer would have
had time to hot-wire the white car and get to the parking lot before Charlotte.

Jared, the bitter janitor, already knew how to hot-
wire. He was a mechanic.

The others might know, too, or they could have looked
up the information online. Helen had seen the step-by-
step hot-wiring instructions on the library computer. A

patron could have looked up that information, but if the person hadn't signed out before their session was up, anyone could have conducted an Internet search on that log-in: Gladys, Blair, Seraphina and Lisa were all in the building. So was Alexa, for that matter. I was busy and distracted, Helen thought, hunting for a new computer mouse, and then filing a report. They could have slipped into the room then.

All I need are their fingerprints. I'll take the prints to Detective Micah Doben, who's investigating Charlotte's murder. He can compare their prints with the print found on the stolen car's steering column.

I won't have to worry about confronting a killer. He can make the arrest and take the credit. I'll take the cash when the killer's caught.

I'll have backup. That's what we had last night when Broker arrested Trey. That's what I'll have today when I go after Charlotte's killer.

I already have Lisa's prints on the smoothie cup. Now I need the other five.

Helen locked Margery's car. She found Jared near the staff door, working on the building's drain spout.

"Hey, Jared," she said. The janitor saluted her with his Coke can, took a last, long drink, then looked around for a trash can.

"I'll toss that for you," Helen said.

"Thanks," he said. "This whole drain spout was about to come loose. I've been wrestling with it for over an hour."

"Looks like you're nearly finished," Helen said.

Jared lowered his voice and asked, "Alexa's not looking for me, is she?"

"Not sure," Helen said. "I'm just getting in."

"I'm running late. I had to fight the traffic all the way to West Broward Boulevard in Fort Lauderdale to pick up a copy of my accident report. The insurance company has been hounding me for it. I thought I'd run in and get it, but I had to wait in line. Took up half my morning and now I'm racing to catch up."

"Your accident with your white truck?" Helen asked. "That happened in Fort Lauderdale?"

Charlotte was run down in Bettencourt, miles away, she thought.

"Didn't I tell you? Happened right around the corner from the Home Depot on Sunrise. Some yahoo came flying around the corner and hit me. Of course, he's not insured. Thanks for throwing that soda away for me. I've gotta go back to work."

"See you later," Helen said, and mentally scratched Jared off her suspect list.

Inside the library's staff entrance, she tossed Jared's soda can in the trash. Jared was such a perfect suspect, she thought. He's bitter enough to kill, he needs money and he knows how to hot-wire cars.

As she passed the break room, Blair and Gladys were chatting. Once again, Blair looked like a librarian stereotype in a baggy pantsuit and a white blouse with a limp bow. A cup of hot tea completed the ensemble.

"Join us, Helen," Gladys said. "The library's new *Economist* arrived and I came in to read it, but I got wrapped up in a conversation with Blair." Gladys had her biker boots propped on a chair. For once, the librarian wore pants instead of a short skirt.

"I was reading the *Library Journal*." Blair held up her magazine.

"What's so riveting?" Helen asked.

"The *Economist* says we have Neanderthal DNA," Gladys said.

"I believe it," Helen said. "I dated a few."

"You and me both," Gladys said, and smiled. "But it's a scientific fact that most of us have one to three percent Neanderthal DNA. Here, you can read the magazine."

She handed it to Helen, leaving more fingerprints on the shiny surface. That was easy, Helen thought. "Thank you so much," she said, then realized she sounded ridiculously grateful for a library magazine.

"You like magazines that much?" Blair said.

"Love them," Helen said.

"Well, I've finished reading mine. I'll lend it to you if you promise to return it. I've marked several reviews of books I want to read." The head Friend of the Library had been amazingly friendly to Helen since she'd been allowed to sort through the Kingsley collection. Helen wondered why. She'd never trust that woman. She was sure Blair had put that rattlesnake in the musty box of books.

Helen held up her fingers in the Girl Scout pledge sign. "I'm trustworthy, brave and loyal," she said, and took the *Library Journal.* "Now I have hours of good reading when I get home. But I should be shelving books."

"There's a full cart behind the checkout desk," Gladys said. As Helen started to leave, the librarian said, "Helen, I've said this before, but I really do appreciate your volunteer work."

"I enjoy it," Helen said.

Oddly enough, she did. As she trundled her full cart over to the shelves, Helen counted the reasons: Shelving was good exercise. It was useful and satisfying. It was soothing to put the books in their proper places, and straighten out the tangles. Like this one: What were three Sandra Brown mysteries doing in the middle of Rita Mae Brown's cozy cat novels? Helen put Sandra after Rita, where she belonged.

I need two more sets of fingerprints, she thought—Alexa's and Seraphina's. Alexa's should be easy. I'll stop by her office for an update. But what about Seraphina, Elizabeth's snarky friend? I remember her looking at the books by the door here.

Helen pushed the heavy cart over to that rarely visited section. The large-print biographies were shelved there, far away from the large-print novels. Seraphina was tall, and Helen remembered her looking at a book at the end of the top shelf. A slim white book with blue writing. There it was, wedged next to a black metal book support: *Seriously . . . I'm Kidding* by Ellen De-Generes.

Seraphina would have had to move the book support to pick up that book, Helen thought. Fingerprints would show up better on the smooth metal book support than the book cover. And the library won't miss it. I have two extra supports on my cart. She switched out the supports, and put the one she hoped had Seraphina's prints on it on her cart.

Nothing left to shelve but two children's books. Helen put them away, then rolled her cart down the dark hall to the library supply room. The oak bookcases Charlotte had used for her makeshift home were shoved against the wall, and all traces of her were gone—blankets, battery-operated TV, even the energy bars.

The library supplies were shelved in front, neat as ever, but now two metal shelves were moved aside so there was a narrow path to the dumbwaiter where Charlotte had hidden the watercolor. Fat dictionaries were piled near the door.

Helen pulled five large manila envelopes off the shelves and labeled them. She put Blair's *Library Journal* in one, Gladys's *Economist* in another and Seraphina's book support in the third.

Two empty envelopes waited for Lisa's smoothie cup and whatever Helen could scrounge from Alexa's office. She put the envelopes in one of the purple Flora Park Library totes stacked on a shelf. There were so many of those floating around the library, the lavender bags were invisible.

Next, Helen called Detective Doben's number at the station.

"Hello?" he said. Helen stayed silent.

"Who's there?" he demanded.

Helen hung up.

If I ask the detective if he wants the fingerprints, he'll

probably say no, she thought. Now I know he's in his office. Hope he stays there until I get to the Bettencourt police station. I have one more stop—Alexa's office.

Helen always felt better when she entered the library director's office. It was so civilized. Alexa wore a striking black suit with a crisp white blouse that emphasized her unusual hair. Once again, she was frowning at a computer, and sipping a bottle of water.

"Hi," the library director said. "Do you have something to report?"

"I will later this afternoon," Helen said.

"Want some spring water?"

"I'll have to take it with me," Helen said. "I need to leave for an appointment."

Alexa turned her back to get a cold bottle out of the small fridge behind her desk, and Helen quickly checked the director's desk for something that would hold a print. There it was. A fat plastic pen.

"May I borrow your pen?"

"That one?" Alexa said, and handed it to her. "It's a freebie. Here, keep it."

"Perfect," Helen said, careful to take it by the end. She could almost see Alexa's fresh prints on its smooth plastic surface. She slid it into the envelope in her purse.

"Were you surprised when Seraphina bought that incredibly expensive car?" Helen asked.

"No. I predicted she'd buy something outrageous," Alexa said. "Retail therapy, remember? I've just about talked her into heading the Flora Park Library Restoration Campaign. I think she'll say yes in another day or so."

"Thanks," Helen said, when Alexa handed her the bottle of cold water. "How about a late lunch at Café Vico this afternoon?"

"The cute Italian restaurant on Federal near Sunrise?" Alexa asked. "I'd love it. I'll meet you there at two o'clock."

"See you there," Helen said.

But first, she had to present her case to Detective Doben. He would find the killer, thanks to her evidence.

Should I order Café Vico's tiramisu or the cannoli to celebrate? she wondered.

CHAPTER 37

· ·

All the way to the Bettencourt police headquarters, Helen debated with herself: Will Detective Micah Doben listen to me? He has to. I'm giving him the solution. Yes. No. What's he gonna lose? But he doesn't like me. Well, he'll like my information.

She pushed Margery's car over the speed limit, in a hurry to get to the police headquarters next to the golf course. Once there, Helen was afraid to park her landlady's car in the lot with the sign warning drivers to beware of the golf balls.

Instead, she parked the Town Car on the street, grabbed her purple tote bag and hurried into the police station, where she told the old, gray cop at the desk, "I have information for Detective Doben about the fatal hit-and-run at Broward and Bettencourt Street."

"Your name, miss?" the cop asked.

"Helen Hawthorne," she said. Now Doben had to come out, she thought.

He did, though he made her wait twenty minutes. Today, the plump, potato-faced detective wore a beige suit with a dark brown shirt and a yellow-and-brown tie. His socks were yellow, too. He also wore a plain gold band and Helen wondered how his wife could let him leave home in that outfit.

"Ms. Hawthorne," the detective said. "You have information?"

"I have the solution to the case, right here," she said, and patted the tote.

"By all means, come in," he said, bowing low. He was mocking her, but Helen didn't care.

Doben led her to the same cluttered cubbyhole with the coffee-ringed table where they'd talked last time. "Now, where's your so-called solution?" he said. His sneer was as ugly as his suit.

"As I told you, Charlotte Dams was homeless and living at the Flora Park Library," Helen said. "She'd discovered a million-dollar watercolor in a book and hid it. She was killed for that watercolor by one of five people connected with the library.

"Since I talked to you, a white car was reported stolen and returned to a strip mall about a mile from that library. The car had been cleaned and polished. Inside that car were white cotton gloves—the kind librarians use to handle rare books."

Helen hoped to surprise the detective with her next bit. "The returned car was impounded by the police for further examination. Was Charlotte Dams's DNA found on the stolen car? Do the white paint chips on her body match the car paint? Was that stolen car used to kill her?"

"You're saying a librarian stole a car?" Helen heard Detective Doben's disbelief.

"Only two of the suspects are librarians," Helen said. "One's a society woman, another is the board president and the third is the head of the Friends of the Library."

"All known car-boosting professions," he said, his

sentence sticky with sarcasm. "Almost as bad as librarians."

"Just because they seem to be nice women doesn't mean they can't commit murder," Helen said.

"But you don't know if they did," Doben said. "You say you have five suspects. Can you narrow the killer down to one person?"

"Well, no," Helen said. "But I have materials with their fingerprints right here in this bag, all labeled. All you have to do is check five sets of prints against the print found on the murder car's steering column."

"Five!" he said.

"Right," Helen said. "I have two sets on two different magazines, a plastic pen, a smoothie cup and a library book holder."

"I doubt those items would stand up to judicial scrutiny," he said.

"Maybe not," Helen said, "but if a set of prints did match someone, it might create enough probable cause for you to obtain a search warrant to get the person's fingerprints for a second test."

He stared at her, stone-faced. Helen babbled on. "Bearing in mind that the US Constitution protects us from unreasonable government search and seizure— I'm not a government employee. I didn't break any laws getting these fingerprints. So this evidence would be hard for a judge to suppress."

Helen smiled. She'd handed him the case all wrapped up in a big red bow. He didn't seem happy with his present.

"I don't need you to quote the law to me, Ms. Hawthorne," he said. "I'm surprised you didn't bring your mouthpiece with you this time. I won't have a civilian—"

"I'm a private eye," Helen interrupted.

"—waste my time," he continued. His voice was low and lethal, his complexion a dangerous red.

"You show up here at this station one more time and I'll have you arrested," he said. "Better yet, I'll have you committed. You can't prove there's any connection between the stolen car and the library, except that it was found in a parking lot a mile away."

"Yes, I can," Helen said. "What about those white cotton gloves left in the car? Librarians use those!"

"So do mimes, Ms. Hawthorne," he said. "But they're smart enough to keep silent."

His laughter followed her out of the room.

CHAPTER 38

· ·

"Y ou want me to do what?" Alexa said. "That's insane."

Helen and the library director were lunching at Café Vico, a pretty Italian restaurant tucked into the corner of a strip mall.

When the elegant Alexa raised her voice, the diners at the next table stared. She switched to a whispery hiss. "I'd have to be crazy to go for a stunt like that."

"Hear me out," Helen said. "It's the only way we'll catch the killer. Someone connected with your library killed Charlotte the ghost."

Alexa groaned as if she'd risen from a tomb, but now the nearby diners were distracted by the arrival of their lunch.

"It's not as crazy as you think," Helen said.

All the way to Café Vico, the private eye had fumed about her encounter with Detective Doben. He doesn't believe me, she'd muttered to herself. He laughed at me. I'll show him.

At a stoplight, Helen looked over and saw the man in the next car watching her talk to herself. She reached

over and turned on the radio, pretending she was singing along with the music.

She'd fled the Bettencourt police headquarters shaking with rage. The old gray cop in the front had grinned
at Helen on her way out, but this time it wasn't friendly.

"My plan is the safest way to catch the killer," Helen
told Alexa. "I've looked at it from every angle."

She had, too. All the way to Café Vico, Helen had
thought about how to trap Charlotte's killer. Then, at
another stoplight, she heard a news story on the radio.
The announcer said: "A successful sting operation by
police resulted in the capture of a drug dealer and sixteen bricks believed to be cocaine, valued at more than
two million dollars."

That was Helen's inspiration. A sting, she thought.
I'll run my own sting, and Alexa will help me.

Helen got to Café Vico first. The restaurant was sweetly
old-school Italian. Outside was a pleasant patio dining
area with plants in pots. Inside, the sunshine yellow walls
were decorated with murals and celebrity photos. Helen
inhaled the scent of buttery garlic. While she waited for
Alexa, she comforted herself with warm rolls dredged
in a garlicky herb dip.

If Doben walks through the restaurant door, I'll
breathe on him, she thought. He'll fall down dead.

Alexa came through the door instead, and all eyes
turned toward her. She waved at Helen, and sat down.
"Don't get too close," Helen said. "I'm on a garlic binge."

"That's why we're here," Alexa said, and Helen loved
her for it. "Pass me what's left of the bread, and we'll get
more." They ordered lunch, too, and wine.

When Alexa's food had arrived—chicken ravioli in
a black-cherry red wine sauce—Helen wished she'd
been more adventurous. Her chicken piccata was deli-
ciously safe.

Helen waited until Alexa had some ravioli under
her stylish belt before she proposed the sting. That was

when Alexa erupted. Several minutes and half a glass of wine later, the library director was calm enough to consider Helen's proposal.

"I'll listen," she said. "But no promises."

"It's simple. We have a conversation in the break room," Helen said. "You and me, talking barely loud enough for the others to hear. In fact, if we lower our voices, their ears will really flap. You know Blair loves eavesdropping."

"But she's—" Alexa protested.

"A good person and a terrific fund-raiser and extremely useful," Helen said. "Today, she'll be even more useful."

"I'm not good at memorizing lines," Alexa said.

"You don't have to," Helen said. "Follow my lead. I'll say that I can prove who killed Charlotte. That I have the evidence to convict the killer in a purple library tote and I hid it in the supply room.

"Then I'll say I've talked with Detective Doben."

"I don't like lying," Alexa interrupted.

"I'm not lying," Helen said. "Where do you think I went after I asked you to this lunch? I talked to the detective at the Bettencourt station."

Alexa studied her face. Helen looked the library director in the eye. Everything she'd said was true.

"I'll say Detective Doben will meet me after the library closes," Helen said, "and that's when I'll give him the evidence."

Now Helen was lying, but Alexa didn't know that.

"I don't want any negative publicity," Alexa said.

"So? You can tell me that," Helen said. "You won't have to pretend to make it up. It's true."

She's buying it, Helen thought. Keep talking. "You know you can't have a killer at your library. You don't want that. It's too dangerous."

"No, I don't," Alexa said. "Especially a hit-and-run killer. That's a cruel, cold-blooded murder, running down that poor young woman like a dog."

Almost got her, Helen thought.

"It's your duty to help capture Charlotte's killer," Helen said.

"Do you really have the evidence to convict the killer in our purple library tote?" Alexa asked.

"Right here," Helen said, and held it up.

Alexa didn't ask what the proof was or ask to see it. Helen thought that was odd, but right now she suspected everyone, even the chic library director.

Alexa says she's neutral about the library restoration, Helen thought, but her architect husband and his firm would make a lot of money building a showcase library in Flora Park. Is that a motive for Alexa to kill Charlotte? I don't know, but then, I don't know anything about Alexa, except for what I can see, that sophisticated shell. But enlisting me to find the killer makes her look innocent.

"So that's all I have to do?" Alexa said. "Talk to you in the library break room and hope the right people overhear it?"

"Yes," Helen said. "But we also need Seraphina at the library. She's one of the suspects."

"Seraphina! But she's Elizabeth's best friend," Alexa said.

"That's what Seraphina says. I'm not so sure," Helen said. "She's sniping and snarky around her friend. She practically ran over Elizabeth, showing off her new car. What kind of friend brags about her money to someone who's broke?"

"But why would she want Elizabeth's watercolor? She can buy anything she wants."

"She likes it. The watercolor struck a note with her. *Muddy Alligators* is not just a Sargent—it's a unique Sargent. It has personal meaning. Seraphina's family has known the Rockefellers for generations. They've visited their estates. The Rockefeller home is one of the few places where Sargent painted in Florida."

"You're the detective," Alexa said, and shrugged.

"But I can get Seraphina to the library easily. She adores tiramisu. This could be my secret weapon to get her to say yes to the campaign."

And if the campaign fails, your husband will get to build the new library, Helen thought.

"I'll order some to go," Alexa said. "How about you? Would you like dessert?"

"Definitely," Helen said. She'd expected to celebrate a triumph at Café Vico. She decided this was still a triumph, just covered in whipped cream.

She savored her creamy dessert, a sweet spot after her harsh humiliation at the police station.

"One more thing before I say yes," Alexa said. "Will you have a gun when you confront this killer?"

"Too dangerous," Helen said. "But I'm armed with pepper spray." She pulled the small container, about the size of a hotel bottle of shampoo, out of her purse. "That way, I can stop the killer, but nobody gets hurt."

"Of course," Alexa said. She looked embarrassed. "I don't know what I was thinking even mentioning a gun."

Lunch was definitely over, and Alexa seemed satisfied with Helen's plan. In the parking lot, she called Seraphina on her cell phone. "Darling, I have a surprise for you. The best tiramisu ever. Join me at my office in half an hour.

"What?" Alexa sounded shocked. "The police wanted to talk to Ozzie? What for? Is he okay? Look, Seraphina, I can get you more tiramisu later. You must be frantic about your boy. Well, if you insist he's fine and you're fine, I'll see you at the library shortly."

She hung up, and said to Helen, "You won't believe this. The police questioned Ozzie. They think he stole a golf cart. A golf cart! Isn't that the most ridiculous thing you've ever heard? He doesn't even golf. She's terribly upset but their lawyer assured her it's just a misunderstanding. Seraphina says she needs that tiramisu.

"We're fifteen minutes from the library," Alexa said.

"We'll start our little play as soon as Seraphina arrives. But if I get her to the library, you have to promise you won't upset our biggest donor."

"Of course not," Helen said. Unless Seraphina's guilty, she thought. Then all promises are off.

"I'll keep the sting short and simple," Helen said. "When I ask for more coffee, it's over."

But it wasn't over, and Detective Doben wasn't finished with her. Helen's cell phone rang just as Alexa was unlocking her car. Helen checked the display and saw Detective Doben's name. Maybe he's changed his mind and wants to see my evidence, she thought.

"I'll take this and meet you at the library, Alexa," she said.

"Ms. Hawthorne," Detective Doben said. "Since you were kind enough to stop by my office, drop off all that so-called evidence and lecture me about its constitutionality, I thought I'd return the courtesy. The Flora Park police told me they found the car thief."

"Car thief?" Helen said.

"You remember the white car that was stolen from the parking lot of Julie's Smoothies. It's in their jurisdiction. I called them to see if there was a connection between that car, which had been in an accident, and the Bettencourt hit-and-run homicide.

"Guess what? Turns out there isn't. They caught the thief. He's a young man with two priors. I'm just calling you out of professional courtesy." His voice was slick with sarcasm. "You wanna get your lawyer to hear this news?"

Helen felt her face turn hot. She gave Alexa a half-hearted wave as the library director drove off.

I've been spectacularly, stupidly wrong, she thought. No one at the Flora Park Library had hot-wired a stolen car and killed Charlotte.

"What about the white gloves?" she managed to stammer.

"His sister is in a high school band," Detective Doben said. "This is his third car theft, and he was determined not to get caught. So he stole the gloves. Should I arrest him for that theft, too? He cleaned the car before he returned it because he thought that would remove the evidence. But he forgot about that one print on the steering column."

"Steering column," she said, her voice as dull as her thoughts, her face red with shame.

"But don't you worry, Ms. Hawthorne. We're giving him the white-glove treatment." Detective Doben's laugh was harsh and mocking.

Then his voice changed to pure steel. "Amateur," he said. "Stay out of my case and leave it to the pros. You don't know what you're doing."

CHAPTER 39

. . . .

Helen had to force herself to slow down on the drive back to the Flora Park Library. She was furious and embarrassed, a bad combination. She wanted to get on I-95 and keep on driving. She wanted to rush over to the Bettencourt police station and punch Detective Doben in the mouth.

But she knew someone at the library had cruelly killed Charlotte, just as the homeless woman was about to start a new life. There was only one way to get revenge on that smug detective—prove him wrong. And that was exactly what she aimed to do.

Helen arrived at the library a minute or so after Alexa parked her car. The library director waited for her by the walkway. "Everything okay?" she asked. "You looked upset when I left."

"I'm fine, thanks," Helen said. "Just a call about a case."

Alexa put the carryout tiramisu in her office fridge while Helen stashed the purple tote in the library supply room, behind the tall wooden bookcases. She took four other totes off the pile and stuffed them with supplies—boxes of marking pens, rubber bands, even packets of white cotton gloves—and set them on other shelves. She made sure the pepper spray was in her pants pocket. Then she cruised the library, looking for her suspects.

She saw Jared sweeping the hall. He was no longer a suspect, but she was glad he'd be nearby if things went wrong. The janitor was strong enough to intervene if there was a problem.

Gladys was at the checkout desk and Lisa was in the break room. The coffeemaker was gurgling and sputtering. "I've cleaned the coffeemaker with white vinegar," the board president said, "and I'm making a fresh pot. You're in time to test it."

"Perfect!" Helen said. Exactly the pretext she needed.

"Pour yourself a cup while I get Blair," Lisa said. "She's been waiting for a good cup of coffee all afternoon."

Helen poured two cups, for herself and Alexa. The two plotters sat down at the table closest to the door. Helen heard footsteps down the hall, winked at Alexa and said in a barely audible voice, "I've got it, Alexa. I've got enough evidence to convict Charlotte Dams's killer."

"Who is it?" Alexa asked. *Creak!* went the hall floor.

"I don't want to alert the killer before Detective Doben gets here," Helen said.

Pop! Rustle. Was that someone's knees? And the rustle of material?

"Who's Doben?" Alexa asked.

You're good, Helen thought. "He's the detective in charge of the hit-and-run murder. I've convinced him that someone connected with the library killed her."

"Where's the evidence now?" Alexa asked.

"In a purple Flora Park Library tote. I hid it in the library's supply room."

Creak! Bless those old floors, Helen thought. They're talking to me.

"Would the evidence be more secure in my office safe?" Alexa said.

"Nope. Too many people know the combination."
Crack!

"That supply room has dozens of purple bags,"
Alexa said. "There's a big pile on the shelf."

"I know," Helen said. "I put mine in a special place.
Like the purloined letter, it's hiding in plain sight, except
it isn't. I hid it behind the tall wooden bookcases." Her
words tasted bitter after the detective's sneery phone
call.

"Helen, that detective isn't coming here during library hours, is he?" Alexa did a good job of sounding
angry.

"Of course not," Helen said. "He promised. I have his
case wrapped up in ribbons—actually, packed in a purple
tote. He'll do what I say. This coffee is good. Want some
more?"

She got up to get the coffeepot and Blair bustled into
the room. "I hope you've left enough for me," she said.
"I'm desperate for a cup of good coffee."

"Me, too," Lisa said, following on her heels.

"I'm sticking with Red Bull," Gladys said. "I need
serious caffeine to keep me awake."

"Did somebody say fresh coffee?" Now Jared was in
the room.

The gang's all here, Helen thought, including Jared
for emergency backup. For everyone to pile in here at
once, they must have been lurking outside the door, listening. Only one person is missing.

That was when blond Seraphina loomed in the doorway, wearing a simple white blouse and expensive designer
jeans.

"Alexa, quit babbling about purple ribbons and coffee. I hope I didn't come all this way for nothing," she
said. Helen wondered if the patrons upstairs could
hear her. Seraphina never said anything softly.

"No, it's in my office," Alexa said.

Helen looked at everyone in the room. They were all
dressed in pants and shirts, as if someone had sent out

a memo. Seraphina's blouse was crisp and white. Alexa had taken off her suit jacket. Her blouse was so expensive it glowed. Gladys's yellow blouse was tight and chic. Lisa's blue blouse was slightly crumpled from her morning walk. Blair wore her usual suit but she'd taken off her shapeless jacket. Her white blouse was tattletale gray, and what it said was "old and cheap." Even lanky Jared wore a long-sleeved khaki shirt.

The trap is baited, Helen thought. Now let's see if I catch a crook.

CHAPTER 40

"Excuse me," the library patron said. "Do you work here?"

"I'm a volunteer," Helen said.

A volunteer on a mission, she thought. I've set up my sting, and my suspects are drifting out of the break room with their coffee. They'll have to move soon if they're going to steal the bag of fake evidence.

My plan is simple: After Alexa and I did our little play, I took a cart filled with novels to be shelved, and rolled it into the reading room.

Now I'll shelve a few books so my five suspects see me at work. Finally, I'll drift down the hall to the supply room and hide behind the bookcases in the back. That way I can watch who comes into the room. When the killer goes for the bag, I'll grab her and start shouting. There are plenty of people around. Jared is still cleaning the hall and he's strong enough to stop her. I should be safe.

Helen didn't even tell the library director her final plans, on the off chance Alexa was the killer. She was in her office now, sipping coffee while Seraphina ate her tiramisu. But either woman could pretend she needed the bathroom and slink down the hall to snag the purple tote with the evidence.

"Well, then you can help me find this novel," the patron said. She was thirtysomething, with straight blond hair, a distinguished nose and very white teeth. Her green eyes would have been pretty if they weren't glaring at Helen.

"I want *Panic*, by Jeff Abbott," Blondie said.

"*Panic*," Helen repeated. That was how she felt. She was panicking. Her chance to catch Charlotte's killer was slipping away the longer she talked to this woman.

"Let's go to the shelves with the A fiction," Helen said.

"I already looked there," Blondie said.

"We'll look again," Helen said. "Just in case."

She frantically pawed through the choices—novels by Rennie Airth, Bruce Alexander, Susan Wittig Albert. No, she thought. Jeff Abbott's novels are shelved before those writers. Ah, Abbott. Here he is.

"I don't see *Panic*," Helen said. But I feel it, she thought. Each second I waste talking to you, I'm losing my chance to catch the killer.

"Your computer says you have it," Blondie said, as if she were holding stone tablets instead of a paper printout. Helen heard a hint of belligerence.

"The computer doesn't show books that are lost or mis-shelved," Helen said. "If it's in the wrong place, we'll have to track it down. That could take time."

"I have all afternoon," Blondie said.

I don't, Helen thought. My sting is falling apart while I stand here.

"How about *Cut and Run*?" Helen said. "Abbott wrote that, too, and it's good."

And it's what I need to do, she thought. Get out of here. Now.

"I've read that one," Blondie said. "I've read them all. I only need *Panic*. I just printed the information off your computer. It says you have *Panic*. There's no librarian at the desk right now. You have to help me."

Helen looked over at the circulation desk. No sign of Gladys. Was she helping another patron—or helping herself to the purple tote?

I have to get to the supply room, Helen thought.

But Blondie blocked her way. She was determined, insistent. She wanted her novel. Blondie stuck to Helen like gum on a shoe sole. The only way to get rid of her was to find the blasted book.

Helen checked all the As and some Bs in the fiction section, in case Abbott's book was mis-shelved. Nothing.

"It's a hardback," Blondie said. "I can't afford to buy hardbacks, but I like reading them better than paperbacks."

Maybe I should hand her twenty-five bucks and tell her to buy the book, Helen thought. It's the only way she'll go away.

"Your computer says two copies are out on loan," Blondie said, helpfully. "But you still have one."

I can slip between the shelves and run for it, Helen thought. But Blondie seemed to read her mind. She shifted to the right and blocked Helen's escape.

"If the computer says the book's been returned, it may be on this cart," Helen said. "It could be the novel hasn't been shelved yet."

She frantically searched the books on the cart while Blondie stood there like a lump.

Help me, Helen thought. This is no time for your impersonation of Lott's wife. I have to run. Start checking these books.

Blondie didn't move. The books on the cart had been alphabetized to make the shelver's job easier. No sign of *Panic*.

Helen was sweating now. Her plan would be in ruins unless she found that book.

"It's a thriller," Blondie said, as if that would help.

"Right," Helen said. She heard a door open in the back hall. Was it the door to the supply room, or one of a dozen others? Was the killer getting away?

"I don't care if it's the gay edition," Blondie said.

"Huh?" Helen said.

"The gay edition," Blondie repeated. "Your computer says it's LGPT. That stands for Lesbian, Gay, Prohibited and Transgender. I don't judge people. It's no one's business who they love." She squared her shoulders, standing tall for gender equality.

Helen felt so relieved she had to lean on the cart. "No, ma'am," she said. "That's not what LGPT means. It stands for *large print*." She rushed over to that section, found the novel and handed Blondie *Panic*. She practically threw it at the woman, Helen was so eager to leave.

"But I don't like reading large-print novels," Blondie said. "They make me look old."

"No, they're good for your eyes," Helen said. "Squinting causes wrinkles." She pushed Blondie toward the self-checkout machine, then pushed the cart around the corner of the bookshelf, where it was out of sight.

Helen ran. She sprinted down the back hall as if it were an Olympic event. She was sure the judges would all hold up their "ten" cards for her speed in the empty, dimly lit hall.

Helen stopped at the supply room, and looked both ways. The hall stayed deserted, except for Jared dust-mopping at the other end. That was reassuring. Help was close by.

She slid inside the dark room. Helen hit her shins on an empty book cart near the door, then carefully worked her way to the back of the room by the tall wooden bookshelves on rollers, bumping her elbows and bruising her knees. She found the tote with the fake evidence, and kept it within sight.

Then she waited in the dark. And wished Charlotte's makeshift home were still there. She'd like a comfortable cushion. Her legs were falling asleep while she stood here. Helen leaned against the hard bookcase, but it offered no comfort. An energy bar would be good, too, she thought. After that huge lunch, she was hungry. And a little bit sleepy.

Wait! Someone was walking down the hall. Now Helen heard the door handle turn. She tensed. Her hand clutched the pepper spray.

The supply room door opened, and the light flicked on. Helen was temporarily blinded. Then her vision cleared and she saw Gladys. Please don't let it be her, Helen thought. I like Gladys. She's crazy-funny. She wouldn't kill anyone, would she? She was so patient with that rude man who didn't like her clothes.

But Gladys had a determined streak, and she was definitely a risk taker. How far would she go to get that red Ferrari? Not to mention those hip clothes? A million dollars could give her the life she wanted.

Gladys took a pack of marking pens off the shelf and turned off the light.

The room was dark.

Gladys was gone.

CHAPTER 41

. . . .

Helen was relieved. But I still don't have the killer, she thought. Who killed Charlotte? The supply room was hot and stuffy. Helen shifted uncomfortably from foot to foot and tried to rest her hip on a bookshelf, but it was the wrong height.

Then she was hit with a blast of light and sound. Helen froze in place, and heard a woman bellow, "Where the hell is that purple tote?" Seraphina. She was loud, even when she was talking to herself in an empty room.

Helen heard her rummaging through the supply shelves like a raccoon in a Dumpster, then the *whump!* of something heavy falling on the floor.

"Shit!" Seraphina said. "It should be here. Why can't I see it?"

Helen's eyes were adjusting to the light. She saw Seraphina pull her cell phone out of her pocket and speed-dial a number. "Alexa!" she said. "I can't find the damn purple tote."

Alexa? Helen thought. Were those two in it together? Had they conspired to kill Charlotte? Seraphina could have killed Charlotte while Alexa helped Phil and me look for the tote. Seraphina's son, Ozzie, rode in his girl-friend's Acura Friday night. Why didn't he drive the nearly new Beemer his mother gave him? Was it in the repair shop? Helen felt for the pepper spray again. Lean, strong Seraphina could easily overpower her without it.

"No, no. You don't have to come to the supply room," Seraphina said. "Just tell me what shelf it's on. You don't know? Why not?

"Okay, I realize you're the director, but I thought you knew everything in this library. Try the third shelf? I'm looking straight at it. Nothing. Sorry to be such a pain in the butt, but my cleaning lady wants one. I gave her a perfectly good Prada tote, only one season old, and she sold it. She wants a purple Flora Park Library tote so all the other cleaning ladies know she works here."

So much for my theory that Seraphina and Alexa are in it together, Helen thought.

"Even cleaning ladies need status symbols, I guess. But I want to humor her. She does windows better than the Flora Park Window Washing Service. Really. You don't have to come. I'll keep looking till I find it."

But Alexa did come to the room. She's a good woman, Helen thought, and Seraphina is a major fund-raiser. She wished she could wipe that last idea out of her mind. She didn't like being so cynical.

The supply room door opened, and Alexa was in the doorway. "There's the tote," she said. "On the third shelf of the third metal bookcase."

She handed Seraphina two bags from the purple pile.

"Thanks," Seraphina said. "If it was a snake, it would have bit me."

Alexa picked up the package of typing paper that had slid to the floor during Seraphina's search, then turned off the light.

Once again, Helen was left in the dark—in more ways than one. Alexa, Gladys and Seraphina are cleared, she thought. That left Blair and Lisa. Unless Jared killed

Charlotte. Did his truck accident really take place in Fort Lauderdale? I never saw the police report. I just took his word for it.

She could hear Jared working in the hall outside the supply room door, his wide, old-fashioned dust mop making clacking sounds with each sweeping movement.

Helen heard voices and footsteps. A woman, but she didn't recognize who was talking. She said something to Jared, then heard his dust mop clacking down the hall. The footsteps were closer now, almost at the supply room door.

Lisa or Blair? she thought.

I don't want Lisa to be the killer. I feel sorry for her, for all she gave up to marry her dream lover, for her lost fortune, for her struggle to care for her ailing mother. Please don't let it be Lisa.

But I know those are all good motives for Lisa to kill Charlotte and try to find the painting. Alexa had to practically throw Lisa out of the library after Charlotte was killed. Only a frantic call from her mother's caregiver made her finally leave.

With a million dollars, Lisa could put her mother into a good home where she'd be watched by professionals. Lisa would even have enough left over for some well-deserved comfort. Killing a homeless woman nobody knew would be easy. Much easier than her current life.

And Blair, she was another one who didn't want to leave the library that evening. Alexa literally pushed her out the door and locked it.

Blair, head Friend of the Library, but no friend to me. Please let it be her, Helen thought. I don't like Blair. She tried to kill me with a rattlesnake. She called Ozzie and he brought one to the library. Then she carefully hid the snake in the box of moldering books. She nearly got away with premeditated murder. She wouldn't hesitate to kill homeless Charlotte.

Helen held her breath.

Eons passed in the stuffy room. Helen recalled her conversations with Lisa, the impoverished board president who'd insisted on a séance. And frumpy Blair, who hated Elizabeth's father because the old boy bought a LeRoy Neiman painting. It was almost funny. But if she had that million-dollar watercolor, she could save her beloved library.

Blair or Lisa? Helen was sure one of them was Charlotte's killer.

Then the door opened, and the light flashed on again. For a moment, Helen was blinded. Now she could make out a tall, lean shape in pants and a long-sleeved shirt. She couldn't move closer to see the person's face or the rolling bookcase might creak.

Was it Blair or Lisa? Helen was dying to peek.

She heard searching, scrambling sounds. She poked her head around the bookcase and saw a slender hand—a woman's hand—pick up a purple tote stuffed with reams of printer paper, then toss the bag on the floor.

The killer, Helen thought, her heart thumping. She's in this room.

She'd been standing too long in one place. Helen's legs tingled unpleasantly with needles and pins. She carefully flexed first one, then the other, while the killer found another tote, this one filled with bags of rubber bands, and threw it down. The killer was getting angry now.

Helen gripped the pepper spray and the evidence tote. She rolled aside the tall bookcase and climbed around it.

"Looking for this?" she asked, and held up the tote.

Helen's eyes widened when she saw the killer standing there. Blair, the head Friend of the Library.

Now that she was face-to-face with Charlotte's killer, Helen was too stunned to speak.

Blair looked surprised, but recovered quickly. "What are you doing back there?" she asked. "Stealing supplies?"

"Catching a killer," Helen said. "You killed poor homeless Charlotte."

"That's crazy," Blair said.

"Is it?" Helen said. "She was run down by a white car."

"So what?" Blair said. "My car was here the whole time. Ask anyone."

"I did," Helen said. "You took a long lunch hour that afternoon."

"So? I'm not an employee," Blair said.

"Exactly why no one would care what hours you kept. But you told Alexa you were staying late because you'd had a long lunch," Helen said. "You listened at the Kingsley collection door and heard that Charlotte had a job interview at Norton Management Associates. Then you rushed over to the building where Charlotte was going for her interview. All the parking spots were taken, so you went to the next lot, and when Charlotte got out of her car, you ran her down and killed her. You hit her so hard, there were white paint chips on her body. Chips that can be traced back to your car."

"My car's in the shop," Blair said. "It's being repaired."

"The police can still find traces of blood and tissue on the undercarriage," Helen said. "And plenty of old paint will remain for a test. The repair shop isn't going to be an accessory to your crime. They'll tell the police the day and time you brought the car in. I bet they took photos of the damage, too—or your insurance agent did."

"Ridiculous!" Blair said, but her voice wavered. She didn't sound so confident now. "Why would I kill a woman who had nothing?"

"Because she had a million dollars," Helen said. "You heard Charlotte say she'd found the watercolor and hidden it. You know every inch of this library. You've gone over it with Alexa, again and again, while the board discussed fixing the floors. You thought if you killed Charlotte, you could come back and search for the painting and sell it. You needed the money to save the library."

Blair hissed like an angry snake. "We're entitled to it,"

she said. "The Kingsley family gave those books away. *Gave them away.*"

She'd said, *We're entitled to it*, Helen thought. Blair's not just the head Friend of the Library. She *is* the library—at least in her mind.

"Finders keepers, I say," Blair shouted.

"The law doesn't," Helen said.

"Just because Elizabeth was the director's friend, Alexa refused to let the library have those books until they were searched," Blair said.

"Elizabeth didn't deserve that money. She's already thrown away one fortune. Why should she have two? She's going to spend it on a crumbling old house. An old house! Elizabeth is only interested in herself. Her house isn't even historic. It's just old. This money could save Flora Portland's life's work, and benefit a whole community. Hundreds of people will be better off because of this library. Living, breathing people."

"Charlotte was a living, breathing person," Helen said.

"She was nobody. She wanted to be a ghost. Well, now she is."

Blair's smile was chilling. She was backing toward the door.

"You're horrible," Helen said. "You tried to kill me. You got that pygmy rattlesnake from Ozzie."

"Seraphina's son wanted to help. You took his mother's job."

Helen moved toward Blair to grab her, but the head Friend pushed over a metal shelf. It landed with a rattling crash, supplies flying everywhere. Helen saw reams of paper, heavy as bricks, burst open and snow down their contents. Paper clips, freed from flimsy containers, turned the floor slippery and treacherous. Bags of white cotton gloves bounced on the floor and metal book supports clanged and clattered.

Helen hoped the noise would bring help. Where was Jared? He'd been right outside the room.

"Don't go looking for the janitor," Blair said. "I asked Jared to run an errand, then told him to buy himself some lunch. He won't be back for at least an hour."

Help is going to come too late, Helen thought. Blair was on her way out the door. Helen had to stop her—now. She had to get through the barricade of the overturned metal shelf and library supplies. The bookcase! The built-to-last bookcase on castors.

Helen rolled the heavy bookcase through the room. The rumbling oak bookcase pushed the overturned shelf out of the way and rolled over the spilled supplies. The old floor was slightly slanted toward the door and the bookcase gained speed. Helen rammed it against the door, slamming it shut and blocking Blair's exit. She held up the pepper spray, but just as she hit the button, Blair lunged forward and twisted Helen's hand, and she got a faceful of spray. Coughing and gagging, eyes streaming, Helen slipped on a pile of paper clips and went down, hitting the hard floor with a *thwack*.

She heard the trapped Blair coughing. She must have caught some of the spray, but she wasn't blinded like Helen.

Helen opened one eye and saw a blurry shape pick up the gigantic hardcover *New Oxford American Dictionary* and hurl it at her. The seven-pound, two-thousand-page dictionary hit Helen in the chest and knocked the breath out of her. She felt a sharp burning pain, and stayed on the floor, dazed.

Blair was getting away. The killer was rolling the heavy wooden bookcase away from the door. Soon she'd be out and gone.

No! That can't happen! Helen struggled to her feet. Dizzy with pain, blinded by the spray, she searched for something to help her stand. She found it. The library cart. A tank with shelves.

Blair almost had the door open.

Helen pushed the cart as hard as she could. Pain seared her chest and she could barely breathe, but the cart connected with Blair's lean body. She pinned the killer to the wall.

Helen felt the pepper spray canister underfoot. Blair was starting to move.

Oh no, Helen thought. You're not getting away. Not after what you did to poor Charlotte. Helen found the canister and sprayed Blair in the face.

"Helen!" Alexa ran into the room. Helen saw the others crowding behind the director. "What's going on?"

"I caught the killer," Helen said, choking and gasping. Despite the pain and dizziness, she couldn't resist the next line.

"Book her," she said.

CHAPTER 42

"Pepper spray!" Alexa said, backing out of the cramped room. "Stay away, everyone. Call 911! Get an ambulance."

The library director half carried Helen to the break room and sat her at the kitchen table.

"Blair is still in there," Helen said. "I sprayed her." Her eyes were streaming and her face was on fire.

"We'll let the police deal with her," Alexa said. "Pepper spray hurts, but it won't kill her. Seraphina, lock the Kingsley collection door and stand guard. Gladys, watch the library. Lisa, hand me that milk in the fridge."

"Milk?" Helen wheezed. She tried to wipe her teary eyes, but Alexa stopped her.

"Don't rub your eyes! That will make it worse. When you said you were armed with pepper spray, I looked up the antidote online, just in case you used it."

Of course you did, Helen thought. If her ribs didn't hurt so much, she would have laughed.

"Pepper spray inflames the capillaries and causes a horrific burning sensation," Alexa said, once again a reference librarian.

Tell me about it, Helen thought.

"Rubbing your eyes will open more capillaries and spread the burning. Lisa, fill a big shallow bowl with warm water and dishwashing soap."

Alexa sloshed cold milk on a clean towel and draped it over Helen's face, then put more milk-soaked towels on her neck, hands, and arms.

Helen gasped out her story through the milky towel: "Blair ran down Charlotte at her job interview—that's why her car is in the shop. She tried to search for the watercolor here but you threw her out."

"Dreadful," Alexa said. "Just dreadful. Why would she do that?"

"She thought the library was entitled to the Kingsleys' million-dollar watercolor and that the money would save this building," Helen said.

"So she killed that poor girl," Alexa said.

"And tried to kill me with the rattlesnake," Helen said. "She admitted it."

The cold milk and Alexa's gentle touch were soothing. "I was wrong about her, Helen. I'm so sorry. Do you feel better?"

"A little," Helen said, her voice raspy as a rusty hinge.

"I wish there was a painless way to fix this," Alexa said. "Next, I have to remove that pepper spray oil from your face. Lisa, where's that bowl of soapy water? Good. Put it right in front of Helen."

Alexa must have tested the water. "The temperature is perfect," she said. "Warm, but not too hot." She took the milky towel off Helen's face, and she tried to focus her weepy, watery eyes.

"You look a little better," Alexa said. "Now stick your face in the soapy water and let the detergent start breaking down that pepper oil."

Helen closed her eyes again, took a deep breath and stuck her head in the water for as long as she could. When she brought her head out, Alexa said, "No, don't wipe it away. Sit there for a minute, and then do it again. Okay, another deep breath. In you go. Lisa, more soapy water."

Helen was relieved to hear sirens. Help had finally arrived. The ambulance crew worked on her pepper-sprayed skin while Alexa told the Flora Park uniform that Blair Hoagland had attacked Helen and killed homeless Charlotte. She also gave him the name of Blair's repair shop so the white car could be impounded.

Helen looked like a rejected library donation: Her blouse was torn at the shoulder and paper clips tinseled her hair, which was drenched with milk and soapy water.

It hurt to talk. But the uniform cop listened as Helen gasped out her story. When he realized that Blair had murdered the Bettencourt hit-and-run victim, he tried to call Detective Micah Doben, but he'd left for the day. Instead, Detective Earline V. Culver took the call.

Helen knew her name only later because she'd kept the detective's card. At the time, Helen had just vague impressions of the woman: sharp-eyed, smart, coal black hair.

Helen was dizzy and her chest felt as if it were wrapped with sharp metal bands. Her eyes still burned.

"You're lucky it wasn't police-grade spray," Detective Culver told her. "That's even worse."

Helen didn't feel lucky. She struggled through her story again until the detective interrupted. "Why are you having trouble talking? Are you hurt?"

"Yes," Helen gasped. "Blair dropped a dictionary on my chest. A big one. About two thousand pages. I can't breathe so well."

"You need to go to the ER," she said. "The ambulance will take you now."

"Call my husband," Helen said, and rattled off Phil's cell phone number.

Helen got to see Blair led away in handcuffs. Alexa was relieved that the head Friend of the Library was taken out through the staff entrance, but the intrepid *Flora Park Gazette* photographer captured the scene.

As four beefy paramedics loaded Helen into the ambulance, she said, "You'll make sure to find the Chevy and impound it at the repair shop, won't you? And test the undercarriage for DNA and blood? And the paint chips—check them against the white paint found on Charlotte's body."

"I know how to run a case, Ms. Hawthorne," Detective Culver said, somewhat sharply.

A worried Phil met Helen at the ER. Her hair was sticky and stinking of spoiled milk. Her eyes still stung, but the pain was bearable. By then she'd been helped into a hospital gown and had a bruise the size of a dinner plate on her chest. "Is that as painful as it looks?" Phil asked.

Helen nodded.

"Your eyes are all red."

"Pepper spray," she gasped.

Phil took her hand and asked, "Are you having trouble talking?"

She nodded again, then said, "Tell me what's going on with Trey."

"Oh, this story is good," Phil said. "Broker—that's Detective Stanley Morgan—executed a search warrant at dawn. Trey lives with his parents, and the cops searched the Lohan family's six-thousand-square-foot house. Which, by the way, is built a lot better than LCC's cheesy rentals.

"The police didn't find anything in Trey's room except a key to an apartment in one of the LCC developments. His father insisted that he gave the apartment to his son, but Broker couldn't figure out what a spoiled rich kid would be doing there—even the cops go into that apartment complex in pairs—so he got another search warrant.

"Turned out the enterprising young man was running a shoplifting ring out of his LCC apartment. Light-fingered residents would go to the big-box stores and steal electronics, household appliances, tablet computers, watches—all the stuff he and his friend Ozzie Ormond were selling at discount prices in Light Up the Night.

"Trey also did a little boosting on his own, stealing jewelry at the homes where he partied. That's where he got the Tiffany bracelet he gave Bree for her birthday.

"He was careful to steal only one thing at those parties, like that Tiffany bracelet. It was expensive, but not especially rare. His drug-addled friends were so out of it, they often didn't miss the item for days, or thought they'd lost it.

"But Trey was desperate. He was deep in debt from gambling, and greedy besides. He broke his own rule at Bree's party. He stole two things: an expensive—and easily identifiable—ruby-and-diamond necklace, and the Coakleys' golf cart with the custom seat cushions. He's going away for a long time."

Helen managed a smile.

"Can I ask you about that Tiffany bracelet, Helen? Your eyebrows went halfway up your forehead when Bree's daddy said he'd buy his daughter one just like it. I gather they're expensive."

Helen nodded.

"How much?" he asked. "Five hundred dollars?"

Helen laughed, then winced. It hurt too much. She shook her head and remembered just in time not to rub her itchy eyes.

"A thousand dollars?" Phil asked.

"Fifteen hundred," she croaked.

"For that little thing?" Phil asked.

Helen nodded again.

"Bet the old boy's sorry he opened his mouth," Phil said. "A fifteen-hundred-dollar bracelet. That was one expensive visit to the cop shop."

Helen tried to smile again, but it still hurt. "What about Snake Boy?" she asked.

"All we can prove so far is that Ozzie Ormond was an accessory in the cart theft, and that's on the security video, but we're still looking. The police are talking to Snake Boy again, and this time, they have a warrant for his apartment. Right now, we can't find any connection between Ozzie and his girlfriend, Chloe, and the theft of the ruby necklace, but we're looking."

That was when the emergency room doctor, a young, coffee-colored man with thick black hair, showed up in Helen's cubicle. He poked and prodded, then sent Helen off for X-rays. An eye specialist examined her and her eyes were rinsed with more saline solution.

Two hours later, the coffee-skinned doctor said, "Your eyes will hurt for another two or three days, Ms. Hawthorne, but there's no permanent damage. You also have a cracked rib. It's painful, but there's not much I can do except give you pain pills. We don't tape up ribs like the old days.

"It's important to keep your lungs healthy. As you heal, practice taking deep breaths. And don't be afraid of taking the pain medication, Ms. Hawthorne, because keeping the pain under control is important for taking strong, deep breaths."

Helen popped two pills under the doctor's supervision, and soon felt like she was flying. By the time she and Phil got back to the Coronado, a sunset salute was in progress, and Helen was feeling no pain. Her sunglasses hid her red eyes.

Margery, Peggy and Markos were sitting at the umbrella table, drinking mojitos and scooping up hummus with pita triangles. Margery and Markos both wore purple shorts, but Helen thought they looked better on the muscular Markos. Margery's tangerine orange manicure was the same color as her glowing cigarette end.

Markos waved them over. "Phil! Helen! I made mojitos and hummus."

"I actually like hummus," Phil said, though he avoided the carrots and celery sticks and heaped only pita on his plate. Phil also took a mojito, but Helen waved hers away. "I'll take a rain check tonight," she said.

Margery looked at her oddly and handed her a bottle of cold water.

Peggy, mojito in hand, said, "I brought home a mate for Pete. Come meet her." Peggy, with her green shorts, red hair and beautiful beak, looked like an exotic bird.

The two Quaker parrots were exploring their handsome new home, a black hexagon pagoda cage six feet tall. Peggy had rolled it out by the pool.

She pointed out its features: "With the rollers, I can bring it outside when the weather's nice. It has two wooden perches, two swings, four stainless-steel cups and a slide-out tray for easy cleaning."

Pete—at least Helen thought it was him—was on the top perch. A second bright green parrot with sober gray feathers on her head looked exactly like Pete, except Helen thought she might be a smidge smaller.

"That's the new woman on the swing, right?" Helen asked.

"That's her," Peggy said.

"How do you tell them apart?" Helen asked.

"You can't, except by a DNA test. I recognize Pete's familiar mannerisms. She's a year old, in her parrot prime."

"Aw," Helen said woozily, and chanted, "Pete's got a girlfriend.

"What's her name?" she asked.

"Patience," Peggy said. "The perfect name for a Quaker parrot. She'll need it to live with Pete."

"Doesn't he like her?" Helen said.

"I don't know yet," Peggy said. "He's been avoiding her. I took a big risk getting him a girlfriend. I wanted Pete to have some company while I'm at work all day and out most evenings with Daniel. I thought another bird would give him someone to talk to. Instead, he's not talking to anyone, even me."

"You've spoiled him," Margery said.

Peggy sighed. "Maybe he's a one-woman bird."

Helen watched the two birds in their new home.

Patience hopped closer to Pete. He backed away and flew down to a lower perch.

"Maybe he's shy," Helen said.

"Maybe he feels trapped," Peggy said. "If he were in the wild, he'd have plenty of space to roam and lots of women. Instead, I've forced her on him. Now he's locked in a cage with a permanent blind date."

"Give them time," Helen said. "It's too soon." She giggled. "It will take time to see if love is for the birds." She laughed at her own joke, way too loudly. The others stared.

"Are you drunk?" Margery said.

"No, stoned to the gills," Helen said cheerfully. "I caught me a killer and Phil broke up a shoplifting ring. It's been a busy day."

"Sit down and tell us," Margery said, puffing on her Marlboro.

Phil guided the giddy Helen to a chaise by the pool, and this time she winced when she sat down. She could feel the pain through the comfortable cloud of drugs.

Helen told her friends about Charlotte Dams's brutal hit-and-run death and how she'd been laughed out of the Bettencourt police station.

"Really?" Markos said. "The cop was that rude to you?"

"Yep. You don't have to be from another country to get bad treatment," Helen said.

She finished with a colorful version of her fight with Blair, and was roundly applauded. They made sympathetic gasps when she whipped off her sunglasses and showed her red, watery eyes.

"Put those things back on," Margery said. "You look like you're bleeding to death."

"I don't feel as bad as I look. But wait—there's more!" she said with a loopy grin. "Phil, tell them what happened with Trey. Markos, you had a part in bringing him down."

Markos smiled. "I'm an operative," he said.

Phil told his story, ending with, "Trey's bonded out for grand theft felony. The police are still trying to figure out if his father is involved in the thefts, since Trey used the family's business pickup to deliver the golf cart to the fence."

"Bet the Lohan family will have an interesting discussion at dinner tonight," Margery said.

Markos started to say something, but they heard a loud *squawk* and looked over at Pete's new home.

"Woo-hoo!" the parrot said. "Hello. Pete's got a girlfriend. Pete's got a girlfriend." His singsong squawking imitation of Helen was eerily hilarious.

"He's talking!" Peggy said. "Look! He's got heart-shaped wings."

Helen saw the bird holding his wings slightly away from his sides, his chest sticking out. From the back, his wings did look like a heart.

"That means Pete's in love," Peggy said. "He's flirting."

"Here's to high-flying love," Helen said. She raised her water bottle and they all toasted.

"Congratulations, lovebirds," Peggy said.

Phil kissed her gently. "That's us," he said. "I love you. We solved two tough cases."

"Three," Helen corrected. "I love you, too."

He kissed her again. The next time she looked up, everyone was gone—Margery, Markos, Peggy and the parrots. It was just her and Phil alone by the pool.

"Let's go home," she said.

"We are home," he said.

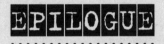

EPILOGUE

. . . .

"Champagne, everybody!" Helen and Phil cried. "The caterers are here. It's a celebration!"

The PI couple was out by the pool, ready for a sunset salute.

A magnum of champagne was sweating in a silver ice bucket, surrounded by six glasses. Three caterers carried out silver trays of sumptuous pink delicacies— smoked salmon, chilled lobsters and stone crabs, their rosy, rock-hard claws dramatically tipped in black— and set them on tables draped in purple.

Margery floated out of her apartment, looking like an exiled queen in a lavender caftan with a striking amethyst necklace. Peggy and Daniel hurried out of her home, breathless and slightly disheveled, but adorably flushed. Markos coolly strolled out of his place wearing tight black jeans and a white wifebeater. Ordinarily, Helen didn't like wifebeater shirts, but Markos's was helping change her mind.

"Did you get him?" Margery asked, and reached for a stone crab claw.

"Finally," Helen said, heaping her plate with cold

lobster, smoked salmon on toast points, and stone crabs with creamy mustard sauce.

"After six weeks and heaven knows how many slippery lawyers," Phil said, "Standiford W. Lohan the Third has been convicted of twenty counts of first-degree felony grand theft."

Daniel, Peggy's lawyer boyfriend, whistled. "He's looking at thirty years."

"And a ten-thousand-dollar fine," Phil said.

"Poor Trey had to sell his Ferrari," Helen said.

"I didn't think they'd ever convict him," Margery said.

"Trey's family has money," Helen said, "but they made powerful enemies. You don't want to mess with the Coakleys. And Trey's shoplifting ring targeted the big-box stores. They were determined to bring him down."

"And his good friend, Ozzie Ormond, testified against him to save his own scaly skin," Phil said. "Snake Boy cut a good deal with the prosecution."

"Trey's father nearly bankrupted himself fighting Trey's charges," Daniel said. "At least that's what I heard."

"He'll make the money back renting those substandard apartments," Helen said.

"Or not," Phil said, stuffing his mouth with smoked salmon. He winked at her, and Helen wondered what her crafty spouse was up to.

"You aren't eating, Markos," Margery said.

"There's so much of it and it's so beautiful," Markos said.

"All of it's healthy, too," Phil said, filling the champagne glasses.

"Almost all," Markos said. "Smoked salmon is a healthy protein and, as a fatty fish, it has the daily allowance for oil. But there are nutritional drawbacks to smoked fish. It's very high in sodium and—"

Margery popped a bite of cold lobster into his mouth and said, "Enjoy! Everybody has to die of something."

"Cheers," Peggy said, and raised her glass.

"To Helen and Phil," the Coronado residents said, and toasted the successful private eyes.

Dave, the crooked owner of Fore! Sale, was arrested for trafficking in stolen property. Many of the pre-owned golf carts in his warehouse showroom were still owned. Dave suddenly recovered his memory and testified against Trey and Ozzie Ormond. He pleaded guilty to a second-degree felony and served two years. He was forced to sell his business. After he left prison, Dave worked as a caddy at the golf course next to his former shop.

Ozzie Ormond, aka Snake Boy, Trey's accomplice at golf cart rustling and the shoplifting ring, cut a deal with the prosecution, and pleaded guilty. He's currently serving five years. Chloe has no contact with her former boyfriend, but Aunt Blair sends him letters from prison.

Police could find no criminal connection between Standiford W. Lohan, Junior, and his son Trey's shoplifting ring. LCC's chintzy "affordable urban apartments" might be a crime, but they weren't a police matter.

Shortly after Trey's trial and sentencing, Phil filed a complaint with the city's code enforcement authority. Trey's father is so busy bringing his apartments up to code, he hardly has time to visit his son.

During the trial, testimony revealed Bree Coakley's wild lifestyle, including the drugs. Her parents were appalled when this information made the news, and their punishment was swift and dire. They cut off Bree's allowance, forcing her to get a job. To escape that dreadful fate, Bree married a lawyer in her father's firm.

Chloe Coakley's parents never discovered her beer-buying scheme for her underage classmates, but they were displeased that her boyfriend, Ozzie, was a convicted felon. She was forced to get a part-time job at a Palm Beach dress shop. Chloe was thrilled with her generous staff discount, until she spent two thousand dollars more on clothes than she made. She was fired for telling a size-eight woman, "The fat clothes are over there."

Chloe's parents insisted on tough love and refused to pay her debts. She now works at a fast-food restaurant and asks customers, "Do you want fries with that?"

Charlee and John, the underpaid Coakley gardeners, took the jobs they wanted in Boca Raton that paid a dollar an hour extra. Ana still cooks her magnificent lunches for the new gardeners. Helen and Phil have a standing invitation to stop by for lunch anytime.

Peerless Point crimes-against-property detective Stanley Morgan turned down a promotion after he cracked the shoplifting ring case. "I'd be a desk jockey," he told Phil over beers. "I'd go crazy shuffling papers and kissing ass. I didn't turn down the raise, though. Another beer?"

Bettencourt detective Micah Doben took a small buyout offer and retired.

Bettencourt detective Earline V. Culver was given a raise for arresting Charlotte Ann Dams's killer. She was promoted to Detective Doben's job after his retirement.

Blair Hoagland, the former head of the Flora Park Friends of the Library, was charged with the vehicular homicide of Charlotte Ann Dams. Her court-appointed attorney claimed that Blair was stressed by the potential loss of her beloved library. She was sentenced to twenty years in prison, three hundred hours of community service, and a five-thousand-dollar fine. Blair might have received a lighter sentence if she hadn't burst into a tirade against the "tasteless" Kingsleys, and the late Davis Kingsley's trashy LeRoy Neiman baseball painting. His Honor was a great admirer of Mr. Neiman's work.

Lisa Hamilton Jackson found a quality nursing home for her mother in Himmarshee, a town in Central Florida's horse country, where the cost of living is considerably cheaper than Fort Lauderdale. She sold her mother's Flora Park home as a fixer-upper and moved to the small town to be near her.

Lisa handles the nursing home's medical billing service and is on the board of the town library. She even has time for some happiness. She's dating a man from one of the first families in Central Florida. Lisa insists that he is not a cowboy, or a cowman, or even a Cracker, but a cattleman.

Seraphina Ormond, Elizabeth Kingsley's friend, was so delighted with the tiramisu Alexa brought her, she promised to spearhead the fund-raising campaign to reinforce the Flora Park Library floors, and kicked it off by donating a million dollars of her own money. Alexa said she'd keep her in tiramisu while Seraphina labored for the library.

Seraphina was grateful for the distraction, after the horror of Ozzie's trial. She raised all the money the library needed for the new floors. She also sweet-talked old Mr. Ritter, who owned two houses in Flora Park, into donating one as the library's temporary home during the construction. Then the dynamo collected enough funds to cover the move. A window nook with Mr. Ritter's wing chair and the latest Sunday *New York Times* were permanently reserved for him.

Seraphina was unanimously elected president of the library board.

When the Flora Park Library finally reopened, Seraphina was honored at a special gala banquet, and tiramisu was served in her honor. Her custom-made gown cleverly hid the twenty pounds she'd gained.

* * *

During the renovation, Paris, the library cat, was the official greeter at the temporary library, a living link to the past and a promise that Flora Portland's library would reopen. The cat has become quite spoiled and now refuses to catch mice.

When the Flora Park Library reopened, the temporary library building became the Flora Park Ritter Center, dedicated to helping the homeless.

Ted, the library's homeless man, now had his own apartment in the center. In exchange, he carefully screens the homeless people who come to the new Ritter Center, and determines who needs psychological treatment, who has outstanding warrants and would be of interest to the police, and who needs a job.

Ted opened a café in the center, staffed by the homeless people he'd trained. He also trains other people to become gardeners and household help, or helps them get grants to finish their schooling. The Flora Park Ritter Center's programs for the homeless offer haircuts, showers, job interview clothes, blood pressure screening and business counseling.

Many Flora Park residents hire the trainees and say they make reliable, affordable live-in staff. The board hired two efficient assistants for Jared the janitor and he enjoys supervising his staff.

The center's new Paris Café is famed for its lattes, and the library staff no longer drinks the break-room sludge. Paris the cat reigns in the café named for her. Charlotte Ann Dams's name appears nowhere in the Ritter Center, but Helen believes it's a fitting memorial to the young woman.

Before Charlotte's body was flown home to her mother in Missouri, Helen gathered a bouquet of sweet-smell-ing tropical flowers from the library garden, and asked the funeral director to put it inside her casket. Charlotte now has Florida with her forever.

Paris may have retired from mouse-catching, but mice still scamper across the old library's rebuilt floors and frolic in its endless rooms. One day, a calico cat appeared at the library's staff door, the spitting image of Flora Portland's pet. She was promptly named Flora and became an organic mouse catcher, though she's partial to treats.

The *Flora Park Gazette* asked Alexa if the calico was the ghost of Flora Portland's pet. "I don't believe in ghosts," the library director said. "It's simply a coincidence that a calico cat happened to show up at the library."

Elizabeth Cateman Kingsley was disappointed that her John Singer Sargent print, *Muddy Alligators*, sold for $850,500 at auction to an anonymous bidder, even though the price was about seven thousand more than the most recent price for a similar watercolor. Elizabeth had been sure that the painting's glamorous, deadly history would bring the price up to at least a million dollars. But art sales are tricky, and once again, Davis Kingsley was wrong. He didn't leave his daughter a million-dollar watercolor after all.

Elizabeth presented Helen with a check for eighty-five hundred dollars.

"What's this?" Helen said. "We have a contract and you owe me ten thousand dollars, Elizabeth."

"I was expecting to recoup a million dollars for the watercolor," Elizabeth said. "Instead, all I'll receive is a mere 850,500 dollars. And you may call me Ms. Kingsley."

"Then I suggest you invest it wisely," Helen said. "And that you write me a check for the correct amount. Otherwise, you may call me Sue."

Elizabeth Kingsley paid in full, and followed the rest of Helen's advice.

Six months after the sale of *Muddy Alligators*, Seraphina Ormond revealed that she was the anonymous buyer of the painting. She donated it to the library. "Consider it a trust fund for any future problems," she said.

The library board gratefully accepted the gift. The "double hanging" gala Seraphina held to install *Muddy Alligators* in the newly renovated lobby, across from Flora Portland's portrait, was the party of the year.

Elizabeth Cateman Kingsley did not attend.

Alexa Andrews, the Flora Park Library director, was extremely pleased with the results of Helen's two investigations. One week after Blair Hoagland was arrested for the murder of Charlotte Ann Dams, Helen stopped by the library to pick up her check and have tea with the stylish director.

Helen enjoyed sipping tea on the yellow sofa in Alexa's office. Paris the cat stopped by for a scratch and danced on the soft carpet, while Helen fed her treats.

Alexa looked like a work of art in a hot-pink suit. She handed Helen the check, then said, "Wait. I have something else for you."

She brought out the colossal copy of Edward S. Curtis's *Portraits from North American Indian Life*.

"This is the book where the watercolor was hidden," Helen said.

"I thought you'd like to look at it now that you have the time," Alexa said.

"Oh, Helen." Gladys waved to her from the checkout desk. She looked street chic in a military-cut jacket, mini, fishnet stockings and her buckled biker boots. "I wanted to thank you for the lovely gift basket of champagne, caviar and bonbons."

"Me?" Helen said.

"There wasn't a card with the basket, but I know

you sent it. I love the Ferrari key chain. That's just the sort of kind thing you'd do."

"I have no idea what you're talking about," Helen said, and winked.

"Yes, you do," Gladys said. "Thank you so much."

Phil was waiting in Helen's apartment when she came back from the library. She was wearing a white blouse and a black pencil skirt, and carrying the massive book. He put his arms around her, and she inhaled his scent of coffee and sandalwood.

"You look like my fantasy librarian," he said.

"I'm not working for the library anymore," she said.

"Sh!" he said. "Don't spoil it. Smart, sexy women are hot. Did I ever tell you my library fantasy?"

He whispered it in Helen's ear, then kissed her. She kissed him back, a long, lingering kiss.

"Let's check it out, book lover," she said.

Read on for a sneak peek at the next
Dead-End Job Mystery
by Agatha and Anthony Award–winning author
Elaine Viets,

The Art of Murder

Available now from Obsidian.

Yep, his hand was on the blonde's bottom.

Helen Hawthorne looked again. She wasn't imagining it: The lad in the lederhosen was definitely lecherous. His hand disappeared behind her skirt, and the cute blonde in the dirndl was smiling.

This painting of rowdy rustics was next to Frederic Clay Bartlett's studio at the Bonnet House Museum. Bartlett was a respected artist who'd studied art in Munich and Paris, a man whose rapturous stained glass intimidated even Louis Comfort Tiffany. But he also painted playful hanky-panky.

"You saw it, too, huh?" Margery said, and grinned. "I told you this was no ordinary museum."

Bonnet House is on Fort Lauderdale Beach, a light-hearted oasis tucked next to trashy tourist shops and grim gray hotels that Helen thought looked like pharaohs' tombs: expensive and dead.

The cheerful pale yellow Bonnet House was Frederic's idea of a Caribbean plantation house. Squirrel monkeys played in the trees, white swans preened in a pond, and exotic orchids burst into bloom everywhere.

"I had no idea a historic house could be fun," Helen

said. "I hate museum house tours. All those dark, gloomy rooms packed with dead people's things."

"Nothing dead about this place," Margery said. Helen's seventy-six-year-old landlady reigned over the L-shaped art moderne Coronado Tropic Apartments. Bonnet House was built around a courtyard alive with green plants and a splashing fountain. "Frederic and his wife, Evelyn, weren't your usual superrich—they both had brains and talent.

"Evelyn Bartlett is my role model," Margery said. "She appreciated good art, good booze, good living and good men. Made it to age a hundred and nine. After a scandalous divorce back in the twenties, she outlived her critics in style."

Margery had her own style and juicy scandals. She'd once been arrested for murder and worn a prison jumpsuit.

Today, her gauzy purple top looked cool in the heavy June heat. Margery wore her gray hair in a swingy chin-length bob. Time had marked her tanned face, but Margery made no effort to remove the lines and wrinkles that proved she'd lived and laughed.

Her silver bracelets jingled slightly, and Helen checked to see if her landlady's hands were twitching. Margery couldn't smoke her Marlboros on this tour.

"I could actually live here," Helen said, surveying Bonnet House as if she were buying it, "and I don't feel that way about most mansions."

Liz, their tour guide, gently herded them into Frederic's towering two-story art studio. Well-bred, well-spoken and gray haired, Liz could have been one of Evelyn's guests.

"Mr. Bartlett had an art studio at every one of his residences," Liz said, resuming her spiel as if turning on a recording. "He painted in this studio from 1921 until the early fifties. It has the clear north light artists love."

The studio's faintly musty smell was mixed with oil paint and a sharp hint of turpentine. A fanciful white fireplace was flanked by two tall white-framed paintings: one of a stylish woman in a golden brown suit and the other an elegant man in a pinstripe suit.

"That's Evelyn on the left and Mr. Bartlett on the right," Liz said. The walls were covered with vivid paintings of the French Riviera. "All of this was painted by Mr. Bartlett. He collected the pottery and sculpture, too."

A striking painting of richly dressed dark-eyed men wearing jeweled crowns and turbans hung above all the art. "That big painting is Persian," Liz said. "Early nineteenth century. Those are courtiers and members of a royal family."

"All men," Margery said. "You know who counted in that bunch."

The studio's mix of paintings and sculpture was striking, sophisticated and energetic. Helen could almost see the boldly handsome Bartlett painting, a romantic figure with slicked-back hair and a mustache, holding his palette like a shield and wielding a brush. He looked like the sort of man who could get away with a poet shirt.

Liz led them through the butler's pantry, painted in Ragdale blue, a once-fashionable bluish turquoise. "This is where Evelyn staged her exquisite meals," Liz said. Next they peeked into the kitchen. "The Bartletts ate only the freshest food. They brought in meat and dairy products from their Massachusetts farm. Their cook, Marie Little, said Evelyn never went into the kitchen. She talked to the cook about the day's meals through the window."

"My kind of woman," Helen said.

Margery checked out the china and Helen admired the German beer steins in the dining room. "Mr. Bartlett collected those during his student days in Germany," Liz said.

"Did he empty them first?" Helen asked.

Liz laughed but didn't answer. Helen wondered if the tour guide had a crush on the long-gone Frederic Bartlett.

As Liz guided the two women from room to room,

they admired the house's whimsical touches: the gilded baroque columns swirled around the drawing room doors, the brightly painted wooden giraffes on a courtyard walkway, the menagerie of carved monkeys, and the lacy wrought iron from New Orleans. They saw Frederic's murals and paintings. Evelyn's colorful, sensual art had its own white-walled gallery in a former guesthouse.

Helen and Margery lingered at the Shell Museum, a thirties bandbox housing Evelyn's shell collection, her Bamboo Bar, and blooming orchids. "At the age of a hundred and one, Evelyn started a new hobby, collecting miniature orchids," Liz said.

"Wonder what I'll be doing at a hundred and one," Margery said.

"Whatever you want," Helen said, tempted by the Bamboo Bar off the Shell Museum. "I like the idea that her husband gave Evelyn her own bar."

"Most men won't even fetch their wives a drink," Margery said.

The bamboo-lined room had four padded barstools, a couch and cocktail table, and a well-stocked backbar.

"The clock is permanently set at five o'clock," Liz said. "This is where Evelyn served her famous rangpur lime cocktail. She grew the limes herself."

Helen wrote down the recipe for Markos, the hunky young waiter who lived at the Coronado. "Maybe he can make it for our sunset salute by the pool," she said.

By the time they were back at the Bonnet House courtyard, Helen felt slightly dazed and dazzled, as if she'd watched Evelyn's and Frederic's star-dusted lives on fast-forward.

The courtyard, sheltered by feathery palms and bright with flowers, was cool even at noon. "I like the giant bird cage," Helen said. The gazebo-sized hexagon cage was a gingerbread confection of pastel wood and screens.

"Mr. Bartlett built the aviary for his wife's pet birds and monkeys," Liz said. "She had macaws, lovely demoiselle cranes, cockatoos and more. The guests would feed the cranes bits of food at dinner."

Helen saw a flock of artists working on the loggia across the courtyard, seated at folding tables. "Is that a painting class?"

"We have lots of classes," Liz said. "That's our oils class. The teacher is Yulia Orel, a local artist who's quite good. Come on over."

Yulia looked artistic, even in jeans. Her exquisitely boned face was crowned by blond braids. Liz introduced Margery and Helen. Yulia nodded politely and went back to telling a slender brunette, "You must use more color, Jenny."

Helen found Yulia's Slavic accent charming. She wondered how Jenny managed to wear white Armani jeans and a navy-striped top without getting paint on her pricey designer outfit.

"No, it's not working," Jenny told the teacher. "I'm going to put this away and forget about it for a week or so."

"I think it's pretty," a blonde with corkscrew curls said. She sat in front of Jenny. Her sturdy body was buried under hot pink, turquoise and yellow scarves, like a sale rack at a beach store.

"I don't want to paint pretty pictures, Cissy," Jenny said. "I want to paint art, like Annabel."

Annabel's nearly transparent skin turned as pink as one of Cissy's scarves, making her dark hair look black. She was about thirty-five, but so thin she looked like she might snap. A lime green cane was propped against her table like an exotic plant.

Annabel shared a table with the only man in the class—reluctantly. She held herself rigid to avoid contact with him but acted as if he didn't exist. Helen wondered why. He looked like a beefy businessman on casual Friday, in khakis and a navy polo that hugged his rolls of fat.

Helen could see the artwork from this angle, the

students' and the teacher's. Annabel seemed better than them—maybe even better than Yulia. She was painting the aviary with bluish gray cranes stalking across the courtyard. At first glance, the painting seemed slapdash, but Helen could feel the movement.

"I'm only a student," Annabel said. "I'm still perfecting my technique."

"Your technique is fine," Jenny said. "You've developed your own voice."

"To develop a voice, you need something to say," the beefy businessman said. Helen noticed his large nose was veined in red. A drinker?

Annabel paled.

"Hugo," Yulia said gently. "In this class, we are free to discuss one another's art, but we do not put down people."

"I don't *put down* anyone," Hugo said. "I tell it like it is."

The class seemed to close in on itself, fighting to ignore Hugo. Yulia examined Cissy's painting of a red hibiscus. Despite the vivid color, the flower was dull and lifeless.

"What am I doing wrong?" Cissy asked, corkscrew curls bobbing, multicolored scarves shaking in frustration.

"You keep flattening your flower," Yulia said. "It looks like a cutout. You're too careful. Be bold! What do you have to lose?"

"Time," Cissy said. "The class is over."

"All the more reason to act now," Yulia said. "I'll stay."

"Next time," Cissy said. "Next time I'll have more courage."

The class began packing up their easels and art supplies. Cissy helped the frail Annabel pack and said, "You really should drink your raspberry tea."

"Later," Annabel said.

Now Yulia took time to welcome Margery and Helen.

"You should join our class," she said. "Painting is relaxing."

Margery shook her head. "No, thanks. I'm not creative."

"What about you, Helen?" Yulia asked.

"I wanted to be an artist when I was a kid," Helen said, "until I discovered I didn't have any talent."

"When you're a child, you have no idea if you have talent," the teacher said. "You can paint for enjoyment. It could help your work. What do you do for a living?"

"I'm a private eye," Helen said.

"Take up painting and you'll see the world differently."

"And it's so romantic here," Cissy said, eyes shining, scarves wafting in the breeze. "Can't you feel the atmosphere? Frederic Bartlett was amazingly handsome—you've seen his photographs. He had three wives and he loved them all. Each woman was an artist in her own way. His first wife was an artist and social activist, his second, a musician and a poet, and Evelyn was a painter and a gardener. It's inspiring here."

Cissy and the others were packed and ready to leave. Annabel took her green cane and her tea thermos. "Don't forget to drink your tea," Cissy reminded her.

Liz the tour guide said, "Helen, Margery, we have one more stop. The tour ends at the gift shop."

"Sorry," Margery said. "I'm dying for a cigarette." Helen was surprised her landlady had lasted more than an hour without a Marlboro.

"We'll walk them out, Liz," Jenny said. "Where are you ladies parked? In the Bonnet House lot?"

"No, across the way," Margery said, "on that vacant lot where those shops were razed. We're parked illegally."

"So are we," Jenny said. "I hope we didn't get towed."

The women walked out together, Cissy carrying both her supplies and Annabel's. How she managed in that welter of scarves, Helen had no idea.

Once they passed through Bonnet House's wrought-iron gates, the otherworldly spell was broken. They were back in modern Florida, surrounded by condos, cars and construction. Jenny surveyed a half-built condo. "They should make the crane the state bird," she said.

Helen was relieved that no tickets flapped on their windshields. The sandy soil was littered with sparkling glass shards and construction debris, and Helen hoped Margery didn't get a flat tire.

"Who has that amazing red Tesla S?" Helen asked.

"Me," Jenny said, nimbly navigating the uneven ground in four-inch heels. "I love it."

"So do I," Helen said. "You're really surefooted. I couldn't walk in this lot in heels."

"You don't need them," Jenny said. "You're how tall?"

"Six feet," Helen said.

"I have to wear heels. I'm only five feet tall."

Jenny and Yulia loaded their cars. Jenny drank the last of her bottled water, while Annabel gulped her tea. "Ick," she said. "I didn't put in enough honey. It's bitter."

Margery lit her cigarette with trembling hands and blew out a plume of smoke like a satisfied dragon.

"You should smoke e-cigarettes," Cissy said, firing up her own e-cigarette. "You won't be so addicted if you vape."

"I like my addictions," Margery said. "I've cultivated them carefully."

That should have stopped Cissy, but she had the fearless fervor of a new convert. "You'll save money," Cissy said.

"I enjoy burning cash," Margery said. Her look should have wilted Cissy's springy blond hair.

Cissy packed the art supplies into her blue Prius while Annabel finished the raspberry tea in her thermos.

"I wish you'd join our class," Jenny said to Helen.

"There's room," Yulia said.

"I'll think about it," Helen said. She was tempted.

"Are you working on a case right now?" Margery asked.

"No," Helen said.

"Perfect," Yulia said. She pulled out her cell phone and said, "Give me your name and address. We meet at ten every morning."

Before she knew it, Helen was signed up for class. Everyone waved good-bye to Yulia.

"That was quick," Margery said. "How do you feel?"

But it was Annabel who answered.

"Terrible," she said. Annabel was as white as milk and trembling. She dropped her cane, then collapsed in the sandy soil.

Also available from
national bestselling author

ELAINE VIETS

The Dead-End Job Series

Shop Till You Drop
Murder Between the Covers
Dying to Call You
Just Murdered
Murder Unleashed
Murder with Reservations
Clubbed to Death
Killer Cuts
Half-Price Homicide
Pumped for Murder
Final Sail
Board Stiff
Catnapped!
Checked Out

Available wherever books are sold or at
penguin.com

facebook.com/TheCrimeSceneBooks